"A fun, ... of magical **Chicago**, *Black Wings* **has it all: a gutsy heroine just coming into her power, badass bad guys, a sexy supernatural love interest and a scrappy gargoyle sidekick. Highly recommended."**
—Nancy Holzner, author of *Deadtown*

AN UNEXPECTED VISIT

"Can I help you?" a voice murmured behind me.

I was pretty out of it, and Gabriel's voice made me jump about three feet in the air—from my knees, no less. I did a kind of jerky half turn and fell to my left side, landing on my elbow so I wouldn't squash Beezle while keeping him out of Gabriel's sight. The impact reverberated through every hurt muscle and bone in my body, and I gritted my teeth as I glared up at him.

"Knock much?" I said.

"The door was open," he said, gesturing down the stairs. He stood in the doorway, looking just as cool and dark and beautiful as he had the day before. He wore the same expensive coat and shoes, and the slightest of creases appeared between his eyebrows as he frowned down at me. "May I ask what happened to you?"

Oh, a giant freaking demon was just here trying to take my heart and bring it back to his master. No big . . .

BLACK WINGS

CHRISTINA HENRY

ACE BOOKS, NEW YORK

THE BERKLEY PUBLISHING GROUP
Published by the Penguin Group
Penguin Group (USA) Inc.
375 Hudson Street, New York, New York 10014, USA
Penguin Group (Canada), 90 Eglinton Avenue East, Suite 700, Toronto, Ontario M4P 2Y3, Canada
(a division of Pearson Penguin Canada Inc.)
Penguin Books Ltd., 80 Strand, London WC2R 0RL, England
Penguin Group Ireland, 25 St. Stephen's Green, Dublin 2, Ireland (a division of Penguin Books Ltd.)
Penguin Group (Australia), 250 Camberwell Road, Camberwell, Victoria 3124, Australia
(a division of Pearson Australia Group Pty. Ltd.)
Penguin Books India Pvt. Ltd., 11 Community Centre, Panchsheel Park, New Delhi—110 017, India
Penguin Group (NZ), 67 Apollo Drive, Rosedale, North Shore 0632, New Zealand
(a division of Pearson New Zealand Ltd.)
Penguin Books (South Africa) (Pty.) Ltd., 24 Sturdee Avenue, Rosebank, Johannesburg 2196,
South Africa

Penguin Books Ltd., Registered Offices: 80 Strand, London WC2R 0RL, England

This is a work of fiction. Names, characters, places, and incidents either are the product of the author's imagination or are used fictitiously, and any resemblance to actual persons, living or dead, business establishments, events, or locales is entirely coincidental. The publisher does not have any control over and does not assume any responsibility for author or third-party websites or their content.

BLACK WINGS

An Ace Book / published by arrangement with the author

PRINTING HISTORY
Ace mass-market edition / December 2010

Copyright © 2010 by Tina Raffaele.
Cover art by Kris Keller.
Interior text design by Tiffany Estreicher.

ISBN: 978-0-441-01963-2

ACE
Ace Books are published by The Berkley Publishing Group,
a division of Penguin Group (USA) Inc.,
375 Hudson Street, New York, New York 10014.
ACE and the "A" design are trademarks of Penguin Group (USA) Inc.

PRINTED IN THE UNITED STATES OF AMERICA

10   9   8   7   6   5   4   3   2   1

For Chris and Henry, who make everything worthwhile

ACKNOWLEDGMENTS

Special thanks go to C. P. Chang, who patiently read each draft and without whose comments and encouragement this book would not have been completed.

A very big thank-you to Danielle Stockley at Ace, who helped shape the final draft and make *Black Wings* the best book it could be.

Much gratitude is due to Cameron Dufty, who gave me a chance in the first place.

Finally, none of this would have been possible without the persistent love and encouragement of my parents, who always believed I could do it.

1

I HATE IT WHEN A SOUL GOES ALL STUBBORN ON ME. It doesn't happen as often as you'd think. Most people understand that they're dead and want to move on. Maybe it's because they think Heaven is waiting for them. Maybe it's because they believe they'll be reincarnated as the Princess of Monaco—does anybody want to be reincarnated as the Princess of Monaco anymore? Maybe it's because they're just tired of this world. When I show up to escort them to the Door, they know why I'm there and they're ready to go. But sometimes, like today, a soul doesn't want to leave its earthly body.

Mrs. Luccardi didn't want to leave her cats—all fifteen of them. People get very attached to their pets. In fact, I've seen a fair number of people more attached to their pets than to their children. I understand that they feel like their little four-legged buddy is part of the family. What I have to make them understand is that they are dead, and can no longer feed, groom, or cuddle little Muffy, Flopsy, or Fido. It can be a delicate job, convincing the recently deceased of their new status.

"Mrs. Luccardi, you're dead," I said. "You can't take care of your cats anymore. Someone else will have to do that now."

I fought the urge to cover my nose as I said this. Mrs. Luccardi was recently deceased and therefore immune to the reek of cat piss that permeated her doily-covered living room, but I was very much alive and getting tired of breathing through my mouth.

Aside from my burning need to breathe air unscented by eau de cat urine, I had two other pressing reasons for getting Mrs. Luccardi out of there. First, I had a potential tenant coming to look at the empty apartment in my building in twenty minutes, and I didn't want to piss off a possible source of income by showing up late. Second, some of Mrs. Luccardi's precious darlings were contemplating her cooling body with "buffet" in their eyes. I did not want Mrs. Luccardi to see her babies gnawing through her flowered housedress to flesh and bone. That kind of thing tends to traumatize the newly dead and prevents an Agent from an efficient escort to the Door.

If the soul doesn't enter the Door, then it becomes a ghost. Agents don't like ghosts. They're untidy. The presence of a ghost means you can't close your list, and if you can't close your list, you have to file extra paperwork to explain why you can't, and I absolutely hate doing any paperwork at all, period. So I really wanted Mrs. Luccardi to leave her carnivorous little fuzzballs and come with me, pronto.

I hadn't even untethered her soul yet. Her incorporeal self floated above the body on the plastic-covered sofa, bound by a thin strand of ectoplasm. I was supposed to cut this strand with magic or my silver knife and release the soul. The knife, along with my Agent status, had been passed to me by my mother when she died.

In life and death, Mrs. Luccardi was a small, thin woman with a head of white curls—the kind of old lady my mother used to call a "Q-tip." She glared at me through red plastic spectacles.

"I don't care if I'm dead, missy. I'm not leaving my babies," she snapped. "Besides, look at you. I'm supposed to believe you're an Agent of death? You're covered in flour."

"I was in the middle of making a pear tart dotted with gorgonzola. You're an unscheduled call. Besides," I said, pointing to my back, "don't you think the wings are a clue?"

She continued to eye me with suspicion. Okay, so a ten-foot wingspan of black feathers probably looked a little incongruous with my "Kiss Me, I'm Irish" apron and my fuzzy blue house slippers. Patrick was always telling me I would have less trouble if I presented a more imposing image, if I looked a little more Reaper-like. I always tell him that it's pretty near impossible to be imposing when you're only five feet tall and generally described by others as "cute as a button."

Of course, if Patrick had shown up for his scheduled escort of Mrs. Luccardi, I wouldn't be here at all. He'd called me fifteen minutes ago, said he had a "personal emergency" (read: a date with a hot guy), and begged me to take this pickup for him. I'd agreed because I owed Patrick a favor or two, but I couldn't be held responsible for my appearance.

"Listen, Mrs. Luccardi," I said through gritted teeth. "You're going to a better place. I'll make sure that someone comes to take care of your . . . babies."

"Oh, no. Harold, my son, will come and have them all taken to shelters. I'm not going anywhere. I have to look out for them." She crossed her arms, set her jaw and looked for all the world like she had no intention of moving in the next millennium. I wondered how, exactly, she expected to prevent Harold from having the cats taken away when she didn't have a corporeal self.

Unfortunately, I didn't have time to argue points of logic with the illogical dead. I glanced at my watch, a slender, silver-linked affair that had been a thirteenth birthday present from my mother. I really had to go. The potential tenant was scheduled to knock on my door in fifteen minutes. It would probably take me that long to fly home.

"Polly Frances Luccardi, will you permit me to untether your soul and escort you to the Door?" I asked.

"No!"

"Polly Frances Luccardi, will you permit me to untether your soul and escort you to the Door?" I asked again.

"I already told you, no!"

I felt the familiar buildup of pressure in my chest that accompanied a magical binding. It was what I imagined it would be like to drown. My lungs and heart felt as though iron bands squeezed my organs; my rib cage felt like it was collapsing. If I asked again and she refused, the binding was sealed. She would never be escorted to the Door, but would haunt this Earth forever.

"Polly Frances Luccardi, will you permit me to untether your soul and escort you to the Door?" I asked. The pressure increased and I gasped for breath.

"For the last time, no!"

My heart and lungs reinflated; my ribs sprung back into place. A surge of power pushed out of my fingertips and snapped the tether holding Mrs. Luccardi to her body.

A lot of Agents untethered agreeable souls using magic, but I didn't like it. I don't know what a binding felt like to anyone else but it made me feel like elephants had been tap-dancing on me. Give me a silver knife and a straight-forward cut any day. Unfortunately, I could only use my knife on the cooperative. No one knew exactly why, but souls that refused the Door had to go through the rigmarole of a binding.

"Polly Frances Luccardi, by your own words and of your own volition, your soul is bound to this Earth for eternity," I said, a little breathless.

"Fine. My babies!" she cried, holding her incorporeal arms out to the cats that were now starting to nibble her corporeal body's ankles.

Whatever. I got out of there before she realized that her little Snoogums was about to make her former shell into breakfast, lunch and dinner. If I had more time, I would have tried harder to convince her to go to the Door. Now I would have to file more paperwork, and Patrick would have to file more paperwork, and he would bitch about it and I would bitch about it and J.B., our supervisor, would be an annoying bastard about the whole thing because he's very insistent on closed lists. But I'd deal with that later. First, I had to get home in time to show the apartment, and I had only a few minutes.

Death is just another bureaucracy, and in a bureaucracy so large, sometimes people fall through the cracks. There are plenty of reasons why people don't get an Agented escort to the Door, and they don't all have to do with kitty love. If a person suffers a violent death, they may leave their body involuntarily—snap the tether that binds them to their mortal self and flee in anguish and madness before an Agent arrives. Sometimes a soul will allow itself to be untethered, come along quietly and then break away from the Agent before they arrive at the Door, fearful of what lies behind it.

Sometimes an Agent is hurt or killed and that person's list may lie dormant for an hour or two until replacements are notified. If that happens, the window of opportunity may close—souls might break their own tethers and wander free, or just refuse to be escorted, like Mrs. Luccardi.

Any of these possibilities creates ghosts, souls that will never pass through the Door. Ghosts have an annoying way of begetting other ghosts, showing up when an Agent is trying to work and convincing the confused deceased that they're better off haunting this mortal coil than taking their chances with the Door.

The thing is, you can't force a soul to be untethered and escorted. The soul has to choose the Door. Like so many mystical things, three is the key number. If the soul is asked three times and refuses the Door, then the Agent metaphorically wipes his hands and the soul becomes a ghost. The Agent is magically bound to leave them alone.

Of course, there are lots of ways around the "asking thrice" rule. You can tell people whatever they need to hear for as long as it takes to get them to agree to be escorted—like Heaven exists and that's where they're going, or they will join their beloved Ethel, or whatever.

I can't attest to the veracity of any of that. All I know is that every Monday I get a plain white envelope in the mail. In that envelope is an ordinary piece of white paper with a typed list. The list has the names, locations and death times of people I'm supposed to escort. I go to the appointed place at the appointed time, take out my knife

and untether the soul. Then I tell them something pretty
and take them to the Door. I don't even know what they
see when they open the Door. My vision goes black as
soon as they touch the doorknob, and returns when they're
inside. The only time I'll get to see what's behind the Door
is when I get escorted there myself, and someday I will.
Nobody outruns death. Not even death's lackey.

I flew in the kitchen window eight minutes late. I own a
brick two-flat in Chicago's west Lakeview neighborhood
and live on the top floor. My wings curled and shrank until
they disappeared into my back. I don't really understand
where they go—I just know that they unfurl when I need
them, and when I don't there are only two long scars that
bookend my spine. A good thing, too—it was hard enough
trying to get through puberty as an Agent of death without
having to explain my big flapping wings to everyone in my
ninth-grade class.

The doorbell buzzed as I pulled my apron over my head
and tossed it on the counter. The pears for the tart I had
been making before Patrick's call had turned brown and
the crust was still rolled out on the cutting board, completely unusable now.

I strode through the kitchen and into the short hallway,
then stepped into the dining room. The front door to my
apartment opened into this room. I tapped the button on
the intercom next to the door.

"Yes?"

"Gabriel Angeloscuro for Madeline Black."

The potential tenant. Goody. "I'll be right down."

I grabbed the keys for the downstairs apartment off
one of the hooks that hung next to the intercom. Just as

I opened the door to head downstairs, I heard a thump behind me and turned.

A small stone gargoyle, about eight inches high, sat perched on one of the dining room windowsills. His face was extremely ugly in a cute sort of way—a kind of strange cross between a cat and a hawk. He had pointed feline ears, a large curved beak nearly as wide as it was long, and slitted cat's eyes. Small bat wings arched from his back. His hands and feet were tipped with curved raptor claws. He crossed his arms over his adorable little Buddha belly and glared at me.

"You look crankier than usual, Beezle," I said.

"Hmph." His voice was two grindstones turning with no grain between them.

"Did you get a look at the potential?"

"Hmph," he said again. He looked supremely pissed off.

"What does 'hmph' mean, Beezle? Did you scope him for me or what?"

He opened his mouth, closed it again, then finally said, "He's a handsome devil; I'll give him that much."

"Oh, that's real useful," I grumbled, and headed downstairs, slamming the front door behind me.

I'd hoped that Beezle would get a sense of the potential tenant's essence for me, so that I would know if he were good, bad or indifferent. Gargoyles can see the true natures of things, which is very handy in a portal guardian. It's always nice to know if the thing that appears to be human standing on your doorstep is a serial killer, a vampire or just the UPS guy. And when you're an extremely single woman living alone, you want to know if the person renting the apartment below you is on the up-and-up or the no-way-in-hell.

My last tenant, Jess, was a delightful widow who had

rented the space for more than ten years. Five months earlier she had moved to Wisconsin to be closer to her grandchildren. I'd done some necessary updates on the apartment and then started advertising, but there had been no takers.

It was kind of weird, actually. Quite a few people had come to look at the place, gushed about the space, promised to bring back a deposit, but nobody returned. And after five rent-free months, I was pretty desperate for a tenant.

I pushed open the door at the bottom of the stairs and stepped into the small foyer. Gabriel Angeloscuro stood on the porch with his back to the main door, a large pane of glass with oak trim. He looked about a foot taller than me, and trim underneath his long black coat. His dark hair was slightly damp from the light October drizzle and curled a little at his neck and ears.

The expensive shine of his shoes made the already shabby paint job of the porch look even worse. Flecks of red paint peeled up under his feet, and I worried that he might catch the fabric of his coat—which appeared to be wool, dry clean only, and sporting a designer label—on a jutting nail. The interior of the building looked pretty good, but it was hard for me to keep up with repairs on the outside—yet another compelling reason to get a tenant and some rent money ASAFP.

For a brief moment I wondered why a man so well dressed would need to rent an apartment at all, much less rent one in my middle-class neighborhood. A guy like that should be in a condo in the south Loop, or somewhere else where trendy people with money bought trendy property. He turned around and met my eyes through the door, and for the second time in the last hour I felt like all the breath had left my body.

Beezle was right. He was a handsome devil. Way beyond handsome, actually. More like the most beautiful thing I'd ever seen in my life. He looked like an Italian Renaissance painter's ideal figure, from his broad forehead and carved cheekbones to the long, slightly arrogant Roman nose and the tiniest of clefts in his chin.

As jaw-dropping as his face was, it was his eyes that were most compelling. At first glance I thought they were brown. But as I looked, and looked, I realized they were closer to black, black like the ocean under the moon, an endless expanse of glinting waves reflecting the sky. There were stars in his eyes, stars and a hint of fire, a sun going supernova a million light-years away.

He didn't move or say a word. I realized that he stood on one side of the door and I stood on the other, and that I held the apartment keys in my left hand and the doorknob in my right. For a second I wasn't sure if I would turn the knob to let him in or hold it fast so that he could never enter. I felt like I was on the trembling edge of something, that if I allowed him to enter my home, my life would change irrevocably.

Then he smiled, the slightest upturn of the corners of his mouth. "Are you going to allow me in to view the apartment, Ms. Black?"

Blood rushed into my cheeks as he politely waited for me to turn the knob. I'd gaped at him like the class nerd panting after the quarterback. So what if he was good-looking? It didn't excuse my rudeness. *Off to a great start,* I thought. At this rate I would never get a tenant.

I opened the door quickly and stepped back to allow him to crowd into the small foyer. He smelled spicy-sweet, like apples and cloves.

"Sorry about that; please come in," I said. I held out my

hand for him to shake. "Madeline Black. I've been a little distracted today."

His own hand was covered in buttery leather glove. He grasped my hand briefly, impersonally, and I wondered why I was disappointed. "Gabriel Angeloscuro."

"Well," I said, trying to pull it together and remember why he was there. "Let's take a look, shall we?"

He nodded and I turned to open the apartment. The two apartment doors sat side by side with the mailbox and a small security light in between. The right-hand door was for the first floor.

The door opened into a small nook before expanding into a long room divided by an archway. The layout was practically identical to my own apartment above.

"As you can see," I said, "this is the living room/dining room area. The floors are the original hardwood and they've recently been refinished."

He walked to the large picture window that faced the street, seemingly not hearing a word I said. "How long have you owned this building, Ms. Black?"

"Nineteen years."

"You seem awfully young to have owned this building for so long."

"I inherited the building from my mother." *After she was murdered.*

"I see." He tapped one of his fingers idly against the glass. "I'm sorry for your loss. And your father?"

"Not in the picture," I said shortly. I had never met the man, never seen a photograph of him. His name wasn't even on my birth certificate. Whoever he was, my mother hadn't thought too much of him. She'd never spoken of him.

"Again, I am sorry to hear that."

This was not a line of questioning that I wanted to

continue. It seemed much too personal for a tenant-landlord relationship. "Those windows were just installed four months ago. They're a lot more energy efficient and they help keep the house warmer in the winter."

He turned away from the window and touched the metal coils of the steam heater that sat directly below the window. He seemed to be refocusing himself, remembering why he was there. "This is an older heating system, yes?"

"Yes, unfortunately, it's much more expensive to replace. It's also unnecessary, since the steam heat keeps the building very warm, even during a Chicago winter. But the kitchen and bathroom have been updated in the last year."

I waved him toward the back of the house. He walked slowly through the empty rooms, his heels ringing on the floor.

"This is one of the bedrooms," I said. A very small room opened off the living room. "There's a large storage space in the closet."

He obligingly opened the closet door and looked inside. "Are those your apartment stairs above this space?"

"Yes," I said. "If you'll come this way, I'll show you the rest of the place."

"It must be difficult," he said as he stood inside the closet and stared up at the diagonal ceiling.

"What's that?"

"Living alone, with no family to help you." He turned to face me and I again had the disquieting sense of falling into his eyes.

"The bathroom is this way," I said, ignoring his comment. I would not be drawn into a personal conversation with a stranger. It would be impossible to explain how Beezle and I had managed to dodge child services for years until I came of age, and it wasn't Gabriel Angeloscuro's business in any case. I'd lived by myself since I was thirteen years old. Yes, it was lonely with no one around except an overweight gargoyle, but I'd gotten used to it. I wasn't used to hot guys prying into my private life.

Gabriel seemed to accept my change of subject and followed me through the rest of the apartment, nodding at the second bedroom, the bathroom, the kitchen.

"There's a small yard out back and laundry downstairs," I said. "You would share both with me. There's also a storage space for this unit in the basement."

He said nothing, only stared out the row of kitchen windows at the small porch, the patch of grass, my scraggly little vegetable garden. I almost hoped he wouldn't want the apartment. There was something about Gabriel Angeloscuro—the familiar way he spoke to me, his disconcerting gaze—that made me deeply uncomfortable.

At the same time, could I afford to wait another five or six months for a better tenant? Probably not. Just because he was handsome and had some boundary issues wasn't a good enough reason to turn him away. If he wanted the place, it would only make good business sense to give it to him—as long as his credit and references checked out, of course.

"I believe I would like this apartment," he said, and then he smiled, showing white, white teeth.

Since an Agent's work is never really done, I had to head downtown immediately after Gabriel Angeloscuro's departure. Paperwork—the bane of my existence—had to be filed in a timely manner or else I would be forced to listen to J.B. rant from now until kingdom come.

"Beezle, I'm headed to the office," I called.

There was a faint grunt from the mantelpiece. The gargoyle was in brood mode and hadn't said a word to me since Gabriel had left. He had, however, seen fit to throw several black looks my way and to mutter imprecations under his breath.

"Whatever," I said. I stepped to the side window and thought about going to the Main Office. As I pictured the building—an unassuming brick nine-story in the Loop— my wings sprouted from my back. I swept out the window and into the morning air.

A handy side benefit of being an Agent is that no one other than the departed can see you when your wings are out. Well, almost no one. Many, many mentally ill people had caught sight of me over the years, as well as any number of folks using psychotropic drugs.

And children. Not all of them, although my mother told me that it used to be that she couldn't pass by a single child without being noticed. If she had to fly by a school playground during recess, she'd cause a riot.

But not anymore. I think children today are desensitized to the possibility of magic and wonder. Most kids I see have their noses buried in a handheld video game or are whining for their parents to buy something for them. Those kids are already too emotionally detached to notice a woman with black wings flying by.

But there are a few still—the ones who read on the playground instead of playing kickball with the other kids, the ones who stare dreamily out the classroom windows during science class, the ones who pretend their closet is a spaceship and their bedroom is the rocky surface of Mars—those kids see me. Really *see* me, and know that I'm not a figment of their imagination.

It took me about ten minutes to get to the Main Office. My wings are a hell of a lot faster than the Brown Line. I landed on the roof of the building. It was one of Mayor Daley's "green roofs," so it was covered in late-season vegetation that was slowly dying off as winter crept in. There was a fire escape door at the back corner of the roof, just above the alley. I pulled out my key, opened the door and clattered down the stairs until I reached the ninth floor.

I pushed into the hallway, a standard office-building, white-walled, gray-carpeted affair. It bustled with Agents and office staff. Most people talked rapidly into cell phones or carried sheaves of paper under their arms. Like I said, death is pretty much a bureaucracy, with all of the attendant paper and bullshit that goes with it. My cubicle was on the fourth floor, so I waited at the bank of elevators with a crowd of other people and crammed in when the doors opened to go down.

When I reached the fourth floor, I stepped out of the elevator and then waited until a small crowd of people emerged so I could blend in. It was childish, but I was trying to sneak past J.B.'s office without him seeing me. He always knows when something is off, and if he saw me, he would ask about the ghost.

J. B. Bennett was the area supervisor for Chicago. Each major city and every rural area has a supervisor, and then there are regional supervisors who oversee several areas. Above the regional supervisors are three managers, and then the president of the Main Office, who answers to the North American Branch Office in Ottawa.

This building controlled the whole Midwest region, so J.B. was one of many smaller fish that longed for bigger things. He was convinced that he was destined for the president's corner office. He was also convinced that if he micromanaged his Agents to death, then he would get where he wanted to be a lot faster.

Every time a soul did not choose the Door, he took it as a personal insult. He treated soul-collecting like a sales job. An Agent had to maintain a minimum percentage of "successes," souls who chose the Door, or else she was forced to write up a biweekly report explaining why she hadn't met her percentage minimum until she brought things up to scratch.

J.B. was also well-known for calling such Agents into his office for no apparent reason and wasting a lot of time haranguing them about their success rate. And he enjoyed assigning extra little tasks designed to irritate the crap out of them. J.B. couldn't fire an Agent who didn't meet his standards—being an Agent was a lifetime appointment— but he could certainly make your life miserable unless you gave him what he wanted.

If ever there were two people who epitomized the saying about oil and water, it was me and J.B. He wanted total submission, a line of orderly soldiers who did exactly as he asked. I wanted nothing more than to be free of him and this miserable job, but I was bound by fate and by magic to stay.

When an Agent dies, the next person in that Agent's bloodline is activated to duty. There is no choice, and there is no escape. The magic in the blood that gives Agents their powers also binds them to the job, and the only alternative is death.

I'd never known an Agent who'd attempted to leave the service, but there were stories—legends, really—of those who had tried. They were hunted down by Retrievers, and when the Retrievers found the errant Agent, no choice was given to them. They were struck down where they were found. They did not enter the Door, nor did they become ghosts. Their names disappeared from the rolls in the Hall of Records. It was as if they had never been.

I had never seen a Retriever. Rumor had it that they were planted among ordinary Agents, living double lives, or that they haunted the upper floors of the Ottawa office, seen only by the highest levels of management. Other Agents didn't believe in them at all, and thought Retrievers were just imaginary bogeymen, stories told to keep Agents from leaving the service en masse.

I was something of an agnostic on the Retriever question. I didn't necessarily believe, but I wasn't willing to take the chance. I wanted to see my mother again someday, and getting vaporized by a Retriever did not seem the best way to do that.

I managed to get past J.B.'s office and into the main room. I had a cubicle tucked in a corner and I scurried past my fellow Agents, most of whom were laboring with their heads bent over forms that had to be filled out in triplicate by hand. Agents possessed some of the most powerful magic in the world, but our data-entry system still hadn't entered the twenty-first century.

I had just settled in comfortably and started to fill out the form for Mrs. Luccardi when the phone on my desk rang. I could see the extension number and I rolled my eyes.

"How does he know?" I asked as soon as I picked up the phone.

"And a very good morning to you, too." J.B.'s secretary, Lizzie, always seemed unruffled. "He wants to see you in his office."

It was just turning out to be that kind of a day. I sighed. "Of course he does."

2

I DIDN'T HATE J.B. HE IRRITATED ME LIKE NO OTHER human being on earth could, however, so I considered it my duty to repay the favor.

J.B.'s office was a tiny two-room space crammed with file cabinets that overflowed with paper. Manila folders were stacked on every available surface, and any leftover space was filled with black three-ring binders. J.B.'s secretary, Lizzie, typed patiently away at some audio transcription as I entered the office. Her eyes were fixed on her computer screen and I could hear the clack of the foot pedal going up and down as she rewound the tape and then pressed down again to let it play. She finished typing her sentence and then looked up at me, pulling her headphones over her frizzy blond hair.

"He'll be out in a minute, Maddy. He's having a quick meeting with Atwood."

"How long has Atwood been in there?"

She glanced at the clock that hung on the wall above my hand. "Maybe five minutes."

I looked at the door that was a few feet behind Lizzie's desk, then up at the clock, watching the second hand. "And three . . . two . . . one . . ."

Right on schedule, I heard J.B. shouting at Atwood. The door muffled his exact words but I didn't need to hear the conversation to get the gist of it. Atwood must have fallen below percentage.

Lizzie looked as if she wanted to say something to defend J.B., but decided discretion was the better part of valor and picked up her headphones instead, nodding at me as she went back to work. A couple of minutes later Atwood came out looking white-faced. He passed me without a word and swept into the hallway. J.B. was right behind him.

The worst thing about J.B. wasn't that he had the world's crappiest personality. No, the real tragedy was that that personality had been shoehorned inside the face and body of a god. Well over six feet with the leanly muscled body of a long-distance runner, he had silky black hair cut ruthlessly short and green eyes that glinted like cut glass. If he'd had even a sliver of sweetness in him, he'd have had women sticking to him like flypaper. As it was, I didn't think he'd been on a date as long as I'd known him.

But then again, neither had I, so I wouldn't be throwing that in J.B.'s face anytime soon.

He stopped as he caught sight of me and smiled with shark's teeth. "Black. Perfect. I need to speak with you about that soul you collected this morning. Get your ass in here."

"Who talks like that?" I asked as I sauntered in behind

him and closed the door. He sat down at his desk. "You sound like a police sergeant from a cop show."

"Sit," he said, ignoring my comment and shuffling things around on his desk.

The quantity of paperwork on his desk was unbelievable. It looked like there had been some kind of paperwork apocalypse. I think the only reason it wasn't on the floor was that J.B. probably thought that paper on his desk made him look busy and paper on the floor made him look like a slob.

"What is it you're looking for? I haven't filed the paperwork yet. I was just filling it out when you called."

I crossed my legs and caught a flash of blue. I noticed that I had never changed out of my fuzzy house slippers. That meant that I had shown the most beautiful human being I had ever seen in person around the apartment while wearing my crummy holes-in-the-soles slippers. And that I had come to work in them. And everyone I worked with must think I am either mentally ill or the world's biggest ditz. I voted for ditz, myself.

J.B. noticed my footwear and raised an eyebrow. I stared brazenly back at him like it was completely normal to wear crappy slippers to work. After a few minutes of playing cowboy, he apparently decided to launch right in.

"What the hell happened with that pickup this morning, Black? And why were you doing it instead of Walker?"

"Patrick had a last-minute emergency," I said, deftly avoiding the first question. "I was able to go instead, so I did. Not a big deal."

"Not a big deal? Not a big deal?" J.B. said.

"I do understand English, you know. There's no need to repeat yourself."

"You lost the soul," he said through gritted teeth. "Since when is that not a big deal?"

"Since when is a person's choice judged null and void by you?" I snapped. "She didn't want to leave her cats."

"You weren't there very long. I don't think you tried particularly hard to change her mind."

I stared at him. "How would you know that? Since when is it your job to monitor the length of time spent on each pickup?"

Something flickered in his eyes, but he pressed on as if I hadn't spoken. "And I know all about Walker's 'emergencies.' If he thinks he can shirk his duties every time he hooks up with some new guy, he's in for a big surprise. And if you keep covering for him, you're going to be spending every Saturday from now until kingdom come in the file room."

"How do you know how long I was at the Luccardi place?" I persisted. I was absolutely disturbed by the thought that J.B., or any other member of the management, was monitoring us that closely. More important, how could they do it? "Did you have some kind of magical LoJack installed on the Agents without our knowledge?"

"Your quota is dangerously low this month, Black. And Luccardi is going to count toward your numbers, not Walker's."

I stood up and put my hands on his desk. "I don't know what you're up to, J.B., but I swear, if I find out that you're illegally monitoring Agents, I will personally ensure that you never get that corner office you want so much."

He looked up at me, sparks in his eyes. "I think we're finished here."

"Not by a long shot," I said, and turned to leave.

"And next time you come in to work, be sure to dress

a little more professionally," he added as I slammed the door shut.

"You're lucky I remembered to take my apron off," I muttered, and headed back to my desk to finish filling out the forms. When I got to my cubicle I looked at the forms, picked them up and then crumpled them into a ball. I wasn't doing anything for J.B. until I found out how he knew I'd spent such a brief time picking up that soul today. Damn the consequences.

A couple of hours later I was at home trying to re-create the pear tart recipe that had been interrupted earlier. I gave up after an hour when I kept forgetting to add ingredients to the crust. I couldn't stop thinking about my conversation with J.B.

The doorbell rang just as I finished washing up my mixing bowls. Beezle still hadn't moved from his perch on the mantel.

"Nice to know you're looking out for me," I said conversationally as I went to the speaker. "It could be anything at the door."

"It's Patrick," Beezle grunted. "And it doesn't really matter what's at the door anymore now that you've let in the devil."

I stopped and glared at him. "Why don't you just tell me what it is about Gabriel that bothers you so much?"

He gave me a cryptic look and crossed his arms.

It was my turn to grumble under my breath as I buzzed Patrick in. He swung the upstairs door open with a flourish. "I have arrived."

"Hooray," Beezle grumbled.

"What's his problem?" Patrick asked as he hung a leather

blazer on the coatrack by the front door and unwound a gray cabled scarf from his neck. Patrick was tall, slim, and had electric blond hair and adorable dimples.

"He's a gargoyle," I said in response, and kissed his cheek. "I didn't expect to see you for a couple of days at least."

"Sadly, Justin turned out to be decidedly not all that," he said. "How was the pickup this morning?"

"She wanted to stay with her cats," I said, rolling my eyes.

Patrick gave me a knowing look. "Did Jakeass chew you out?"

"And how," I said fervently. I debated telling Patrick about my suspicion that J.B. was monitoring us, but decided against it. I wanted to look into things further myself before getting Patrick—or any other Agent—alarmed. "He's probably going to take a bite out of your ass, too."

"Well, it's nothing you and I haven't seen before."

"Class troublemakers," I said, and grinned.

He grinned back. "Can we have pizza and beer? I need cheese and mushrooms and alcohol, and possibly some zucchini fried in large quantities of oil."

"I don't have any beer," I said.

"Then let's have pizza and whatever you have. I'm buying," he said firmly. Patrick was independently wealthy, which had something to do with his father making brilliant investments and passing on that talent to his only son. He'd offered to invest some money for me, but as I pointed out to him, you had to have something to invest in the first place.

"I think I have milk and chocolate syrup," I replied.

"I can't imagine anything better," he said, and slung his arm around my shoulders.

Pizza, chocolate milk and my best friend. I couldn't imagine anything better either.

A couple of hours later Patrick left to walk the six or so blocks to his home, both of us somewhat sedated by the large quantities of food we had consumed. I waved at him from my front window, which gave me a view of the residential street on which I lived, although the enormous oak tree in the parkway blocked the view. The rain had blown through and left a clear, almost perfect autumn night. The window was cracked open about an inch and I could smell cool air and the faint scent of smoke from someone's fireplace. It was past eleven and the streets were quiet save for the hum of traffic from nearby Addison Street.

The time spent with Patrick had taken my mind off J.B. and Gabriel Angeloscuro, but I found my worries nagging at me again almost as soon as he disappeared out of sight on the street.

Beezle had barely spoken to Patrick, which was unusual since Patrick was about the only person in the world Beezle would deign to speak to other than myself. He wouldn't tell me what was bothering him specifically about Gabriel, and I wasn't about to let his vague pronouncements of doom stop me from taking on a badly needed tenant.

I made a note on the pad next to the phone to call Charlie McGivney the next day. He was a P.I. I knew who ran background checks on potential tenants for me at a nominal fee.

The phone rang, making me jump about twenty feet in the air. Beezle shifted restlessly on the mantel, his ears cocked forward.

"Hello?"

Nothing. Only the crackle and hiss that sounded like someone on a cell phone out of range.

"Hello?" I asked again.

". . . ddy?" A fragment of voice came and went so quickly I wasn't sure I'd actually heard it.

"Is someone there?"

Another hiss, and a pop, and then, "Maddy! I need you!"

I frowned at the receiver. "Patrick? What's wrong? The connection is terrible."

". . . ner of Ravenswood and Grace."

"What?"

"I'm at the corner of Ravenswood and Grace, and I'm headed back your way!" He sounded out of breath and completely terrified.

The phone clicked and went dead.

I stared in astonishment at the phone for a moment. Patrick wasn't prone to melodramatic fits. I dialed his cell number back and listened to several rings before his voice mail clicked on. I hung up the phone in frustration, hurriedly pulled a black sweater over my jeans and T-shirt and yanked on a pair of black Converse sneakers.

"Where are you going?" Beezle asked.

"There's something wrong with Patrick," I said as I grabbed my keys and cell phone from the basket by the door.

"I'm coming with you," he announced.

"Why?" I asked, pausing at the open threshold.

Beezle never wanted to go anywhere. Gargoyles are homebodies, preferring to stay near the portal they guarded. Over time, their soft flesh hardened until they were near-permanent fixtures of the building. A gargoyle could get up and fly away if it liked, even after it turned to stone, but most didn't want to, or maybe they just lost the knowledge. Beezle was still pretty active for an old gargoyle, but as a general rule he didn't leave the house unless I was going to Dunkin' Donuts, and only then to make sure that I got enough Boston Creams.

"Can't I just want to get some fresh air?" Beezle asked mysteriously.

"No," I said. "But I don't have time to argue with you. Come on."

I walked back to the mantelpiece and picked Beezle up, resting him on my right shoulder. His claws dug into my sweater and his wings fluttered against my ear as he settled himself in.

Ravenswood and Grace was only a few short blocks from my building. I shivered as I walked, picking up the pace. The temperature had dropped to the low forties, far too cold for a T-shirt and sweater. Beezle's warm, heavy little body snuggled closer to my neck.

My eyes moved all over the street as I walked, looking for Patrick. There was nothing and nobody out. I saw the blue glow of televisions filtering through mini-blinds in several windows, but no one out taking their dog for one last walk or coming home late from a liquid business meeting. Everything seemed unnaturally still.

I turned onto Grace and hurried toward the El. The Brown Line and the Metra commuter train both ran parallel to Ravenswood on this section of their tracks. There was a Metra overpass bridge right at the corner from where Patrick had called. A large warehouse that tenanted an assortment of small businesses took up most of the south side of Grace and a couple of small-frame houses were on the opposite side.

I slowed as I approached the corner. I couldn't see Patrick anywhere. It belatedly occurred to me that it was deeply stupid to walk out into the night and the quiet with nothing to protect me except one overweight gargoyle and a cell phone that may or may not be charged.

"So where is he?" Beezle whispered.

"How should I know?" I tried not to show how disturbed I was. Patrick had said that he was on his way back to my house. We should have run into him already.

I heard a sound, a flutter of movement like flapping wings, and then a wet, sucking noise. I turned toward the sound and saw the faintest of movements below the overpass.

"Don't go in there," Beezle said, gripping my shoulder tighter with his claws.

"Why?" I asked, walking toward the bridge anyway.

"There's something in there," he said. "I can't tell what it is. I can only sense that it isn't natural."

Beezle sounded frightened, not exactly an everyday occurrence. There isn't much that can frighten a gargoyle. I paused, and listened, and in that moment of silence there was a voice so soft that I wouldn't have heard it if I wasn't straining.

"Mad . . . dy . . ."

"Patrick!" I shouted, and plunged into the dark.

3

"NO, DON'T!" BEEZLE CRIED.

But it was too late, because there, crumpled on the ground, was a body. I ran toward it.

"Patrick!" I screamed again. *Don't let it be him. It can't be him.*

Then I noticed the shadow. Just barely silhouetted by the streetlights on the other side of the overpass, something huge and dark crouched over Patrick's limp body. The dark form turned its head toward me. Red eyes gleamed in the darkness. I froze as it sniffed the air.

A deep rumbling began to echo in the quiet. It was a sound that held no joy for the listener, a sound that grated against your spine and the insides of your teeth, that scraped the backs of your eyeballs. It was, I realized with a start, the sound of the creature laughing.

"You," it purred, and its voice was more horrible than

its laugh, a black velvet thing with razors underneath. "I've been waiting for you."

It stood to its full height, well over eight feet, and took a step toward me. I heard claws dragging on the sidewalk while my mind began to gibber. Beezle frantically implored me to move, to run, but I couldn't. Those red eyes held me, just as Gabriel's eyes had, except there was no pull of mystery and romance this time. There was only death.

The thought of Gabriel—a little non sequitur from my brain when I was about to get eaten alive—jolted me out of the monster's burning gaze. It was still several feet away, apparently savoring the kill. I could smell the brimstone of its breath, and something else. Something like burnt cinnamon. And that smell made me pause again. That scent—I remembered it. It had been all over my mother when I had found her, dead in an alley. Only a few blocks from home. Only a few blocks from here.

"Maddy, come on, come on!" Beezle shouted. He was off my shoulder now, wings flapping, claws tugging at my sweater like he was trying to pick me up and carry me away.

"You," I said, addressing the thing before me. I had the slightly hysterical thought that our conversation thus far had been less than scintillating. "I remember you."

It paused. I still couldn't see the features of its face, but I sensed that it smiled. Sweat pooled at the base of my spine.

"Do you, now?"

"Yes," I said. "You killed my mother."

A chuckle. "And a very tasty morsel she was, too."

The sly remark filled me with rage. That was my mother it was talking about. My mother, whom I'd loved more than anyone, had been nothing but a bar snack to this . . . thing.

I felt the familiar burn of magic in my chest, filling up

my throat, pulsing on my tongue. But I couldn't control it; I didn't know what to do with it. I'd never called magic for anything but soul release, and I wasn't sure how I was calling it now. I gasped for air and flung my hands in front of me.

A ball of blue fire hovered above my palms for a split second, then flew where the monster's chest should have been. I still couldn't see much more than a huge black mass. The ball exploded and the monster howled its rage. The combined force of exploding magic and angry monster breath flung me backward through the air. I smashed into the stop sign at the corner and crashed to the ground. The last thing I remembered was knocking my forehead against concrete.

I don't know how long I lay there before I realized that Beezle was tapping my cheek with one little finger, his anxious face very close to my nose. It made me cross-eyed to look at him.

"Maddy?" His voice was low and urgent.

"Ugh," I said.

"Are you okay?"

I took a moment to assess things. My ears rang, my vision blurred and every part of my body ached. It felt like I'd been hit by a train, or possibly an airplane.

"I hurt all over," I whimpered, and then I turned my head to the side so I could vomit.

Beezle tactfully flew a few feet away until I was finished being sick. "Can you stand up?" he asked.

"Working on it," I said, and laid my cheek against the cold sidewalk.

I must have passed out again. I had a vague sense of being lifted very gently. I heard Beezle and another voice fading in and out, although I couldn't understand what they were saying. I wondered who was talking to Beezle. Most people thought he was just a statue, or maybe a stuffed doll. It sounded like they were arguing. The arms that held me gripped me a little tighter. I felt safe and warm, so I let go into the darkness again.

I went further, falling, falling, falling through darkness, back to the beginning. And there was a girl, and her name was Evangeline, and I saw her, and I was also a part of her.

At first Evangeline thought he was something she dreamed. He came to her as she lay under the half-moon in the cool of the midsummer evening. Her mother snored away in the hut and Evangeline, unable to sleep, had felt the stars calling her and gone out to listen to them.

The warmth of the earth cradled her, and the grass stroked her long black braids with loving hands, and the stars told her their secrets in whispers. Her fingers pressed into the earth and she closed her eyes and opened herself to everything.

Then she heard the great leathery flapping of mighty wings. Evangeline opened her eyes to find the dark angel blocking out the sky, and all she could see was his awful beauty, haloed in starshine and moonlight, and his black, burning eyes. He whispered her name, and his voice wound into her ear and down her throat and under her ribs, and she knew what he had come for. She opened her arms to him, and his smile dazzled like the Morningstar and he enfolded her in his great black wings.

Evangeline woke the next morning to the sound of her mother's voice. She was on her own pallet, her hair still braided and not undone by a lover's hands, her shift clean and unstained by the grass and the earth. She sat up as her mother told her to get a move on, there were chores to do, and she wasn't a princess who could laze around all day. So she rose, and felt herself all over as she washed her arms and legs with a washcloth from the bucket. Her body did not feel different, and she thought he must have been a dream, and her chest ached a little at that. But she put on her day dress and walked out barefoot to fetch some wood so her mother could bake bread.

Evangeline's mother had sharp eyes and a sharper tongue and she saw her daughter moving soft-legged and dreamy-eyed, and thought that it was time to go to the bone-counter and have a match made. She knew that when girls got that look you had to take them in hand and tie them to a husband before they got ideas about flowers and handholding, ideas that had them skinning off their shifts with the first sneaky-eyed and sneaky-handed boy that came along.

Evangeline walked behind the hut toward the river to collect the branches that fell from the trees hunched over the bank. As she passed the place where she had dreamed of the dark angel coming to her in the night, she saw that the grass was tamped down, as if someone had lain upon it. Her heart quickened, and she knelt in the grass and ran her fingers across it. As she did she remembered a Morningstar smile, and she saw three drops of blood on three blades of grass. She pressed her hand to her belly, listened, and heard the fluttering of tiny wings deep inside. Evangeline smiled, and stood, and went to the river to collect wood.

All day she smiled a faraway smile, and her sharp-tongued mother said sharp things to her more than once so that Evangeline would pay attention to her chores. Evangeline would start and remember that she was kneading bread, or stitching a blanket, but after a while she would forget again, and smile her faraway smile, and her mother would have to use her tongue as a lash.

And all the while that Evangeline remembered her lover, her mother watched her and thought again that she needed to get to the bone-counter sooner rather than later. So after supper was finished, she told Evangeline to wash the stewpot; she was going to the bone-counter. Evangeline hummed a little noise, and her hand moved forgetfully inside the stewpot, and her mother went to the bone-counter with fear in her heart that her daughter may have been lost to her already.

The bone-counter was a thin brown man with thin white braids and a long thin nose. He sat in front of his hut all day rolling the bones and reading them for the villagers. He knew all of the signs and portents, and whether that year's crop would be good or bad, or if a woman would birth a boy or a girl, or if the wind might shift and bring the sickness from the Forbidden Lands, as it sometimes did, though not very often anymore.

He also knew all of the old stories, how a long time ago there had been great, shining cities of stone and metal, and there had been noise and people crammed together, and all of these people were connected by roads. Then one day the Great Powers had grown angry and destroyed all of the cities. There had been a great burst of flame, and a white cloud of ash in the air, and then another, and another. And afterward many people got sick and many people died for many years to come. Evangeline's mother had seen some of these roads once, when she was young and her family had moved from one village to another. They were cracked and filled with grass and trees, and they had felt strange beneath her feet.

Evangeline's mother went straight to the bone-counter's hut, and did not stop to visit with the other women of the village that she passed, but the women wondered at the look on her face, and began muttering among themselves about the cause. One word passed their lips again and again—"Evangeline." For all of these women were mothers, and knew that mothers looked that way only when their daughters had made them heartsick.

The bone-counter sat cross-legged and stern-mouthed, and when he saw Evangeline's mother coming he knew that the signs he had read that morning were true, though he had prayed otherwise. Evangeline's mother looked up from her worrying hands and saw the bone-counter's sad eyes, and fear took root in her, spreading from her heart and hands to her belly and brain and into her knees, and she fell upon them in the dirt before him.

He told her that he had woken that morning with terror in his mouth, and he had gone to the bones, which had revealed to him a vision of Evangeline enfolded in great dark wings. At this Evangeline's mother felt the fear in her heart burst and bloom and change. She was gripped by anger and shame that her daughter had seen darkness and welcomed it, thereby putting them all in danger.

The bone-counter said, "You know what must be done."

And Evangeline's mother nodded, and stood, and went to find strong men to carry the wood.

In the hut Evangeline dawdled and dreamed and thought of black, burning eyes, and felt the fluttering deep inside, a whisper in her blood. She sighed and put away the stewpot, and as she did she heard his voice in her ear, like a caress, saying, "Come to me. Come to me. Come to me."

She spun in circles, arms outstretched, wanting him again, only him, and cried, "Which way?"

He did not speak again, but she saw in her mind ash-and cloud-covered gray mountains, and a twisted tree with white branches clawing at the sky. Evangeline said, "I'm coming to you," and she pulled the thread from her braids, releasing her black hair, and removed her day dress and shift, and that was how her mother found her, naked and pale and burning as if lit from within by the light of the Morningstar. Her arms were outstretched, and her eyes were closed, and Evangeline's mother felt shame and rage break upon the surface. She closed one hand around Evangeline's wrist and Evangeline opened her eyes, and her mother saw gold fire in green depths, and her doom.

Outside the men stacked the wood on the pyre and the bone-counter said prayers to the Great Powers and the women muttered like magpies and said, "Evangeline," "Evangeline," "Evangeline." They all waited for her mother to bring Evangeline from the hut so they could burn her and purify the land before the crop was tainted. And in their secret hearts they were glad that it was not their daughters who had brought this shameful curse upon the village.

Then there was a scream, and the smell of smoke and scorched flesh, and from the hut Evangeline's mother burst forth, her body covered in silver flames. Evangeline followed, her face all angle and bone, and her eyes burning fiercely in their sockets. Though she was thin, so thin, with tiny bird bones in her wrists and ankles and neck, the women shrank from her blazing eyes, but the men saw her white skin and black hair and wanted her. They rushed to grab her, to take her and keep her, and the bone-counter cried out, but their need pulled them to Evangeline. Where they touched her, their hands were lit by silver flame, and soon the air was filled with black smoke and cries of anguish.

Evangeline walked forward and the crowd parted around her. At the edge of it stood the bone-counter like a strong tree in a battering wind, stony-eyed and grim-jawed. He waved a staff covered in feathers and he spoke words of magic and power to subdue her, but Evangeline did not notice or care. She knew only that she needed to find her lover, and that this man stood in her way.

She closed her eyes, and those around her breathed a sigh of relief, for her eyes were too terrible and beautiful to look upon for long. She raised her arms to the sky and her face turned up to the rising moon, and the villagers were transfixed by her stillness. The bone-counter whispered his magic words and invoked the Powers and waited for Evangeline to be struck down. And in that stillness came the flapping of wings, thousands of wings, and Evangeline opened her eyes and smiled.

The creatures came from the sky on black wings, red-eyed and sharp-clawed, and they screamed horrible cries of joy as they closed upon the villagers. The bone-counter had only a moment to wonder why his power had failed him before his tongue was torn from his mouth and his eyes were pulled from their sockets and his belly was split and spilling.

And Evangeline walked, destruction following in her wake. She did not notice. She did not care. She was looking for someone, and she could not stop walking until he was found.

Smoke curled from her footsteps, and behind her were screams and flames and rent flesh, but they were distant to her, something already past. She looked ahead.

The sun scorched the sand and rocks and Evangeline's bare skin. Her belly rounded and swelled, and her white skin grew brown. She carried a water jug from the *village that burned behind her, but even that was only for the child, for she cared nothing of her own discomfort. She swallowed some water, and her lover's son flapped his wings inside the taut and straining mound of her belly.*

Two thousand miles had passed beneath her feet, and many villages, as she left the green lands and walked into the desert. She walked, searching for her lover, every step bringing her closer to ash- and cloud-covered gray mountains—the Forbidden Lands. Evangeline walked, always hearing his voice in her ear: "Come to me. Come to me. Come to me." She did not care where her steps led her so long as he was there at the end of it all.

And then one day she woke to find his voice no longer in her ear, and she looked over the horizon and saw the jagged fingers of a white tree reaching to the sky. Beneath the tree there was a dark shadow haloed in starshine, and Evangeline no longer felt the sand of the desert beneath her feet as she ran. For three days and three nights she ran, the horizon always just out of reach, until on the fourth day great mountains suddenly loomed before her, and there was the tree, with him beside it.

"I have come to you," she said.

His smile dazzled like the Morningstar, and his great black wings opened, and Evangeline went into his embrace. He closed his arms around her, and his wings beat around them, and the wings in her belly beat in time, and he lifted her up and carried her away, and she lifted her face to the brightness of his kiss.

The next morning I woke in my own bed. I'd had a dream, a vivid dream, about a girl called Evangeline, but the memory of it slipped away as I lay in the hot autumn sunshine pouring through my window. Darkness and blazing eyes mixed in my head with a monster and the smell of burnt cinnamon, and fire pouring from my hands.

Somehow I had survived, and someone had brought me home. That same someone had bathed me, twisted my long black hair into a single braid, put me in a clean nightgown, changed my bedsheets and bandaged the palms of my hands. Since I wasn't close enough to anyone who could have performed such intimate services for me, I was more than a little freaked out.

"Beezle!" I shouted. He flew in through the bedroom door so quickly he must have been hovering in the kitchen just outside.

"Maddy," he said. "How are you feeling?"

"Better," I said, surprised to hear myself say it. I felt . . . rested, more rested than I had felt in a long time. "But how did I get here? Who brought me home?"

Beezle looked surprised. "No one brought you home. You brought yourself home."

"No, I didn't. I remember someone picking me up and carrying me. I could hear you arguing with him."

"With who?"

"Whoever carried me home, Beezle! Why are you acting like you don't remember this?"

"Well," he said slowly. "Maybe because it didn't happen?"

"Who were you talking to, then?"

He looked affronted. "I don't talk to any humans except you. And . . ."

"Don't you think I'd remember coming home, taking a shower, braiding my hair? I never braid my hair."

"You did last night. I mean, you did seem pretty out of it, but you told me that you were okay to walk home."

"You're telling me that I got up and walked home and did all of those things?"

"Yes."

"Why are my hands bandaged?"

"Burns," Beezle said, and he frowned at my palms as if they offended him.

"From what?"

"That ball of fire you conjured up. The burns were there when we got home. You put some cream on them and wrapped them up."

I didn't remember doing any of it, and I was certain I'd heard another voice. My head started to ache as I strained to remember.

"How did you do that, by the way?" Beezle asked, and his voice sounded funny.

"Do what?" I asked.

"Call up nightfire."

I stared at him. "Nightfire? What the hell is that?"

"Funny you should mention hell," Beezle muttered.

"What's that supposed to mean?" I asked.

"Nothing," Beezle said, shaking his head. "Anyway, how did you call it?"

My brain felt a little fuzzy around the edges. "I have no freaking clue. I didn't even know that Agents could call nightfire."

Strangely, Beezle looked relieved by this pronouncement. "So what happened, then?"

"I don't know. That thing was talking about Mom . . . talking about eating her as if she were an hors d'oeuvre. And I just got so angry. All of a sudden I felt all this power build up inside and it hurt me to keep it there, so I let it go. Wait," I said, remembering why I had been below that overpass in the first place. "Wait. What happened to the monster? To Patrick?"

"The monster . . . ran away," Beezle said. There was something about the way he said it that made me think he wasn't telling me the whole truth. But before I could pursue that line of inquiry, he spoke again. "Patrick was dead, Maddy. He was dead before we even got there."

I slumped back onto the pillow and felt tears burn the backs of my eyes. I swiped at my face with an impatient hand. "Did I just leave him? Did I leave his body there?"

"I don't think there was much of his body left."

I closed my eyes in pain. "Very tactful."

"I'm sorry," he growled, and it looked like he meant it. "But you were out of it. You couldn't have helped him even if you'd tried."

"He was my friend, Beezle. Pretty much my only friend. I can't believe I would just walk away from him, no matter how 'out of it' I was. And why was that thing after him in the first place? It doesn't make any sense unless . . ." Realization dawned. "Unless it was after me, and it used Patrick to get me there. Which would mean he died for me, because of me."

Beezle looked at me sternly. "I know what you're thinking, and you just get it out of your head right now. Your mother charged me with your protection and you are *not* going haring off to find Patrick's killer."

"That thing didn't only kill Patrick. It killed my mother. And I've spent a lot of years wondering what happened to her, and why no Agent ever came for her soul."

"How do you know that no Agent came for her?" Beezle asked, watching me carefully.

"I checked the Hall of Records. Every dead soul is

recorded there, and so is their choice. My mother's soul isn't there. No Agent came for her, and if she wandered the Earth, she would have come to me. I know she would have."

Beezle looked at me with something like pity in his eyes.

"Don't lecture me," I said, holding up a warning hand. "You loved her, too. It's the only reason you stayed to watch over me."

He looked away and grumbled something.

"What?"

"I said, Katherine Black was special."

"Yes, she was. And I'm going to find the thing that killed her and Patrick. And when I do, I hope I can call up that nightfire again. Because when I find it, I'm going to make sure it dies screaming."

4

I DRESSED, PULLING ON A PAIR OF FADED BLUE JEANS,
a long-sleeved black T-shirt, and a pair of ankle-high black
leather boots with chunky treads. My wardrobe mostly
consists of jeans, cords, black tops and black shoes. I don't
want to have to think about coordinating anything, so it's
best if all of my clothes are already coordinated when they
come out of the closet. Besides, what color is more appropriate for an Agent of death than black?

I had a soul to pick up at ten forty-three P.M. tomorrow—
James Takahashi at the corner of Clark and Belmont.
Other than that, I had the next couple of days completely
free. Free except for a few niggling little details—like
running a credit and background check on Gabriel Angeloscuro, finishing up the recipes for the article on pears that
I was writing for a magazine that featured low-fat cooking, checking the Hall of Records for the whereabouts of

Patrick's soul, and finding my mother's killer. Just an ordinary day's work.

I contacted Charlie McGivney, the P.I. who'd agreed to handle the background checks for me. I read him Gabriel's information from the apartment application. The application was written in a freakishly neat print, almost like a typewriter. Charlie said he'd get back to me in a day or so. One task down.

I yanked on my black peacoat and called to Beezle, who was doing his broody thing on the mantelpiece again. "I'm going to see J.B."

"What for?" he grumbled.

"So I can find out what happened to Patrick," I said. "I need a pass from him to get into the Hall of Records."

"But you hate J.B., and he hates you, so why should he do you a favor?"

"I don't *hate* him."

"Yes, you do," Beezle insisted.

"No, I don't. I just find him to be a little smug. And condescending. And annoying."

"And your boss."

"That, too," I said as I stepped to the side window and thought about going to the Main Office. As I pictured the building, my wings sprouted from my back.

I wasn't really sure how I would convince J.B. to give me a pass to the Hall. We hadn't exactly ended our conversation on a high note the day before. And in addition to all of my other worries, I was still bothered by the fact that he seemed to have at least one Agent under surveillance. Something else to add to my to-do list.

Lizzie frowned at me when I walked into J.B.'s office. "Do you have an appointment, Maddy?"

"No, but I'm sure that he will relish the opportunity to shout at me for no apparent reason."

"Maddy," she chided. Lizzie was maybe ten years older than me, and she tended to use every one of those years as an excuse to act vaguely maternal. "You shouldn't talk that way about Mr. Bennett. He is your supervisor."

"Okay, okay," I said, holding up my hands in surrender. After all, I wasn't there to give Lizzie a hard time. "Is he in?"

"I'm sure he can see you," she said, and announced my presence over the intercom.

"Send her in," J.B. barked.

I tried to put on my nice face. I needed something from J.B., and I wasn't going to get it from him by giving him an attitude. But then he ruined everything by acting like J.B.

"I noticed that you haven't filed your paperwork for the Luccardi incident yet," he said before I had even finished shutting his office door.

Paperwork, I thought. *I'll take that paperwork and shove it up your . . .*

I took a deep breath to clear my head. No use letting him make me angry.

"Patrick is dead, J.B., and I need a pass to get into the Hall of Records." I hoped that I looked contrite and harmless instead of annoyed and murderous, which was how I generally felt in J.B.'s presence.

"You know you don't have the authorization to go poking around in there. What the hell are you talking about?"

"Patrick? You know, Patrick Walker? My friend, one of the Agents under your supervision? He was murdered by some big scary thing last night at Ravenswood and Grace. I want to find out what choice he made. If he's wandering the Earth, I need to talk to him about the monster that killed him."

He stared at me dumbly. "Are you taking drugs, Black?"

"What?"

"Walker's not dead."

"Yeah, he is. And you should know about this, because an Agent would have gone to collect his soul. And there should have been the activation of the next closest relative in his bloodline."

"But none of that happened, Black. I don't have any paperwork here; ergo, Walker is not dead." He said this with the ringing finality of a true believer at a tent revival.

"J.B.," I said, striving to put a note of patience in my voice when I wanted to shake his complacent self silly, "I saw his body. I saw said big fucking scary thing that killed him. It almost killed me. And I want to know what happened to his soul."

J.B. gaped at me. "Did you have a bad dream last night or something?"

"No!" I shouted, getting frustrated. "It happened, J.B. Just the way I told you. And this monster—whatever it is— it was stalking Patrick. He knew it was coming after him. He called me to ask for help. And . . . J.B., I'm pretty sure that this is the thing that killed my mother."

I'd never seen J.B. look uncertain before. It softened his face, loosened the tension creases around his eyes. "Black, your mother . . . That's . . ."

"Just check, won't you? You can find out in a few minutes if Patrick's dead or not," I pleaded.

He hesitated, but something in my face or voice must have told him that I wouldn't leave until he checked. He picked up the phone on his desk and dialed out.

"Hall of Records," he said. He watched me with a

strange look in his eye. I couldn't decide if he felt sorry for me or he thought I'd lost my marbles. Probably a little of both.

"This is J. B. Bennett, Area Fourteen supervisor. Can you verify the death of one Patrick Walker in Chicago last night?"

I leaned forward in my chair, gripping the seat with my hands. J.B.'s face changed as he listened to the person on the other end of the line. In about three seconds he looked thunderous, an expression I was very familiar with.

"What the hell do you mean he died last night? He was an Agent, for chrissakes! I should have been notified so I could activate a new one! I want to talk to your supervisor, young lady."

"J.B.," I said, flapping my hands to get his attention. "We don't have time for this."

He held up a finger to shush me. "Well, you tell him to contact me as soon as he's done."

He slammed down the phone. "Just what in the hell happened last night? That little ditz in the Hall of Records told me that Patrick's file shows his death but not his choice. I don't know who they're hiring down there these days. Faeries, probably. Flaky little things. Lord knows they're better than the gnomes, but flash something shiny in front of them and they lose all sense of focus . . ."

J.B. continued to rant while I absorbed his words. Patrick's file showed his death but not his choice. My mother's file had shown her death but not her choice. That monster . . . Just what had it done to their souls?

"J.B.," I said. "Focus. We have a big problem here."

"Yes, we do. Someone needs to take those Record Keepers in hand."

"Fuck the records."

He looked astonished, like I had just sworn in church. J.B. loves nothing if not order. Then he recalled that he was supposed to be the boss.

"Listen, Black, your attitude is way out of line . . ."

"I'm trying to tell you about a killer monster and you're worried about my attitude. Why do you always worry about the stuff that doesn't matter?"

"What matters more than the official reprimand that I'm going to write up on you as soon as you leave this office?" he asked, his eyes as cold as ice.

"Patrick's file shows his death but not his choice."

"So? Some idiot in Records didn't enter the information."

"No," I said slowly. I thought of the sound that I'd heard beneath the overpass as the monster stood over Patrick's body. A kind of sucking sound. I thought of the odd records that showed two deaths with no choices. "That thing that I saw last night . . . I think it ate his soul."

"There's no such thing as a soul-eating monster, Madeline," J.B. said with the long-suffering tone of someone speaking to a moron.

"You're an Agent," I said, matching my tone to his. "You know that the world isn't what it seems to be. You've seen vampires and werewolves and faeries and ghosts. You have wings! Why is it so unbelievable that there is a monster out there eating souls?"

"Because there aren't any records of such a creature. Because all those other creatures you mention have had their souls collected by an Agent at death." He had returned to his normal smug look, the one that made me want to punch him in the face.

"What if this creature doesn't have a soul itself, and that's why we have no record of it?" I didn't really know where I was going with this. It sounded crazy and illogical to me, too, but I had seen the monster. I knew it had done something horrible to Patrick, to my mother. Maybe it hadn't sucked out their souls, but it had done *something*, something that had affected the way their deaths were entered in the Hall of Records.

I didn't want to be alone in this. As infuriating as J.B. was, at least he had some authority and resources that I didn't have. He could help me—if he wanted to.

"Look, Black. I know you and Walker were close and that you will miss him terribly. Heck, I'll miss him. Despite his screwup this week, Patrick was an excellent Agent. But," he said, leaning back in his chair and folding his arms behind his head, "whatever the circumstances of his death are, they're none of your business. Your business is to collect souls and file your paperwork. End of discussion."

"You know what, J.B.?" I said, my temper flaring. "You're pathetic. There's a freaking monster out there eating your Agents' souls and all you're worried about is another report. Well, I hope you don't think it or any other piece of paper is going to get you that promotion that you are so desperately seeking. Everyone, including upper management, thinks you're a giant pain in the ass."

J.B.'s face had lost all color by the end of my little monologue. "Get out," he said through gritted teeth.

"Gladly." I stormed out of his office, knocking over a chair as I went. It was immature but doing it made me feel better.

I fumed all the way home. It was absolutely typical J.B. to care more about reports than people. And while he was being a total ass, my chances of getting *anyone* with authority to listen to me were slim to none. Even worse, the likelihood of getting a pass to the Hall of Records was now infinitesimal.

I really wanted a crack at those records. There might be other cases like Patrick's and my mother's, cases of an Agent who died with no records showing his choice. Information like that might give me a clue of how to find this creature.

There was a monster running loose but I had no idea what it was, no idea how it chose its victims and nobody to help me. I was a soul collector and a recipe writer. I'd never conducted an investigation of any kind and I didn't want to fumble around trying to find answers while this thing chewed through the population.

As soon as I flew through the dining room window, Beezle clambered in behind me.

"What is it?" I said. "You look more out of sorts than usual."

"That person was here," Beezle said darkly.

"What person?" I said, going to the answering machine to check for messages.

"Angeloscuro," he spat.

I turned to look at Beezle, my finger hovering over the PLAY button on the machine. "That's quite a lot of venom for a man you barely know."

"I know enough," he said.

Something in his tone made me wary. "What do you know? You told me that there was nothing special about him when he first arrived."

"No, I didn't say that," Beezle said.

"Yes, you did. I asked you if you'd scoped him out for me and you didn't tell me anything."

"I told you he was a handsome devil," Beezle responded, crossing his arms over his chest.

"A fact that I figured out within three seconds of laying eyes on him. So what if he's handsome? You have some objection to a handsome man living downstairs?"

Beezle clamped his jaw shut and closed his eyes.

"Whatever," I said, hitting the PLAY button on the machine. There were two messages, one from Charlie telling me that Gabriel's references had checked out. That was fast. Really fast. I hadn't expected him to get back to me until tomorrow at least.

The second message was from Gabriel, asking if his application had been accepted. Even when tempered by the coldness of a digital machine, the sound of his voice made me shiver.

Beezle's prejudices and my own mixed feelings notwithstanding, I knew I was going to accept Gabriel as a tenant. Frankly, I needed the money and no other potential client had returned with a deposit in all the time the apartment had been advertised. I chalked up my misgivings to nervousness about being attracted to him.

Attraction was not something I had a lot of experience with. I spent so much time alone as an Agent, rarely mixing with non-Agents, and I never dated. The job just wasn't conducive to a normal social life. How do you explain to your date that you have to leave the movie for fifteen minutes as the hero is about to rescue the damsel because you have to pick up a soul that just had a heart attack while driving on Lower Wacker?

I called Charlie back, thanked him and promised to pay his bill as soon as I received it. Then I called Gabriel. He had a cell number listed on his application and he picked up after the first ring.

"Gabriel Angeloscuro."

Damn, his voice was sexy. The wing scars on my back

were tingling and all he'd done was say his name. I felt like a quivering maiden in a romance novel.

"Mr. Angeloscuro, this is Madeline Black. I'm calling about the apartment?"

"Yes, Ms. Black?"

"Your application was accepted, so if you'd like to come by and drop off a deposit and first month's rent, I can give you the keys. You can move in anytime."

"Is today at four P.M. an acceptable time?"

"Yes, that would be fine. See you then." I hung up before he could speak again. Three minutes of conversation with him made me want to run for the shower and turn the water to icy cold.

Beezle glared at me as I placed the phone in the cradle. "I hope you know what you're doing, Maddy."

"Getting some income, that's what I'm doing."

"At what price?" he asked.

"Beezle, if there's something really wrong with Gabriel, then why don't you tell me what it is instead of making these ringing pronouncements of doom?"

He threw his clawed hands up in disgust and flew out the window, presumably to return to his nest over the front porch. I put Beezle's mood swings out of my mind as I contemplated my next move. I needed to get into the Hall of Records. In order to do that, I needed a pass, because my level of clearance didn't give me authorization. In order to get a pass, I needed to kiss J.B.'s ass. Right. Not in this century.

That left less-than-legal means of entry. I was pretty sure that I didn't have an undiscovered talent for breaking and entering. I'm very much on the clumsy side and I didn't know the first thing about lock-picking or avoiding security equipment. What I did know was a very powerful witch who lived in Lincoln Square who could sell me an amazing concealment charm that would help me get in and out of the Hall undetected.

I gave her a quick call and she agreed to have one ready for me the next day at a rather exorbitant price. It was a good thing that Gabriel was coming by with a rent check.

My investigation seemed stalled until I could get into the Hall, and I didn't want to pace the house and think about the creature when I couldn't do anything about it right then. I decided to spend the afternoon working on pear recipes for my article. In order to bring in a little income I work as a freelance food writer and recipe developer, selling articles to different magazines. Agents who work directly for the bureaucracy, like J.B., pull in a regular paycheck, but everyone else is on their own.

My Agent status prohibited me from getting a job that required regular hours. As with dating, a boss probably wouldn't understand if I rushed out in the middle of a departmental meeting. Most Agents find jobs with flexible hours or work from home, the way I do.

For the next few hours I put all thoughts of Gabriel, Beezle and the possibly soul-sucking monster out of mind and lost myself in the kitchen. When I next looked up, the buzzer was ringing insistently and it was four o'clock already.

"Crap." I had meant to quit working a half hour before Gabriel arrived. I wanted to have the new lease printed out and everything ready to go for him.

I yanked off my apron as the doorbell continued to sound and hurried to the stairs instead of buzzing him up. Beezle was nowhere to be seen, which surprised me because I figured he'd be lurking around to glower at Gabriel while the lease was signed.

I pushed open the door at the bottom of the stairs, expecting to see Gabriel standing in the foyer. Instead, J.B. stood just outside the exterior door. He gave a little finger wave when he saw me. I could hear my buzzer still ringing upstairs although he stood outside on the porch and the doorbells were inside.

"Must be broken," I mumbled as I pulled open the exterior door. "What the hell are you doing here?"

"I take that to mean you aren't happy to see me," J.B. said.

"Am I supposed to be?" I asked, crossing my arms and leaning against the doorframe. "Have you come to apologize for being a total jackass today?"

He smiled winningly. "I'm sorry for being a total jackass."

I pushed away from the door and gaped at him. "Are you sick? Maybe take a wee too much cough syrup?"

"No, why?" he said, continuing to beam. His smile was a little disconcerting. He looked like a game show host.

"I've never heard you apologize for anything to anyone. I might need to send out an interdepartmental memo to commemorate the occasion."

He spoke in a low, confidential tone. "Look, Maddy, I really need to talk to you. Can I come in for a little bit?"

I narrowed my eyes at him. Something was wrong here. J.B. never smiled, he never apologized and he never, ever called me Maddy. I shifted my weight, considering him, and that was when I saw Beezle. His little body was crumpled facedown on the porch a few feet behind J.B.

"Beezle!" I cried, and shouldered J.B. aside, kneeling on the peeling wood of the porch. I lifted the gargoyle very gently in my hands and turned him over. There was no visible sign of damage on him but his breathing was very shallow.

"Well, I was trying to get inside, but having you outside is an acceptable substitute," J.B. said behind me, and he kicked me in the side of the face.

5

STARS EXPLODED AS I TUMBLED DOWN THE PORCH stairs and onto the walkway. A metallic taste filled my mouth and I spat blood as I rolled to my back. I could feel more blood dribbling down my chin. I'd lost Beezle during my gymnastics routine and I tried to sit up, groping the ground for him.

"What the fuck?" I said to J.B. as he walked slowly down the stairs toward me. His eyes were alight with madness.

"Oh, little girl, if you knew how long we have been seeking you," he said, and his voice was very, very different from J.B.'s voice.

He didn't look very much like J.B. either. The irises of his eyes had expanded to cover all the white, and changed from J.B.'s bottle green to a fiery orange-red. The pupils slitted, and his teeth . . . Well, suddenly he seemed to have far too many and each one was far too sharp.

He stepped over and kicked me in the face again. I whimpered as my head slammed to the pavement. I wondered listlessly where my neighbors were. It was after four o'clock. Weren't people supposed to be on their way home from work and school? Why was everyone just letting this thing beat the crap out of me in the middle of the street?

The thing-that-was-not-J.B. bent over me, yanked me up by a handful of my sweater and put J.B.'s face close to mine. I could smell brimstone on its breath.

"I will be honored above all others once I bring my master your heart," he said, showing me a strange sigil that was burned into his other hand. The sigil looked like an ampersand with the bottom loop cut off halfway.

All I could muster at that moment was some spit and bravado, so I hocked a mess of blood on his face. "Sorry, bud. Whoever sent you here is going to be disappointed because I'm keeping my heart right where it is."

"Whoever sent me? You mean you do not know the sign of my master, Focalor?"

"Why would I know another freak like you?" I asked, and kneed him in the balls.

He dropped me to the ground and yowled in pain, which accomplished what I had wanted—to be released. Unfortunately, the abrupt landing also made my head explode, so I was unable to take advantage of the opportunity to get away before it grabbed me again.

"Can it be?" he hissed, and his saliva spattered on my face. My skin burned where the moisture touched it. "You do not know your father is the sworn enemy of my master?"

Something of the blankness and confusion I felt must have shown in my eyes because the monster started to laugh. The sound of its laughter made me nauseous.

"You don't know. You don't know who you are. And—"

He took a long sniff, closing his eyes to savor it. Then he opened them again, and his smile widened. "You're a virgin."

"That's private," I muttered, my face coloring. *Unbelievable,* I thought. I was on the verge of having my heart torn out by some bad guy's lackey and I was embarrassed because he knew that I was the last virgin over the age of thirty in the United States. But I was having trouble thinking straight. I knew I should do something. I just didn't know what.

"Oh, your heart will be a pretty prize indeed," he said, and he pulled back his arm. His fingernails lengthened until they looked like the sharp, curved claws of a tiger, but they were as black as obsidian.

So this was it. My heart would be torn out by those claws in a second. I was going to die. And Beezle . . . What would happen to Beezle?

"Mom," I whispered.

"Your mommy isn't going to come for you, little girl," he said, and he plunged his hand toward my chest.

An instant before he touched me, a blast of blue flame came out of nowhere and hit the monster in J.B.'s face. The last vestiges of the glamour fell away just before his body went up in flames with the frightening rapidity of a nuclear blast. I saw a seven-foot demon, red-skinned and bat-winged, looking like a Doré engraving from *Paradise Lost.* He howled in rage one moment, and the next instant, he was gone. Nothing remained except a scorch mark on the walkway.

I lay there for a few moments, wondering what had just happened, who had rescued me and how on earth I was going to get back up the stairs when I felt like I'd been boxing with a rhinoceros.

As I looked up in the sky and contemplated these things, I finally noticed that a thick black fog had surrounded my property. It was as if the house had been encased in an opaque bubble. Now that the creature was gone, the fog slowly dissipated. At least that explained what I had perceived as lack of caring on the part of my neighbors. They hadn't been able to see the big nasty kicking the crap out of me.

"Beezle," I said, and sat up abruptly. That was a bad idea. I didn't just see stars. I saw galaxies, and the galaxies spun and whirled in a way that made vomiting the only plausible option. I breathed slowly in and out through my nose until the queasiness passed, then pushed up from the ground using my hands until I was in a squatting position. I wasn't sure if I could get all the way up to standing.

A host of new aches and pains screamed and shouted for attention. My ribs felt bruised; my face was swollen; my skin still burned where the demon's saliva had touched it. I ignored all these things and focused my blurry eyes so I could find Beezle.

I squinted until I could see more or less clearly. I spotted Beezle, lying on his belly in the middle of the front lawn. I crab-walked to him very slowly and picked him up, turning him over and cradling him in my hands.

"Beezle," I whispered. "Beezle, please be all right."

He made no noise or movement except for the shallow little puff as his chest moved up and down. At least he was still breathing. But what was I supposed to do for him? Beezle had never been sick or injured, and I didn't know anyone else who had a gargoyle.

I carefully rose to my feet and limped to the porch with agonizing slowness. Grasping the railing, I pulled myself up the porch stairs and stumbled through the front door into the foyer. The downstairs door stood open, the way I had left it when I'd hurried down expecting Gabriel. I frowned and glanced at my watch. It was half past four, well beyond the time I'd expected him. Maybe the creature's spell had somehow kept him away from the house.

"And why are you worrying about that now?" I muttered, hauling myself up the stairs with one hand on the railing and one hand cradling Beezle. When I cleared the last stair my breath was coming hard and my ribs were on fire. I pushed my front door open, light-headed, and sank to my knees.

"Can I help you?" a voice murmured behind me.

I was pretty out of it, and Gabriel's voice made me jump about three feet in the air—from my knees, no less. I did a kind of jerky half turn and fell to my left side, landing on my elbow so I wouldn't squash Beezle while keeping him out of Gabriel's sight. The impact reverberated through every hurt muscle and bone in my body, and I gritted my teeth as I glared up at him.

"Knock much?" I said.

"The door was open," he said, gesturing down the stairs. He stood in the doorway, looking just as cool and dark and beautiful as he had the day before. He wore the same expensive coat and shoes, and the slightest of creases appeared between his eyebrows as he frowned down at me. "May I ask what happened to you?"

Oh, a giant freaking demon was just here trying to take my heart and bring it back to his master. No big, I thought. I shifted a little so that I rested on my forearms, legs stretched out behind me, and looked up at him. I really wanted to stand up because I felt it would be better for my dignity, but Pain and Weariness were ganging up on Dignity, and it decided to retreat in self-preservation.

"I had a little accident," I said.

"I see that," Gabriel replied. He looked at me expectantly, and when it became clear that was all the information he was going to get, he said, "I have the rent check."

"Right. The rent check. Can you give me a second?" I asked.

"I will wait in the foyer." He turned so quickly and moved so silently down the stairs it was almost as if I'd imagined him.

"Okeydokey," I said. "That was awkward."

Beezle hadn't moved through all of this. His breath still came steady but shallow. I had no idea what the creature had done to him or how to fix him. I needed to get rid of Gabriel quickly so I could figure out how to help Beezle.

I heaved to my feet, trying not to cry out as all my aches and pains flared anew. I staggered into my bedroom and laid Beezle gently on my pillow, covering him up with a bit of my flannel blanket. Then I went into the bathroom to wash my face. I felt grimy.

I glanced in the mirror to check the damage, and my mouth dropped open. Both of my eyes were puffy and purple. Dried blood and dirt encrusted my chin and my right cheek. My left cheek was bruised where the demon had kicked me. The demon's saliva had left a spattering of burn marks all over my face, each one no bigger than the size of a small pebble. I lifted my shirt and found my torso covered in black-and-blue marks.

Gabriel had certainly handled my appearance with composure. If our situations had been reversed, I would have called 911 instantaneously. I looked and felt like I needed professional medical attention.

"He is very, very cute, but very weird," I said as I attempted to wash my face gently with a washcloth. I could do nothing about the bruises or the burns right now but I could at least present myself with a blood-free visage.

And then I slowed, the cloth dropping from my hand into the sink. Why was I worried about how I looked? What the hell was it about Gabriel Angeloscuro that seemed to distract me? Why was he blithely accepting my explanation of my injuries? And just what did a guy who dressed like a broker want with me and my crumbling two-flat?

Something about that thought seemed to clear my head, almost as if fog was literally being blown away in my brain. In its place came rushing all the doubts and questions that I had dismissed. Gabriel clearly had money, but he wanted to rent here instead of buy somewhere nicer. Was he a drug dealer? On the lam from the government?

He'd asked a lot of personal questions during the tour of the apartment and I let them pass without my usual attitude. Why? If J.B. had been half as intimate, I would have bitten his head off, partially masticated it and then handed it back to his flailing body.

And what was up with Beezle? Why did he dislike Gabriel so thoroughly? Why was he so damn mysterious when I asked him about Gabriel? It was almost as if . . . as if . . .

My thoughts strained for the answer. The sensation was painful, physically painful. There was a snap in my head and I blinked, and when I looked in the mirror a little blood leaked out of my right eye, like a ghastly tear. But I remembered what I hadn't remembered before, the sound of Gabriel's voice in my head when I fell into his eyes, his voice telling me that he meant no harm, and to accept him, and not to ask questions.

And Beezle—he must have bespelled Beezle to keep him from telling me the truth about Gabriel. That was why

Beezle had been so mysterious. He would never have willingly concealed the truth about anyone from me.

I felt rage rise up in me, rage like I had never felt before, and it scorched the air around me. He had violated me, crawled inside my head and made me compliant. Underneath the rage there was a sick, scared feeling, but I pushed it away. My hands crackled as electricity jumped from finger to finger.

I turned, ready to rush out of the apartment and down the stairs, ready to hurt Gabriel as terribly as he had hurt me. But he was already there, in the doorway of the bathroom, looking calm and knowing. Before I could direct a blazing bolt of magic at him, he put his hands on my wrists.

"Don't do something we'll both regret," he murmured.

"What?" I said through gritted teeth. "Like bore a little hole in your brain, like you did to me?"

"I did not expect you to remember so soon. Truthfully, you should not have remembered at all. Your mind is very strong."

His face was very close and I was careful not to look directly into his eyes. I did not want to fall into starshine again and have my will sucked out of me. The pressure on my wrists was firm, but he wasn't hurting me. I struggled even though it was clear he could hold me there all day without sweating.

"Didn't expect me to remember that you violated me?" I spat.

The little crease between his brows appeared again. "I did not mean to violate you. I simply wanted you to . . . accept me."

"You put a geas on Beezle so that he wouldn't tell me what you were." My breath came hard and fast. It hurt to breathe like that, with my ribs bruised from the fight with the demon and all that anger and magic crackling inside me. My skin felt tight and hot. I didn't know how Gabriel could stand so close to me. The magic surged beneath my skin like a live thing.

He moved closer, to gain a better grip on my struggling, and suddenly the bathroom seemed far too small. My nostrils filled with the scent of apple and cloves. "Yes, I put a geas on the gargoyle."

"That's faerie magic," I accused.

"I am no faerie."

"Well, what are you, then? And what do you want with me?"

"Your father sent me," Gabriel said, and the world tilted.

All the magic inside me deflated in a rush, leaving me sick and dizzy, like a hangover. My knees buckled and Gabriel grabbed me by the shoulders before I fell down and cracked my head on the bathtub.

"My father," I said. "That's the second time today that someone has mentioned my father. A man I've never seen or heard about until today. I thought he was a deadbeat, or maybe just dead. My mother never mentioned his name."

"I believe," Gabriel said, "that Katherine Black was attempting to protect you until you were old enough to understand."

"Understand what?" I asked. I didn't want to hear the answer. Everything was changing, too fast. But I also needed to know, and I would not allow Gabriel or anyone else to keep it from me. This was not the time to be a scared child, and the magic that had surged inside of me flickered in acknowledgment.

Gabriel shook his head. "It is too soon. You do not trust me. I have failed him."

"Understand what?" I asked again, and this time there

was no mistaking the command in my voice. Gabriel looked up, surprised. He searched my face, and I met his eyes without fear. I saw a star shooting across the deep canvas of black, but I did not fall in. He would not be able to take me that way again.

"You are truly his daughter. It is there in your eyes," he said, and he turned me gently to face the mirror again, holding me there with his hands on my shoulders.

But he didn't need to hold me. Shock rooted me in place as I saw the same field of stars in my own eyes that I had seen in Gabriel's.

"It's a trick, a glamour," I whispered, and I reached toward the mirror to touch my own reflection.

"It is your destiny, revealed to you at last," he said, and his hands fell away from me as I trembled and turned to him.

"Who am I?" My voice sounded childish, afraid.

"You are the only human child of a cherubim of the first sphere, a chief of the Grigori, Lord Azazel."

6

GABRIEL SAID THIS AS IF HE EXPECTED ME TO KNOW what it meant.

"A cherubim . . . An angel?" I asked. I thought of those fat little angels on greeting cards holding red bows.

Gabriel smiled, the slightest upward quirk of his lips. "Azazel was once an angel. But his fall came long ago."

"A fallen angel," I said. I knew I sounded like an idiot, but the revelation was a lot to process. Thoughts bounced around my head at random. Patrick was dead. I had a monster to catch and a concealment charm to pick up. Beezle was sick, maybe dying. And my father was a fallen angel. Plus, James Takahashi's soul was going to be departing its body around ten forty-five P.M. tomorrow. In all of the commotion, it was easy to forget that I actually had a job to do.

"Yes."

"And you're here because . . . ?"

"Your father sent me to protect you until he can call you home."

"And home would be . . . ?"

"In Morningstar's kingdom."

"Morningstar, right," I said faintly. I had a vague memory from a *Sandman* comic that I'd read once. My mother had never been big on religious education. "Morningstar is Lucifer?"

Gabriel nodded.

"So his kingdom is Hell?"

"I suppose that is a name that mortals give it. Although mortal descriptions are generally inaccurate."

"Oh, really?" I raised my eyebrows at him. "There was a guy here earlier—he kicked the shit out of me, by the way—and he looked awfully like a 'mortal's description' of a demon. Horns and claws and everything."

"I said mortal descriptions are *generally* inaccurate," Gabriel murmured.

"I really need a drink of something. Something that has alcohol in it." I pushed past Gabriel and into the hallway, striding toward the kitchen with my thoughts chasing one another around my brain.

It was hard to come around to the idea that my father, whom I'd always considered your usual deadbeat, had missed my childhood because he was busy doing . . . whatever it is that fallen angels do. Tempt people, maybe? Was my dad hanging on street corners and in bars, holding out an apple to unsuspecting humans?

I stood in the middle of the kitchen, staring blankly at my refrigerator.

"This is why I wanted you to accept me before you learned the truth. Your father said you would react like this," Gabriel said from the doorway.

I looked up at him and blinked. "I don't have any wine, or tequila, or anything else with alcohol in it."

Gabriel sighed, muttered under his breath, did a funny little finger wave and suddenly there was a bottle of red wine uncorked on the counter. He had even put a glass next to it.

I looked at him, then picked up the bottle. "Elysian Fields cabernet sauvignon?"

He sketched a little bow.

"Thanks for the magical bottle of underworld juice, but I have chocolate somewhere, and it will do in a pinch." I started rummaging in the cabinet above the sink.

He frowned. "You do not want the wine?"

"I've read enough faerie tales to know that only the deeply stupid take food or drink from supernatural beings," I said, pushing aside a couple of bags of granola and cursing. Where had I put that damned candy?

"I told you I am not a faerie," Gabriel said, and he sounded a little affronted.

"Yeah, but you didn't bother telling me exactly *what* you are, did you?" I said, and my voice rose. "Dammit, Beezle, did you eat that chocolate again? I told you, that's for emergencies only . . ."

My voice trailed off as I remembered what had happened to Beezle.

"Can you fix him?" I demanded.

"Fix . . . ?" Gabriel asked.

"Beezle. My gargoyle. The big, horned sweetheart who made mincemeat of my face hurt him, and I can't tell how."

Gabriel looked uneasy. "Show me."

I led him into the bedroom. A couple of hours ago, the mere thought of Gabriel's presence in my bedroom would have sent me into raptures, but now I could see him only as a Beezle-savior.

Gabriel leaned over Beezle, who was still and quiet on my pillow. The gargoyle had never looked so small to me, or so frail. I ached for his eyes to open so he could give me his best basilisk glare, or to hear him complaining about the sparrows nesting in his perch. I wrapped my arms around myself and watched as Gabriel laid two gentle fingers on Beezle's chest, then lifted the gargoyle's eyelids.

Gabriel murmured something that sounded vaguely like Latin. A little ball of blue flame appeared in the palm of his hand. The room suddenly smelled like a freshly baked apple pie. He turned his palm over and placed his hand on Beezle's chest. The flame slid smoothly under Beezle's gray skin and for a moment, nothing seemed to happen.

"Well?" I asked impatiently.

"Wait," Gabriel said. His voice was calm but his eyes looked worried.

Beezle arched his back and took a great gasping breath. His eyes flew open and he coughed so hard that it seemed his chest would break open from the force of it.

"Beezle!" I shouted and took a step toward him, but Gabriel held his arm up to restrain me.

"Wait," he repeated, and when I started to jostle past him, he grabbed both of my arms and held me in place.

Beezle coughed and coughed, a terrible choking sound, and his eyes rolled in his head. Then a great cloud of black smoke spewed out of his mouth, a malignant thing that seemed to have glowing red eyes in its depths. For a moment it hovered above him.

Then it seemed to sense the presence of other people in the room. The cloud turned, spotted me and gave a sickening howl. It rushed toward me with the unerring precision of a bloodhound and the speed of a laser beam.

Gabriel shouted, "No!"

Beezle cried out, "Maddy!"

I thought, *He's all right.* Then the cloud flew into my nose and my mouth and my ears and my eyes and it burned its way into my body. For the second time in two days I felt myself falling, and falling, and the darkness hurried to me, and in the darkness she was there again.

Evangeline woke in darkness, and knew something was wrong. She did not feel the Morningstar's presence beside her, where he had always been since the day she had come to him. Her hands went to her belly, now as big as the mountains that loomed above the Valley of Sorrows, and she felt the comforting flutter of wings. Her children—for she now knew there were two—were still safe inside her.

But they would not be for long. The day of her lying-in was coming soon, and something was wrong. She was in darkness, and beneath her she felt the shift of dirt and damp, and heard the scuttling of small things. How she had come here she did not know. She was suddenly gripped by fear, for she knew that her love would not have released her willingly, and she had a brief vision of his glorious strength struck down.

She shook the vision from her eyes. In her heart she would know if Lucifer was dead, and her heart told her that he still lived. But her heart did not tell her how she had come to this strange place, or why.

Evangeline remembered going to her bedroom in the palace to rest, and Lucifer had followed her as he always did, so that he could love her before she slept. And afterward she had slept while he held her in his arms.

And then she had awoken in this place, and there was no memory of what came between.

There was a scraping and a scratching from above, and a sound of something heavy being lifted, and the grunts and gasps of he who lifted it. She pushed heavily to her feet, her mountain of a belly before her, wanting to do credit to the Morningstar and hold her head high. But a blazing shaft of light appeared when the trapdoor was pulled away, and she covered her eyes with her arm.

"She has awoken!" a voice called, a male voice, nearly as beautiful as her love's, and she thought this must be another of the fallen.

Hands reached down and roughly grasped her beneath her shoulders and pulled her through the door, and she had no time to make herself dignified, for those hands covered her eyes with a strip of cloth, and she was pushed forward and told to walk.

She did not want to cry, or to show fear, but she trembled deep inside, and her children felt her tremble and they tumbled about inside her, fluttering their wings.

All around her was the murmur of beautiful voices, like the pealing of silver bells, and then there was one voice that rose above them all, a voice even lovelier than the others, a voice that spoke of the Morningstar's destruction, and Evangeline as the agent of that destruction. They would murder her love and her children for their own power, for their own pettiness. They would keep her alive long enough to birth the children and then they would be sacrificed. Evangeline felt her heart falling away, the blood draining from her face, and the darkness rising up to meet her once again.

And then I was flying up, and up, and up, and my eyes flew open, and Gabriel's mouth was on mine, but he wasn't kissing me; he was saving me. He sucked the great black cloud into his own body, and as he did I saw his face contort in pain. I felt the last of the cloud clinging to the inside of my throat but Gabriel pulled air until those tiny wisps emerged, and then he fumbled in his pocket for something. I saw him take out a small, carved wooden box and then exhale the cloud into it. I could hear the thing inside the cloud screaming in fury as Gabriel closed the lid.

He looked exhausted. His dark eyes shone in the whiteness of his face and he inhaled and exhaled deeply, like he had just finished a hard run. He cradled me in his arms, and our faces were very close together.

"Maddy?" Beezle said, and I realized that the gargoyle sat on my legs.

"What a really weird family we are," I said without thinking, but before I could be embarrassed about it, Gabriel laughed, and Beezle crawled up from my lap to wrap his little arms around my neck, and I decided that instead of being embarrassed I would just be grateful.

"Thank you," I said to Gabriel.

He nodded, the ghost of a smile still on his face. "Of course. I was not sure what Antares had done to the gargoyle until I saw the curse emerge, but I am glad that I was able to reverse it."

"'The gargoyle'!" Beezle said crossly. "I have a name, devil."

"Antares?" I said. "Is that the guy who was here earlier?"

"Yes," Gabriel said. "He is your half brother, but he despises your father and he has sworn allegiance to Focalor, one of Lord Azazel's enemies."

"Uh, excuse me?" Beezle said, releasing my neck long enough to wave his clawed hands in Gabriel's face. "I thought you put that geas on me so I wouldn't tell her all this crap. I thought that she was 'not ready for the knowledge.' Now you're just going to spill everything without preparing her?"

"She has broken the spell on her mind. There is no point in continuing the pretense now," Gabriel said. "She already knows about Azazel."

"She already knows . . . I thought we agreed that I would be the one who told her?"

"I did not make any such agreement," Gabriel said serenely.

"You know that you implied it, you . . ." Beezle began.

"Hey," I said, snapping my fingers in Beezle's face. I didn't know what bothered me more—the fact that I had a demonic sibling or that my companions were talking about me like I was an infant. "Sitting right here. Not that the idea that I have a fallen angel for a dad and a really ugly half brother isn't shocking as hell. I mean, I would have probably enjoyed a little bit of prologue to that information. And that reminds me, Beezle—just what did you do with the emergency chocolate?"

Beezle looked abashed, but before I could berate him for eating all the candy, Gabriel asked, "What happened to you when the nuvem entered you?"

"The nuvem?" I asked, avoiding his question. I didn't know why, but I wanted to keep Evangeline to myself for the moment.

"It is a kind of demon that is also a curse. It was meant to bind the gar . . . Beezle," he amended. "It would have accelerated his progression to stone and then bound his powers so he could no longer protect this building. To you it would have seemed like he was dead."

"Why didn't Antares just kill him, then? Not that I want

anything to happen to you, Beezle," I said, cuddling him close to my cheek.

"Gargoyles can't be killed," they both said together, and Beezle glared at Gabriel.

"Why is that?"

"Because a gargoyle is a protector. It is bound by its magical gifts to protect its domicile eternally. A gargoyle may sleep, sometimes for many centuries, but its powers will always be present and aware of any threats. By binding Beezle's powers, the nuvem was coming as close to killing him as it could," Gabriel said.

"Why is all of this happening now? Why are monsters and demonic half brothers coming out of the woodwork just when you show up?" I said.

"An excellent question," Beezle said, giving Gabriel a smug look. "It's almost as if you led them here."

Gabriel narrowed his eyes at Beezle. "You know full well, gargoyle, that I was sent here by Lord Azazel to protect Madeline. Perhaps he read the signs and knew that danger was imminent."

"Or perhaps he manipulated it that way so that she would come running to him," Beezle muttered.

"And why would he want that?" I asked, and tried not to let that long-ago hurt show. "He never wanted me before."

"To Lord Azazel you are valued above all things," Gabriel said.

"He has a funny way of showing it," I said.

"There are many things you do not know about your father," Gabriel said.

"Why don't you enlighten me?" I said. "I'd like to know something about this . . . angel that gave me half his genetic material and then took off for parts unknown."

"You should not speak of Lord Azazel in this manner," Gabriel said, and his eyes were icy cold.

"Why not? To me he's just another deadbeat dad," I snapped back. It infuriated me that this stranger should know more of my father than I did.

"Not unlike your own father," Beezle murmured maliciously to Gabriel.

"What about his father?" I asked. Underneath my curiosity about my father was an interest in Gabriel, who had demonstrated some powerful magic but carefully avoided all questions about his origins.

"My lineage is not at issue here," Gabriel said firmly, and something passed between him and Beezle.

"What do you know, Beezle?" I said, frustrated beyond belief. I stood and paced across the room, away from Gabriel. He stood up and leaned against the countertop, his expression relaxed but his eyes tense. "Why won't you tell me? I am sick of being in the dark."

The gargoyle's expression closed suddenly, as if he realized that his dislike of Gabriel had led him to say too much. Gabriel glared at Beezle, his lips white and furious. I looked between them, both of them closed-mouthed and tight-faced, and pretending that I wasn't there and hadn't heard a thing.

The fury that roared up inside me was so sudden I gasped. Just as had happened before, I felt magic crackle inside me, and when I spoke, there was a power in my voice that made them both turn and look at me with wary eyes.

"I . . . am . . . tired," I said carefully, so they would understand. I could feel the magic jumping inside me, wanting to break free, to burn. "I am tired of being afraid and unsure, of having my mind and will taken from me."

Gabriel had the grace to look slightly abashed, although

he said nothing and still watched me with caution in his eyes.

"I am tired of having my ass kicked by all the freaky monsters coming out of the woodwork. But most of all, I am tired of being treated like a child. You both have information that I need, information that I need to survive. You both know more about the magic inside me than I do. You both insist on keeping things from me as if I have no right to know. I do have a right to know. You will not keep me ignorant anymore," I said, and the command in my voice was apparent even to me. Electricity crackled in my fingertips. "You will tell me what I want to know. Everything."

Gabriel still said nothing. He stood preternaturally still, as if he feared one small movement would set me off. Beezle fluttered near me, his grindstone voice trying to soothe. "Maddy, you don't know what you're asking . . ."

"*Do not* treat me like a child," I thundered, and the house actually shook. Glasses in the cabinet knocked together and I heard a few of them shatter. The magic inside me felt like a living thing, harsh and wild, and it wanted to come out. It wanted to burn, and it didn't care who was in the way. A tiny part of me was frightened, frightened of the power inside me, and I wondered if I could control it. My skin felt stretched, barely able to contain what was inside me.

"Maddy," Gabriel said, and his voice was so soft, so gentle. The voice of an angel. "Don't."

He hadn't moved a centimeter. His hands were open at his sides, no threat to me.

"Don't," he said again, and the magic inside me stuttered and pulled back for a moment, confused. "You will hurt yourself. You will hurt Beezle. You would never be able to live with yourself if that happened."

Beezle. The small part of me that was afraid remembered Beezle, not as an obstacle to information but as my friend. My only friend. My family. I didn't want to hurt him, and the magic keened a little at that. It wanted to hurt. It wanted to burn.

"Beezle," I said, breathing unevenly. The magic was held at bay, for the moment, but I could feel it straining and snapping like a dog on a leash. "Tell me who he is."

7

GABRIEL LOOKED AT BEEZLE. I LOOKED FROM FACE TO face, and something passed between them. Gabriel still looked angry, and also vulnerable, and Beezle looked disappointed and tired. But there was resignation there, too, in both their faces. I had won. The magic dwindled inside me, down to a candle flicker, and waited.

"I have to go back a little," Beezle said, apologetically.

"I don't care how far you have to go back," I said. "As long as when you're done I know everything."

"Be careful what you ask for," Gabriel said, and his voice was silky and dangerous again. "It may not be knowledge that you want."

"I may not want it," I shot back, "but I have to have it. Like I said, I'm tired of getting beat up by things I don't know and don't understand."

A gamut of emotions ran through his eyes, too fast for

me to read, and ended with something that looked like regret. I didn't know if he regretted not protecting me better, not telling me sooner, or that I was about to discover things he'd rather keep hidden. Probably it was a little of all three. But I did know that I couldn't afford to feel badly about it. Whatever Beezle was about to tell me could save my life the next time that creature came hunting for me.

"Long ago," Beezle intoned, and he sounded so stiff that I giggled. He glared at me and I pressed my lips into an appropriate imitation of solemnity.

"Long ago," Beezle repeated, "before the Fall, a group of angels were sent to Earth to watch over humanity, and they were known as the Grigori."

"Grigori," I muttered, trying to remember. I looked at Gabriel. "Didn't you say something about my father and the Grigori?"

He nodded his head, keeping his eyes on me the whole time. "Lord Azazel is chief of the Grigori, and Lord Lucifer's right hand."

"Ahem," Beezle said. "Do you want to hear this or not?"

I mimed zipping my lips together and indicated that he should continue.

"Azazel is a Grigori, and so is Lucifer, and Focalor," Beezle said. "Soon after they came to Earth, the Grigori became enchanted by the beauty of human women and began to lust after them. They lured the women to them by teaching humans forbidden things, such as the making of weapons of war, and the signs of the sun and the moon, and the resolving of enchantments. The Grigori took these women as their wives, and soon the women bore children, a race of giants called nephilim.

"The nephilim were true monsters. Each one killed its mother as it was born by clawing through her womb. Not one of them had the angels' beauty. Each grew to more than eight feet tall, with clawed feet and fingers and great razor teeth. Each had some magic passed to it from its father, but the magic was always tainted and twisted inside it."

"Tainted and twisted, how?" I asked.

"Well," Beezle said, and he looked at me very steadily now, gauging my reaction. "Lucifer, for example. He was one of the angels of death, who retrieved souls from Earth for entry to Heaven."

Something was nagging at me, but I was distracted by Beezle's last statement. I felt a little like a magpie, chasing after the next shiny object. "Hold on a second. Heaven? Like the pearly gates and Saint Peter and all that jazz? Are you telling me there really is a Heaven? It's not a just a story that we tell the dead to get them to come with us?"

"Well," Beezle said. "There is something like what you would consider Heaven. There are also other choices. Isn't that what you do when you retrieve souls? You bring them to the Door so that they can make a choice?"

"Yeah, but I never thought there was an honest-to-goodness biblical-type paradise behind the Door."

"I don't think this is the time to debate theology," Gabriel said. "I believe you were about to tell Madeline of Ramuell?"

"I thought you didn't want me to know anything of this at all," I snapped, annoyed at his insistence that Beezle stay on track. "Who died and made you the hall monitor?"

I felt like I was on to something that no other Agent had known before. The moment of blindness when the Door opened was a deep-rooted source of frustration for many Agents, especially at the beginning of their careers. To have so much power over a soul at death and then to be unable to see where they go . . . The thought of solving the mystery was tantalizing.

"The de— Gabriel is right," Beezle said hastily. "This is not the time for this discussion."

"And when is the time, Beezle?" I said, angry again. The magic inside me surged up, as if it had only been waiting for my call. "What will it take for you to tell me everything I need to know? Does that monster need to kill me first?"

"The mysteries of the Door are not for humans to know," Gabriel said, and I could see the stars flaming in the darkness of his eyes.

"Well, I'm not entirely human, am I?" I shot back.

"You are part human, and that is enough," Gabriel said, with a ringing note of finality in his voice. "This information will not protect you from the creature, nor will it help you defeat him."

The magic inside me sang out, and I wanted to fight. But I reluctantly conceded that Gabriel was probably right. He and Beezle certainly knew more about the monster than I did, and I would have to settle for getting the information that I needed right now. My magic slunk down again, disappointed.

These surges of power made me nervous. They frightened me, and I wasn't certain I could control them. Something else to discuss with Gabriel and Beezle—*after* I had the answers I needed.

Beezle read concession in my face and went on. "Well, anyway, Lucifer. He was one of the angels of death who retrieved souls. But his magic, when rooted in the monstrous form of his nephilim child, was twisted. Lucifer's son, Ramuell, does not retrieve the soul after death. He sucks it from the living body of a human being, and the soul never moves on, but lives forever, imprisoned in Ramuell's body."

As Beezle spoke, the gears in my head turned and

everything clicked into place. "Ramuell is the creature that killed my mother and Patrick."

"Yes," Beezle said, watching me steadily.

"My mother's *soul* is trapped inside that thing for all eternity."

"Yes."

"And what if I kill him?" I said through gritted teeth, and the magic zipped through my blood, alight with lust at the thought of death. "Will I free my mother? Will I free Patrick and any other soul trapped inside him?"

"We don't know," Gabriel said quietly. "No one has ever killed a nephilim before."

"Why the hell not?" I shouted. "Obviously they're monsters, and you and Beezle and probably every angel and demon in the world knows about them. So why hasn't anyone gone nuclear on them and rid the world of their presence once and for all?"

"The Grigori saw the nephilim and knew they were monsters," Gabriel said. "But they were also the Grigori's children. The children of nightmares, yes, but their children nonetheless. The Grigori had never had children before—no angel had. They could not bear the thought of killing their own offspring. So they bound the nephilim in the Valley of Sorrows for all eternity."

"Well, obviously their *binding* didn't take. What the hell is Ramuell doing rampaging around Chicago? How did he break free?"

"We are not entirely sure," Gabriel said, frowning. "If he had simply broken free—an unlikely event, as all of the Grigori poured their power into the binding of the nephilim—then he would simply kill and destroy until he was captured again. I do not believe that Ramuell is 'rampaging,' as you put it. These attacks appear to be controlled in some way. Lord Azazel has long suspected that someone, an enemy of Lucifer's, is controlling Ramuell and using him for their own purpose."

"What *purpose*," I said, and I could taste the magic on my tongue, hungry and eager, "would it serve to kill Katherine Black? How would she be a threat to Lucifer?"

"We don't know," Gabriel said again. "But Lord Azazel believes that your mother's connection to him was one reason she was targeted."

I felt a little hysterical. "So because my mother made the mistake of falling in love with my father, she was murdered and her soul is trapped forever inside this nephilim, which no one knows how to destroy?"

Beezle nodded, and I had never seen his face as heartbroken as it was now. "As Katherine died, she performed a binding to protect you from Ramuell, using her own life force as a sacrifice. She suspected that Ramuell would come for you sooner or later. There is a circle of protection approximately one-quarter mile around this building. It does not protect you from all threats, but it will keep you safe from Ramuell. He cannot enter the circle. That is why he had to lure you out the other night, using Patrick to draw you to him."

I felt sick. My mother had sacrificed herself for me, kept me safe long after she was gone. But there wasn't time to dwell on that now. There was something else bothering me; the first question that I had asked hadn't been answered yet.

"So tell me," I said, and I was proud of the control in my voice, "just what are you, Gabriel? Why did my father think that you were the only one who could protect me from Ramuell?"

Beezle looked at Gabriel, whose jaw was clenched. There were meteors exploding in Gabriel's eyes.

"It is your secret to tell," Beezle said, and he bowed his head.

"And it is not the time to tell it," Gabriel said. He held up a hand to stop the protest on my lips. "It will not help you find Ramuell."

"But it will help me know if you are to be trusted," I said.

"You will have to trust that Lord Azazel knew what he was about when he sent me, and that the gargoyle would not allow me here if he thought you would come to harm."

I looked at Beezle, who shrugged and said, "I don't have to like him, but what the devil says is true."

I didn't trust my father, and I wasn't sure that I entirely trusted Gabriel, but I knew that Beezle would never put me in harm's way. If Gabriel was really a threat to me, Beezle would never have let him walk through the front door in the first place, geas or no.

"You will tell me," I said to Gabriel.

He nodded. "When the time is right."

I didn't like the sound of that, but I figured I had been given more than enough information to go on for now. At least I knew what I was up against. Lucifer's child.

Lucifer . . . the dream that I'd had of Evangeline. She had been pregnant with Lucifer's child. Was that Ramuell inside her? Was the nephilim somehow sending me these visions, confusing me, trying to lure me to it by making me sympathize with its human mother?

I wondered if I should tell Gabriel and Beezle about my dreams. But I held back. My magic was whispering in the back of my head, telling me to wait, that it was not yet time.

I still needed to get into the Hall of Records. I needed some way to track Ramuell, and the only way I could think to do that was by finding his victims. That, or perhaps the witch that I was supposed to meet for the concealment charm could make me a tracking spell. The problem was you usually needed something personal for a tracking spell, and if I could get close enough to the monster to draw a hair or prick its finger, then I wouldn't need the stupid spell in the first place.

I realized suddenly that I was exhausted. The revelations of the last twenty-four hours and assorted beatings I'd taken were catching up with me. Gabriel seemed to sense that I'd had enough.

"I will return to you tomorrow," Gabriel said, and sketched a little bow before sweeping out without another word.

"We'll be waiting with bated breath," Beezle muttered as the front door closed.

"I need popcorn," I announced.

"Dinner of champions," Beezle said, and hitched a ride on me into the kitchen.

I took a package of popcorn out of the pantry and stuck it in the microwave, noticing as I did that the microwave clock said it was five forty-seven.

"I can't believe this day isn't over yet," I groaned, resting my elbows on the counter and dropping my head into my hands. Beezle scrambled down from my neck and onto the counter, his claws clicking. "When is it okay for me to go to bed and pretend the last two days never happened?"

"Huh," Beezle said, hunched in front of the microwave and focused with a predator's intensity on the popcorn bag turning on the glass plate. The only food that Beezle liked better than chocolate was popcorn.

"Beezle," I said. "How come you never told me about my father?"

The gargoyle dragged his eyes reluctantly away from

the popcorn bag, which had started to pop. His face was a mixture of shame and defensiveness. "I wanted to," he said.

"But . . . ?" I asked, rotating my wrist in a circle to indicate that he should go on.

"Your mother asked me not to tell you anything unless it became necessary."

The microwave beeped, indicating that the cycle was complete. Beezle scurried out of the way so that I could get the popcorn out of the microwave and put it in a bowl.

"Define 'necessary,'" I said as I took two handfuls of popcorn and put them on a napkin.

He watched me take my serving of popcorn with greedy eyes. "You know . . . if Azazel showed up, I was to tell you everything. Other than that, Katherine left it to my judgment."

"And your judgment was to keep me completely in the dark, even after I made nightfire? I'm sure that most gargoyles would consider that a 'necessary' moment."

He looked abashed, but there was a defensive note in his voice as he said, "I was already under that devil's geas when you manifested nightfire. I couldn't tell you anything that would reveal him or your father."

I looked at Beezle carefully, trying to decide how angry I wanted to be about his withholding information from me. Beezle loved me, I knew he did, but he had loved my mother far more. If she had asked him to keep a secret until he turned to stone, he would have. I could be as upset and angry as I liked, but the fact that his loyalty was to Katherine and the promises he made her wouldn't change. I sighed as I handed Beezle the rest of the bowl and he stuck his face so far into the popcorn that all I could see were the tops of his ears.

There would be no talking while Beezle was eating, so I decided to eat a little, too. I was pretty sure that I hadn't eaten all day. After two kernels of corn I realized that my head was still too sore from Antares's beating to chew anything. When I tried to crunch down, a bolt of pain ran from my back teeth up to my eyeballs. I dumped the rest of the popcorn back into the bowl. I could see Beezle's whole face now. His jaws worked with grim determination on the remaining few handfuls at the bottom. I decided I wasn't that hungry after all.

I was definitely tired. Everything that I had learned in the last couple of days weighed on my heart. Patrick's death and avenging my mother had been shunted aside by Antares, Gabriel, Lucifer, and my father, the fallen angel. And even with all of this happening, I still had my job to do. People don't stop dying just because an Agent has personal issues, even if those personal issues are increasingly apocalyptic in nature.

I could infer without any help from Beezle that Gabriel had been sent to me because Azazel was clearly having troubles of his own, and his enemies would want to use me to get to him.

Case in point: my darling half brother. And Antares was probably going to take it very personally that he hadn't been able to rip my heart from my chest on the first try. He just seemed like the type.

Thoughts of being a pawn in a looming demon war made me want to swallow a jar of antacids, so I pushed that aside for the time being and tried to concentrate on what I needed to do immediately.

"Beezle," I said, tapping my finger on the counter. "Tomorrow I want you to go with me to Greenwitch's."

Beezle licked the greasy butter film off the bottom of

the bowl before he spoke. "I don't do things or go places. I stay here and guard the domicile. That's the duty of a gargoyle."

"It wasn't the duty of a gargoyle the night Patrick was killed," I reminded him. "Besides, I want you with me for a while."

"What for?" Beezle said crossly. You'd think he hadn't come as close to dying as was possible for a gargoyle. He was just as much of a crab as usual.

"First, because I might need more information as you deem it 'necessary,'" I said with a meaningful look. "And second, I want to know that you are safe. So you stay with me."

"Right, because anyone looking at you would immediately think 'safe,'" he grumbled, but he looked secretly pleased.

I carefully touched all the tender places on my face, and realized that no amount of makeup could cover the damage done from demon saliva. I wanted a shower, though, to wash off the general ickiness of my encounter with Antares.

"Besides," Beezle said. "What do you want to see Greenwitch for? Like you haven't had enough supernatural incidents this week?"

"I need to get a concealment charm from her so I can break in to the Hall of Records," I said.

Beezle snorted. "Are you stupid or just acting like it? What makes you think the charm will get you into the Hall? Besides, the last thing you need right now is an encounter with a witch."

I shut the bathroom door firmly and turned on the shower, drowning out the sound of his voice. It sounded too much like the one in the back of my head, and I didn't need the warning in stereo.

8

THE NEXT DAY I SLEPT AS LATE AS POSSIBLE AND PUT-tered around the house until it was time to head out to Greenwitch's. I had a brief thought that maybe I should tell Gabriel where I was going—I did have his cell phone number—but then I decided that it was daylight and I was a big girl. I didn't need my father's errand boy leaning over my shoulder everywhere I went, no matter how cute he was. I had my late-evening soul pickup—one James Taka-hashi at the corner of Clark and Belmont—and I was going to get the charm a few hours beforehand. I hoped she'd had time to finish it up, because after my pickup I was planning on trying my break-in plan.

Not that I had much of a plan. Mostly it involved hop-ing that I could find the necessary keys to the Hall once I got into the building. J.B. had a set that he kept with other important keys in his desk, and I just had to hope that he didn't bring them home with him every night.

A little after seven o'clock I stood at the door of Ms. Greenwitch's garden apartment just off of Lincoln Square, a gentrified neighborhood a little north of where I lived. Greenwitch was her real name, and perhaps it wasn't coincidence that she was also a bona fide witch. It was likely that the power in the blood had led to the naming of one of her ancestors as Greenwitch, and the line had been marked by both their name and their abilities ever since. My mother had occasionally used her services, and I had maintained the acquaintance because it is handy to know a witch. Occasionally Agents need charms of protection when our duties lead us into dangerous areas, like vampire nests or faerie rings. Vampires aren't put off by the cloak of invisibility around an Agent, and if they're hungry, they'll eat anything.

Beezle was perched on my shoulder trying to look unobtrusive. Gargoyles don't make great accessories, and he'd flat-out refused to hide in my coat. We'd gotten quite a few strange looks from passersby on the street while we waited. Of course, it's possible they weren't staring at Beezle but at my mangled face. No adults said anything, though. People tend to avoid contact with strangers, and they didn't want to look too closely at Beezle. One kid had pointed at us and said, "Look, Mommy, a rat!" before his mother averted her eyes and hurried away. Beezle was beyond thrilled about that comment.

"What kind of a foolish child would mistake a gargoyle for a *rat*?" he said, puffing up with injured dignity.

After several minutes of knocking and waiting, knocking and waiting, the door finally opened to reveal a very tall and athletic woman in her fifties, with her silver hair in a close-cropped pixie cut. Her eyes were a pale gray, so light that she almost looked blind. Her face was all strong lines and planes, and that face told you she was not to be trifled with. She was dressed in a slim-fitting black bodysuit.

"Good evening, Ms. Greenwitch," I said.

"You interrupted my nightly yoga practice," she said. Her voice was low and husky, like Kathleen Turner's. "Come in."

She closed the door behind us as we stepped down the stairs into a short hallway. The white walls were covered in black-and-white photographs of trees. Ms. Greenwitch led us to another small room just a few steps down the hall. There was a closed oak wardrobe, a long oak table and little bunches of herbs drying on hooks in the ceiling. It was as clean as a hospital surgery room. She waved fingers covered in silver rings at my face. "I've got a healing charm for that."

I was tempted, since I knew Ms. Greenwitch's charms were spot-on and it would not only take away my pain but make me a little less obvious in a crowd. "How much?"

She named a price that was three times what I had in my pocket.

"Just the concealment charm, please," I said, and Beezle snorted.

Ms. Greenwitch shrugged and went to the wardrobe. She took a key from a silver chain around her neck and unlocked it, carefully opening the door in such a way that I couldn't see the contents inside. A moment later she closed and locked the door again and handed me a small paper bag, which I pocketed. I handed her the wad of bills from my pocket and she unrolled the cash, carefully counting aloud until she was certain I hadn't cheated her. Not that I would dare. You don't want a powerful witch pissed off at you. You might wake up one day and find your mattress had turned into a bed of scorpions, or that lightning was suddenly attracted to you every time you stepped outside.

She nodded and I assumed that meant she was satisfied. "Thanks for the rush job," I said, holding out my hand.

She grasped my hand firmly for a shake, and suddenly she went rigid. Sweat broke out all over her face as her skin blanched white as paper. I tried to pull my hand away so I could help her to a chair—I thought she was about to faint, or maybe having a heart attack—but she gripped my fingers tighter, so tight that the pressure hurt. Beezle dug his claws into my shoulders and hissed. His wings rose from his back like an angry cat's fur.

"Ms. Greenwitch? Are you all right?"

Her eerie gray eyes were wide and staring and fixed on mine. When she spoke it was through clenched teeth, almost as if the words were pouring unwillingly from her mouth.

"You are the last. He is coming for you. In smoke and flame, he is coming for you. There is only death in his wake and the heavens will pour fire, and all that you are will be destroyed." The pupils of her eyes widened, until there was only a thin ring of gray around the black, and she stumbled back, releasing my hand.

"Get away from here," she spat. "And never return."

I had never really been friends with Ms. Greenwitch, but I was a semi-regular client and I'd always thought we'd at least had a decent business relationship.

"What just happened?" I asked, confused beyond measure.

"Get *out*!" she screamed, and her face was drawn in lines of desperation. Her eyes went to the small window near the ceiling. All that was visible through the glass were the bars that protected the basement-level apartment and the cement gangway that ran along the side of the building.

I reached for her—to comfort or calm her, to try to figure out what the hell was going on—and she threw her hands forward, blasting me in the stomach with a punch of magic. The force sent me into the hallway, crashing into the wall. Beezle clung to my neck like a needle in a pincushion and I felt little rivulets of blood running from the places where his claws dug in. There was a strong scent of sage and thyme in the air as I struggled to my feet. It felt like a few new friends had been added to my very bruised ribs. I was getting really, really tired of getting beat up.

"Right," I said, flicking my fingers in salute at her. It hurt just to do that. "Leaving now."

"You stay away from here, Madeline Black," she called after me, her voice shaking. "Keep your cursed blood out of my path."

Cursed blood? I mouthed to Beezle as we walked up the stairs. He shrugged. By the time I got to the front door, I was gasping for breath even though the flight of stairs wasn't very long. I stumbled out onto the street and stood on the sidewalk for a moment, trying to remind my lungs that they liked oxygen and they should take all of it they could get.

"You need to take up running or something," Beezle said. "And maybe lay off the desserts for a while."

I smacked the side of his head, and the movement pulling on my ribs caused me to see stars. "I'm not out of breath because I'm fat, Beezle. I'm out of breath because I've gotten beaten up three times in the last couple of days."

"Three?" he asked.

"Ms. Greenwitch, Antares and Ramuell. You know, the

soul-sucking demon I have sworn to destroy because he killed my mother and Patrick."

"I forgot about that," Beezle said, with a little note of wonder in his voice. "It seems like a long time ago. But, you know, you probably could stand to lose a few . . ."

"Beezle, if you finish that sentence, I will never buy popcorn again for the rest of my life."

He snapped his jaws shut and crossed his arms, going into broody mode.

I walked very carefully down the sidewalk, intending to disappear into a nearby alley that ran underneath the El tracks and unobtrusively push out my wings. Ms. Green-witch lived a few short blocks from the Western El stop, and a steady stream of late commuters flowed past as I shuffled my way down the street. Most of them appeared not to notice the gargoyle glaring from my shoulder, and the early-autumn darkness did a fair job of disguising my bruised face unless I passed directly beneath a streetlight.

A young woman and man, both of them in their late twenties, went by. They were dressed like young professionals, just off work. She carried the cardigan that matched her short-sleeved sweater over one arm, while he had a take-out bag in one hand and a leather messenger bag slung over the other shoulder. A bottle of wine protruded from the top of a slim paper bag that she had tucked inside her oversized tote. They looked tired but anticipatory, the way that people do when they're almost home from work and they know they can put on their comfy socks and be with the one they love.

The two didn't even notice Beezle and me as we passed. I felt a stab of jealousy, a tiny flutter in my stomach. I'd always accepted that it was my fate to be an Agent. I'd had no choice in the matter. I could do my duty kicking and screaming, but I would still have to do it all the same. And being alone, without a person with whom to share the wine and takeout, that was part of the package, too. There was no other way to be when you were an Agent. My mother had taught me that.

Of course, Mom had her little fling before you were born, didn't she? an insidious voice whispered in my head.

I tried not to think about it, because if I thought about it too closely, I'd realize that I was angry with her. Angry with her for loving a fallen angel. Angry with her for not telling me about my father, for not preparing me for the day when demons would come knocking at my door, for not helping me learn what to do with the magic that was bound up inside me.

So I wasn't going to think about it. I squared my shoulders and marched into the alley, and Beezle shifted on his perch and muttered, "What's the matter with you all of a sudden?"

"Nothing," I snapped as we passed beneath a streetlight and into a patch of darkness. No one could see me once my wings emerged, but there was no point in freaking out the nice commuters by disappearing from sight in front of them.

I closed my eyes, thinking of home, and as my wings unfurled I caught a whiff of burnt cinnamon. My eyes flew open just as Beezle cried, "Maddy!" and I saw Ramuell's gaping maw open before me. I felt his hot breath scald my face and I shot upward in an explosion of black feathers before he could close his mouth around my head.

The monster roared and stood to his full height, slashing at my legs with his scarlet claws as I flew up. I managed to tug away, flapping my wings desperately and blasting him in the face with a blue ball of nightfire. Ramuell released me, howling and clawing at his eyes. I zipped out of the alley and realized that my left pant leg had ripped open. The inside of my leg burned where the claws had rent my flesh and blood was running into my left boot, soaking my sock. The burning acid ran up my leg, traveling through my bloodstream, contaminating everywhere it touched.

I arrowed toward home with desperate speed, looking once over my shoulder to see if the creature was following me. There was no sign of it. It had disappeared as cleanly as if it had never been there.

"What the flaming hell was that all about, Beezle?" I shouted. "How did it just appear out of nowhere? How come people weren't screaming and yelling at the sight of it? It had to get into the alley from somewhere, and it wasn't there when we went in—I'm sure of that."

Beezle said nothing, just clung to my neck even tighter. The burning acid in my leg had spread to my hips, and my stomach, and my chest. I slowed my speed as I saw the familiar rooftop of my house. My lungs felt tight and my vision blurred.

I aimed for the kitchen window and was off by a hairs-breadth, slamming my shoulder into the window frame and tumbling end over end to land flat on my back. The breath whooshed out of my body as from a deflating balloon. Beezle had released me before my swan dive and now he fluttered above my face.

"Maddy, Maddy, are you all right? Your leg doesn't look so good," he said, and I could hear the anxiety in his voice.

I tried to focus on his face, to tell him that I was all right, but everything looked like it was covered in thick fog. My lips and tongue and throat felt numb, and in my pain-filled haze it seemed somehow that my blood was moving more slowly, that my heartbeat was winding down like a clockwork toy.

"Maddy, say something," Beezle pleaded. I could feel his little clawed hands on my cheeks as he pressed his beak against my nose. "Maddy, please get up. Please speak to me."

You never say please, I thought, but it was too much effort to say the words. It was hard to focus on Beezle's cat eyes, so I let my eyelids drift closed.

"No, no, you wake up right now!" Beezle said, and I could feel his hands shaking me ineffectually. It seemed like his voice was at the other end of a long tunnel, pleading and angry at the same time. I wanted to pat him on the back but my hand wouldn't move.

"What has happened here?" Another voice, silky and dangerous. Gabriel.

"Ramuell," Beezle said. "He slashed her."

Gabriel said nothing, but suddenly his hands were on my leg, pulling away the tatters of my jeans. I heard the sharp intake of his breath but it echoed oddly in my ears.

"You have done a very poor job, guardian," he hissed, and I thought vaguely that he had never sounded as frightening as he did now. "I only hope that I am not too late."

His arms went under my shoulders and knees, pulling me to his chest. I wanted to see his face, but I couldn't open my eyes. I felt very far away, floating.

"And what of you, protector?" Beezle spat back. "Isn't that why Azazel sent you here? To keep her safe?"

"Quiet," he said, and I felt a strange warmth emanating from his hands. "The venom is everywhere now. I have only a little time and I need to concentrate."

The warmth from his hands spread through his arms, and his chest, and it burned hotter and hotter. It was like standing too close to a furnace. The heat grew more intense, and it hurt. I wanted to scream but the noise wouldn't come out of my mouth. Everywhere Gabriel touched me, the heat touched me, too, and it was like wildfire in my veins, burning away the acid.

And then his mouth was on me, too, at my throat, and my cheeks, and on my eyelids. And where his lips moved he left a trail of flames behind. He whispered against my mouth, "You have to live," and then he was kissing me, and his kiss was like the heart of the sun. The fire careened in my veins, scorching, burning me clean and whole. I felt my legs again, and my arms. Then my lungs inhaled and exhaled, and my heart resumed its regular beat.

The heat subsided, and my eyes flew open. Gabriel's mouth whispered across mine once more, and then he pulled away, and he smiled. His dark eyes were lit by starshine, and I felt I was falling again into the heart of the universe. Not by some spell of Gabriel's, but by my own foolish wants and needs. He had kissed me to save me—this much I understood. But my heart, my very lonely heart, ached for what I had never known before.

Gabriel must have seen something in my own eyes. His smile faded and his expression flickered, unreadable, and then he carefully released me, placing me in a sitting position on the floor. His hand rested against the small of my back, making sure that I didn't fall backward again.

I looked away from him. I didn't want him to see how the little rejection had hurt me. My body felt remarkably whole, like it had the morning after Ramuell's first attack. I suspected that if I looked at myself in the mirror, I would find all my cuts and bruises were gone. "Thank you," I whispered, and my throat felt rusty and unused.

"You are welcome," he said softly, and there was something in his voice that hadn't been there before.

I whipped my head back to look at him, but whatever I thought I'd heard wasn't there in his face. *Stupid, stupid, Maddy,* I thought. *Did you think he was going to fall madly in love with you after one kiss?*

No, my life was no fairy tale. I was not a princess woken from sleep by her true love. I was an Agent, the daughter of a fallen angel, and he was . . . whatever he was, but certainly not normal or human.

I shook my head, glanced at my watch and remembered that I still had a duty to perform.

"Well, this has been fun, kids," I said. "But I've got a pickup to get to shortly."

I wobbled to my feet and grabbed the counter as my vision spun in circles.

Gabriel put his hand on my shoulder. "You are in no condition to go anywhere."

I shrugged off his hand. "I just need a minute."

"You look like you need more than a minute," Beezle said.

"No," I said, shaking my head. "I need a shower, and some food, and I'll be fine."

"I will go with you," Gabriel said.

"I don't think that will be necessary," I said. I wasn't sure that I wanted him around. I didn't want to make a fool of myself in front of him. Still, he was the one who had kissed me in the first place, so maybe he wouldn't object if I flirted a little in his direction.

And should you really be thinking about a supernatural romance right now? I chided myself. I had to keep my head in the game or Ramuell was going to eat me alive—literally.

"I must confer with Lord Azazel," Gabriel said. "Then, whatever activities that you have planned for the evening, my lady, I will be at your side."

"'My lady'?" I said. "Since when am I your lady?"

"You are the daughter of my lord; therefore, you are my lady. Forgive me for not addressing you so sooner."

"Are you crazy?" I asked, totally unnerved by his sudden formality. I was no one's boss. I could barely control my own small life. "Don't even think about acting like you're my servant."

"When you are ready to leave, I will accompany you," he said. "I will retire downstairs for the moment and confer with my lord."

He headed out of the kitchen and down the short hallway. My shout stopped him at the door.

"Wait," I said. "You need the keys. And what are you going to do in an empty apartment for the next half hour?"

A ghost of a smile flickered across his face. "I do not need the keys, and the apartment is not empty."

"It isn't?" I was confused. I didn't want him to leave, even if he was only going downstairs. I didn't want this sudden feeling between us, either. Was this what normal people felt like?

"No, it isn't empty," he repeated. "After all, I do have a little magic of my own."

9

FIFTEEN MINUTES LATER I STEPPED OUT OF THE shower and wrapped a towel around my body. Gabriel had healed my injuries, but my jeans had been mutilated beyond repair and my skin had been covered in flakes of dried blood. Cleaning up had been deemed prudent.

As I walked into the bedroom I saw Beezle exactly where I'd expected him to be—perched on my dresser, arms crossed, opening and closing his wings in an annoyed little metronome. He narrowed his cat's eyes at me as he took a deep breath to begin his tirade.

"Don't even start with me, Beezle," I said mildly as I pulled my underwear from the top drawer. Basic, boring black cotton bra and basic, boring black cotton underpants.

"You don't know what you're getting yourself into," Beezle snapped. "I see that look in your eye."

I crossed to the closet and pulled out a black turtleneck

sweater and jeans. Basic, boring. Black and blue. I looked critically at my wardrobe. Didn't I have anything to wear that wasn't completely drab?

"Madeline, are you listening to me?" Beezle asked.

"No," I said absently, pulling on my clothes. Maybe after I got paid for my current writing assignment I could go out and buy a few new things. Maybe something red. Red would probably look nice with my dark hair and eyes.

Beezle launched himself from the dresser as I sat on the bed to pull on my boots, which looked mighty crummy after a couple of days of stomping in alleys and bleeding on the leather. As I finished tying the left lace Beezle came to a halt, hovering in front of my face.

"Now, you listen here, Madeline Black," he said, stabbing a little claw in the direction of my nose. "Whatever ideas you have in your head about Gabriel, you had just better get them out right now!"

"And what makes you think I have any 'ideas' at all?" I shot back, annoyed. Gabriel may not be perfect. I may have had doubts about his motivations and his actions. But I was attracted to him. That much I could admit to myself. And I had been so alone for so long. I wasn't about to let Beezle take that away from me just because he didn't like the fact that Gabriel was fallen.

"I told you," he said grimly. "I've seen that look in your eye."

"I doubt that very much. I've never had anyone around to put that look in my eye."

"I didn't say I'd seen it in your eyes," he said. "I remember Katherine mooning about just the same way that you are now. And may I humbly remind you that Katherine's romance with Azazel was not the smartest thing she had ever done."

I stared at him, stricken. "So what are you saying? I should never have been born?"

"No, no," he backpedaled hastily, waving his arms. "Of course not. But it is very likely that her death was caused by her relationship with Azazel. I don't want to see you fall into the same trap."

I tried to put aside all the raw emotion that I had been carrying around the last couple of days—the lust, the longing, the anger, the hurt, the sense of betrayal by all and sundry. The flayed nerve that was the source of magic deep inside me. When I sifted through those things, looked at them critically, I could agree with Beezle. I was a mess right now. My life had changed too much and too quickly, and I hadn't exactly responded like a mature adult. Maybe I wasn't examining Gabriel close enough. Maybe I was letting myself get sucked in by his beauty, by my needs.

"My lady?" he called, knocking on the front door and opening it. "Are you ready to leave now?"

The sound of his voice made my body pull tight like an arrow about to be loosed.

"Maddy," Beezle pleaded. "Please think about what you are doing."

I heard Gabriel call me again and I patted Beezle on the cheek. "Don't worry, Beezle. I promise to be careful."

Careful. I would be careful. But I hadn't promised to stay away.

At ten thirty-seven Gabriel and I stood on the corner of Clark and Belmont, watching the teeming masses of humanity rush to and fro. The buildings and the people reflected the constant state of flux that was any Chicago neighborhood. This particular corner had been something of a punk mecca—the Dunkin' Donuts on the northwest corner of Clark had been affectionately known as the Punkin' Donuts for years. Behind it stood the Alley, once a tiny purveyor of Gothic and punk fashion, now a venerable old Chicago institution that took up several of the buildings on Clark and Belmont. The Alley still hawked Doc Martens, plaid pants and black satin corsets, along with bondage gear, vibrators and just about any other accessory required for the young and alternative, who still flocked to this neighborhood in droves despite the increasing gentrification.

On the opposite corner, a Starbucks packed with the young and the fashionable bore a sign that proclaimed NOW OPEN 24 HOURS. The sidewalk was covered with scaffolding that wrapped around the corner, protecting pedestrians from falling debris as the building next door to the Starbucks was renovated.

Farther west on Belmont were an independent video store, a used bookstore, a Japanese goods emporium, several fashionable boutiques and a Middle Eastern take-out place called Sinbad's that had the best falafel and hummus in the city, as far as I was concerned. East and closer to the lakefront was Boys Town on Halsted, with its strip of nightclubs and open-late eateries.

The proximity of this intersection to such a variety of businesses, restaurants and people, as well as the convenience of three bus lines and a major El stop, meant that Clark and Belmont never slept. Even at ten forty-five on a weeknight, there was still a snarl of traffic, buses trying to negotiate in and out of bus stops while car drivers cursed through their windows, cabbies zooming to pick up and drop off fares without any regard for pedestrians, cyclists or inanimate objects. People stepped off the sidewalk willy-nilly and crossed portions of the four-way intersection, not bothering to wait for the crossing signal.

Gabriel and I leaned against a storefront on the northeast corner and watched the crowd of neo-Goth and emo kids lurking in the small parking lot of the Dunkin' Donuts, sharing cigarettes and coffee cups. Students and young professionals intent on their laptops could be seen through the window of the Starbucks.

"How will you know which is the man you are looking for?" Gabriel said, his eyes roaming the crowds of people. He was definitely taking his bodyguard duties seriously tonight. He gave off a take-one-step-closer-and-I-will-show-you-Armageddon vibe that had people veering around us on the sidewalks. I don't think he was aware of what he did.

"Whenever I have to pick up a soul, I just know it's them," I said simply.

"There is nothing to signal you?" Gabriel asked.

"If you mean a rotating blue light and siren, or maybe a flashing arrow announcing, FRESH SOUL RIGHT HERE, then no," I said, amused. "There is a kind of signal, I guess. It's more like a knowing, like I sense that they are in my presence and then my whole being just kind of locks on them. I never really thought about it before. It's always been instinctive."

We fell silent for a few moments. Gabriel scanned the crowd for threats—although I could have told him that if Ramuell showed up, we would definitely notice—and I scanned the crowd for James Takahashi. My mind wandered a little as we waited, and then a thought occurred to me.

"Gabriel," I said.

"Hmm?"

"When you say that you are consulting with my father, how is it you do that? Do you have some kind of special way of communicating with him?"

Gabriel frowned and looked at me. "What do you mean?"

"Well, how do you get in touch with him? Are you performing some kind of spell?"

He looked very amused as he pulled something out of his pocket and held it up to me. A tiny little silver cell phone.

"Uh, okay," I said, a little embarrassed. "I guess your cell plan really has great network coverage if you can get a cell signal in the pit."

"Lord Azazel lives in Minnesota," Gabriel said absently, and returned to his bodyguarding.

"Minnesota?" I asked. My father lived less than seven hours away from me? "How can that be?"

"He lives in Minneapolis," Gabriel clarified, and looked at me. I must have looked as stunned and confused as I felt. "Lucifer's kingdom is metaphorical, not literal. The fallen are scattered throughout the world, maintaining different bases of power for him."

"And my father lives in Minneapolis," I repeated.

"Yes."

"And where does Lucifer live?"

"Los Angeles."

I let out a laugh at that. "Of course he does."

Just then I felt a little twinge in my consciousness and I turned away from Gabriel, my attention absorbed by the mass of people moving back and forth in front of me.

"What is it?" Gabriel asked, sensing the change in me.

"He's here," I said, and a second later I found him.

He looked about seventeen or eighteen, with dark, almond-shaped eyes and dyed white-blond hair that was cut short all over his head except for two long hanks in the front that brushed the tops of his cheekbones. He was tall and his scarecrow limbs were clad in what I thought of as mall punk—red plaid pants covered in zippers, baggy black T-shirt, surplus combat boots. There was a messenger bag imprinted with a skull and crossbones slung over his shoulder and he read from an obviously well-used copy of Dostoevsky's *The Idiot* as he walked. A half-burnt cigarette dangled from his bottom lip.

I could see what was going to happen. Takahashi walked and read, heading south on Clark only a few steps from the intersection. On the west side of Belmont, a few feet from where Gabriel and I stood, a cabbie dropped off a fare and prepared to pull through the intersection just as the light flashed yellow for a second or two before changing to red.

The cabbie, being from Chicago, was not about to let a little thing like a red light impede his forward motion. Takahashi glanced up from his book long enough to verify that the crossing signal showed WALK, and then went back to reading as he stepped into the street. I felt the wings pushing out of my back. If anyone had looked at me at that moment, they would have seen me wink out of sight, almost as if I had never been there.

Time slowed down. Takahashi took a drag from his cigarette. The cabbie accelerated through the intersection, jabbering into a cell phone headset as he went. My feet left the ground. Beside me, I felt Gabriel rise up as well. I glanced at him briefly and noticed that his wings looked a lot like mine. I returned my gaze to the happenings below as we floated over the street and waited.

The taxi slammed into the boy with a screech of brakes.

Dostoevsky went flying in a burst of pages. I saw Taka-hashi's left leg crushed beneath the front passenger-side wheel. The bumper slammed into his head. It was almost as if he'd been sucked underneath the car rather than hit by it, like the car was vacuuming him off the street.

Blood pooled. Bone crunched. People screamed. The cabbie sat in the taxi, eyes bulging, hands shaking. Some-one ran to check Takahashi's pulse. At least fifteen people called 911, and another fifteen started telling whomever they had been chatting with on their cells that they had just seen a guy get smashed by a cab right in front of them.

I waited, Gabriel hovering patiently beside me. In a moment, Takahashi exhaled for the last time. His soul drifted out, looking confused as he saw his own crushed body. I lowered down to him until we were at eye level. His eyes widened when he saw me. After a moment he looked resigned.

"Are you here for me?" he asked.

"Yes," I said simply, and held out my hand.

He reached forward to place his hand in my own, and that was when everything went horribly wrong.

A woman screamed, a piercing, unending wail, and all three of us turned in the direction of the noise. Ramuell stood in front of the Starbucks, looking comically out of place next to the familiar logo. Next to him a young woman wearing a thick cabled sweater and carrying a latte had her mouth open in a wide *O* as she screamed. It was the first time I'd seen the nephilim in anything but complete shadow. Under the harsh glare of the streetlamp he looked like a 3-D nightmare.

He was at least nine feet tall, and red all over, like the red of human muscle beneath the skin. The color gave the nephilim a raw, oozing appearance. Black claws, thick and

curved, protruded from his fingers and curved black horns
rose from his head. He smiled at me, and showed a mouthful of jagged teeth as sharp as Sweeney Todd's blade. As
we watched, frozen in horror, Ramuell casually back-
handed the woman next to him. The screaming abruptly
stopped, drowned in a noisy gurgle as the nephilim's claws
sliced her head from her body. The shock was too much for
her soul and I saw her snap her tether the moment her soul
left her body. Ramuell snatched the loose soul and shoved
it between his teeth. The woman's soul screamed on, the *O*
of her mouth disappearing beneath the nephilim's horrible
grin.

"No!" I shouted, the magic rising up in me furious
and hungry. I fought for control as people started to run,
knocking one another over in their haste to get away from
the monster. I didn't want the magic to overwhelm me; I
didn't want to make a mistake and hurt an innocent.

Beside me Gabriel unleashed a blue bolt of nightfire
and Ramuell snarled, batting at it as if it were a softball. It
missed the creature's chest but burned the palm of his hand
and he howled in pain and fury. He charged at Gabriel, who
left my side, engaging Ramuell in combat. Gabriel shot
more nightfire at him, and Ramuell parried with magic of
his own. Balls of lava appeared at the creature's fingertips and he launched them at Gabriel, who neatly dodged
every attack. As I watched, sickened and struggling with
my unstable magic, the lava that missed him landed on
whatever was nearby. It burned through the roofs of cars
and smashed easily through shop windows. It melted the
face off one man, and left others screaming in the street,
holding fragments of limbs.

All around me souls broke free of their tethers, but there
were no Agents in the vicinity to collect them except me.

That terrified me nearly as much as Ramuell's presence at Clark and Belmont in full sight of screaming civilians. The lack of Agents meant that these deaths were not meant to be; they were out of sync with the order of the universe.

All deaths are predicted and managed by the bureaucracy that employs me. For this many people to die unexpectedly meant that something was very, very wrong about Ramuell's presence here—and not just for the obvious reasons. Somehow the nephilim and his master had managed to fly under the radar of even the micromanaging Agency.

Beside me I felt James Takahashi tugging at my hand. I turned and saw his soul had gone pale with fear.

"Come on, come on," he said, and I realized he wasn't trying to pull me from the scene. He was trying to get me to release him so he, too, could run away. My fingers had tightened in a death grip around him as I fought to control my magic. I didn't want to accidentally unleash an explosion that needlessly killed everyone in the intersection.

"No," I said, feeling helpless and torn. I needed to help Gabriel. I needed to try to capture these poor lost souls winging free of their bodies all around me. "I have to make sure you get to the Door."

"Lady, that thing is going to eat me," he pleaded, using his right hand to try to pry my fingers off his left.

"No, he's not," I said firmly, and I felt something settle inside me. The magic was still there, churning and hungry, but I was in control. And I would do my job. I would help Gabriel fight Ramuell, and I would bring Takahashi to the Door. "You are not going to be eaten. You are going to have a choice, the way you are supposed to."

"And what about the lady who got eaten up by that monster?" Takahashi shouted. "What are you going to do about her?"

"Set her free," I said, and there was something in my look or my voice that convinced Takahashi that I meant it. He stopped tugging, and I slowly released the pressure of my fingers on his hand.

"How are you going to do that?" he asked.

The magic flared up inside me, knowing what I wanted, eager to help me do it. "I'm going to kill the nephilim and release all the souls he has eaten."

Takahashi looked doubtful. "If you say so."

I nodded. "I do."

I let go of him, trusting him to stay put. His soul was still tethered to his body—somehow neither the shock and horror of his death nor the shock and horror of the nephilim had managed to terrify him into breaking free.

While I'd been negotiating with Takahashi and trying to get myself under control, Gabriel and Ramuell had nearly destroyed the intersection. Most of the people were gone now—fled down the street or inside the nearest buildings. A row of terrified faces peered just above the lower sill of the coffee shop window. Several bodies lay on sidewalks or on the street. A few people had been blasted as they'd attempted to flee their cars, and their bodies hung half-in and half-out of their vehicles.

Gabriel and Ramuell seemed to have fought to a stand-still. The nephilim stood on the north side of Clark, Gabriel on the south side, like Old West gunfighters waiting for the cue to draw. Ramuell's body was dotted with burns, places where Gabriel's nightfire had splashed against the red skin. The burns were dark purple and oozing.

Gabriel seemed blessedly unhurt, although it looked liked he'd lost a few feathers from his wings. They fluttered in the wind that always seemed to blow from the east, from the lake. Both Gabriel and Ramuell breathed heavily—I could see the quick little puffs of steam from Gabriel's mouth in the cold air, and hear the faint snort that came from Ramuell with each exhalation.

Far away a siren screamed, and behind me the El rumbled, reassuringly normal, into the Belmont station. Soon people would leave the station. Some of them would walk this way. Gabriel and I had to get Ramuell away from here before the nephilim took the lives of any more innocent bystanders.

My wings rustled in the wind, and it sounded as loud as a gunshot to me. Both Gabriel and Ramuell turned to me at the same moment. Ramuell's eyes burned red, a deep red like the coals at the bottom of a fire. Gabriel's eyes blazed, too, but not with the starshine to which I had become accustomed. Looking into his eyes was like staring into the heart of the sun. I squinted against the glare, and for a minute they both looked so alien, so hostile, that I was scared of both of them. My heart stuttered in my chest, and I realized I wasn't any hero. I was just plain Maddy Black, caught up in things I didn't understand, and I was afraid.

And then Ramuell spoke, and his voice was the sound of dead things scraping over rock.

"Well, well, if it isn't my dessert," he said, and he smiled, and his smile was a horror to behold.

Even in the momentary paralysis of terror, I felt anger rise up in me. This monster was not going to gobble me up without a fight. My magic surged up and made little crackles of energy jump from my fingertips. I felt uncomfortably full, my skin stretched tight, my ears humming with electricity.

"Well, well, if it isn't Lucifer's least wanted," I said.

Ramuell's burning eyes narrowed to slits as he turned to

face me more fully. "Watch yourself, little girl. There are lots of ways to prolong your inevitable death."

I looked once at Gabriel, gave an infinitesimal nod, hoping he would understand what I wanted. A narrow crease appeared between the twin suns.

"You know what, Ramuell? I've been through a lot in the last couple of days, and I'm not really in the mood to banter with Hell's castoff," I said, and as I did my feet left the ground.

"Bitch," Ramuell snarled. "I will make you suffer far more than your mother."

The mention of my mother nearly arrested me. My heart sang out in pain at the thought of her suffering at the hands of this beast. But I didn't want to be drawn into an emotional quagmire that could trip me up or slow me down. I concentrated on the people in the here and now, the living and dead that I needed to save, and that helped steady me.

"You'll have to catch me first," I said, and I blasted Ramuell with all the magic that was poised and waiting inside me. It came out in a streaming blue mass of sulfur and electricity—nightfire.

I caught Ramuell by surprise, and the nightfire poured over the nephilim in a continuous stream. Gabriel added his magic to mine, flying closer to hover at my side. His nightfire and mine mixed together like winding ribbons, my magic a darker blue than his.

While the nephilim roared in pain, he made no effort to dodge the nightfire or bat it away, nor did he attempt to defend himself by blasting us as he had done previously. Ramuell seemed paralyzed by our combined efforts. But the outpouring of magic, so strong a few moments before, started to become difficult to maintain.

"Be careful," Gabriel shouted. "You're using too much of your own essence."

"I don't know how to control it," I said desperately. I felt a little woozy, like my blood sugar was low. I shook my head to clear it. "It doesn't matter. We have to get Ramuell away from here before he kills anyone else."

Gabriel nodded. "I can use my magic to bind him if you can keep him distracted for a few more moments."

I wasn't sure how long my magic could hold Ramuell, but I knew I wasn't about to let him go now that we had him in our sights. If I had to pour out every last drop of myself in order to defeat the monster who had eaten my mother's soul, I would.

Gabriel eased away from me, pulling the nightfire back. I held Ramuell now. It was my magic alone that kept the nephilim from breaking free.

Sweat poured down my face, stinging my eyes. My hands were before me, and nightfire poured from my fingers in a continuous flow of magic. Deep inside, down under my ribs, the place where I felt the source of my magic flow twinged like a rubber band pulled to its breaking point. Ramuell hadn't moved. He still stood howling in the middle of the street, accepting my punishment without attempting to defend himself.

Gabriel hovered a few feet away, his lips moving, his eyes closed. He seemed to have drawn into himself, pulling up power from a well deep within.

I tried to concentrate on the source of magic inside me, tried to level off the flow of power so that I could sustain it long enough to help Gabriel bind Ramuell. But even as I struggled to control it, I felt something snap inside me, and the nightfire pouring from my fingers abruptly ceased, as if someone had shut off a spigot.

I gasped, and Gabriel's eyes flew open. Ramuell smiled, even though the flesh of his chest and shoulders was burned through to the organs. I could see shiny, squishy things pulsing beneath a lacework of crisped and blackened skin. Then he blasted Gabriel with a ball of white fire. The force of the blast pushed Gabriel across the intersection and smashed him into the Dunkin' Donuts sign. Sparks of electricity shot into the air as Gabriel's limp body hit the sign with enough force to buckle it in the middle. He dropped to the ground and lay quite still.

I had no time to think or to respond. Ramuell leapt across the distance separating us and snatched me out of the air, landing lightly on his clawed feet. He held me by the shoulders as though I were a child, my feet dangling. I kicked out at his stomach and felt the toe of my boot connect with one of those soft and exposed organs. Ramuell grunted and gripped my shoulders tighter. I felt his claws cutting into me, and the familiar acidic burning that followed.

In a few minutes I would be dead, one way or another. Either Ramuell would eat me or the acid raging through my body would consume me. My blood pounded in my ears, but I dimly heard people screaming. The people from the El. The ones I had tried to protect, tried to keep from Ramuell. I had no magic left, and there was no one to help me. They would surely be eaten alive if they didn't get away.

Ramuell chuckled, a hideous sound that started deep in his chest and rumbled to the surface. I tried to kick him again and he deftly held me away from him so that I was just as ineffectual as the child I felt like at that moment. I couldn't punch or kick him. My magic was gone. My only weapon was my silver knife, and I couldn't reach inside the shaft of my boot to get it. I'd thought I'd come here to gather a soul, not battle a nephilim.

"Nothing to say, little girl?" Ramuell sneered, his terrible face leaning close to mine. His teeth snapped very close to my nose and I flinched subconsciously, which made Ramuell laugh harder. "Not going to fight, or think up clever retorts? Not going to beg for your life, the way your mother did?"

The acid burned through me, making me feel weak and dizzy. I fought to stay awake. I didn't want to be a comatose hors d'oeuvre during my last moments on Earth.

"My mother . . . never begged . . . for anything," I said. My tongue felt thick in my mouth.

"Oh, yes, she did," Ramuell said, lowering his voice to a conspiratorial whisper. "She begged for her life and the life of her mewling brat. She begs for it even now. I can hear her, inside me, with the others."

And for a moment, I thought I could hear her, too, hear her soul crying out in anguish, trapped somewhere inside the nephilim's body. The thought filled me with despair. I couldn't even keep myself alive after my mother had sacrificed herself for me. Soon I would be one of the screaming souls imprisoned inside this monster.

But even as I smelled the sulfur-and-burnt-cinnamon stink of Ramuell's breath, felt its heat on my face as he opened his mouth to consume me, something in me cried out. I wasn't going to let the nephilim destroy me, and as I thought it, a blast of white heat exploded inside me and pushed out through every inch of skin. I felt scorched by the force of it and closed my eyes as light exploded all around me. Ramuell screamed, a scream of pain and horror like I had never heard before. The nephilim dropped me to the ground and I opened my eyes.

I saw it for only a second. The magic that blasted out of me had seared away the nephilim's skin completely wherever he had touched me. His hands were little more than dangling slabs of meat, and when he locked eyes with me, I saw fear in the red depths.

Then I saw—but I couldn't have seen—a hole appear behind Ramuell, like the surface of reality had been rent open. The nephilim stepped back into the swirling darkness and was swallowed up, the hole closing neatly as if it had never been there.

I had a moment to wonder what had happened to James Takahashi, and then the burning in my blood consumed me, and I closed my eyes.

10

WHEN SHE AWOKE SHE WAS AGAIN IN DARKNESS, IN *the trap that they had enclosed her within. The memory of that beautiful voice speaking of the death of her Morningstar, the death of her children, was almost enough to make her fall away again. But she hardened herself, for she would need all of her wit to escape with her life and her children.*

She was not without power. When the Morningstar had planted his seed inside her, he had given her some of his own magic, to protect her and their children. Evangeline had not used this magic since she had blazed the path from her village to the Forbidden Lands and the arms of her lover. And the creatures that she would fight were not frail mortals, but angelic beings with powers of their own.

Still, she must fight. If she was to return to Lucifer, she must fight.

She lay in wait, tiny, still, like a mouse in a hole, until one of them came for her. She closed her eyes so that she would not be blinded by the creature's light. She waited while it hauled her roughly through the door. Then she opened her eyes, and she saw its face, a face very lovely, a face very surprised when white flame burst from within her and burned it away.

Evangeline did not take in her surroundings longer than to determine the way out. There were no other creatures in the room, and she hurried forward to the only door, the wings in her belly fluttering in delight. She felt the magic of her children bubbling up inside her, wanting to break free, and she knew that she had not long before they would be born.

At the door she came to a long hallway, white and smooth and faced by a row of gilded windows, and there was only one way out and one way forward. Another of the creatures stepped into the hallway before her, and the white flame burst from her again, and not a trace of her captor remained.

The Morningstar's children bounced and fluttered, and Evangeline felt a pain in her side, and a wetness between her legs. She knew she had but little time. She stepped through the door, and into a large and airy room.

A collection of the creatures was there, all gathered in perfect beauty, but Evangeline did not notice and she did not care. The Morningstar's children were coming, and she had to return to him.

The creatures turned, and all but one froze in surprise. She looked at Evangeline with great green eyes, and Evangeline saw knowledge in them, and saw the creature alight on downy white wings a moment before the flames burst from her for the last time.

Evangeline's captors and her prison blasted away in an instant, leaving her alone in the glare of the sun, her feet in the sand, the jagged peaks of mountains all around her. She fell to her knees, crying out, and placed her hand over her belly. Little wings pushed beneath her skin, as she lay on the sand, her face in the sun, and waited for her children to come forth.

I woke in my bed to find that for the second time in a week I had been cleaned and dressed in my pajamas. Again, Gabriel seemed partial to the only nightgown that I owned—a virginal white cotton lawn that made me look like a sacrifice about to be laid on an altar. I don't know what had possessed me to buy it in the first place.

My long hair had been neatly braided down my back, and that, more than the fact that he had seen me naked twice now while I slept, made me blush. I felt my face warm all the way to the tops of my ears. There was something disturbingly intimate about the thought of his hands carefully braiding my hair.

The room was almost fully dark. A thin shaft of light pushed through the curtains from the streetlamp in the alley behind my building. The digital clock on my bedside table read 3:18 A.M. The window was slightly open and I smelled the cold Chicago fall night—a mixture of car exhaust, fallen leaves and a lingering whiff of smoke from someone's fireplace.

I saw Gabriel in the weak glare from the streetlamp, sitting in a hard-backed wooden chair pilfered from my kitchen. He'd moved the chair very close to my bed. I slept on my left side so when my eyes opened I faced him. I could brush his knees with my hand if I stretched my arm out. His head was tipped forward and rested on his chest, and he snored softly.

It hadn't occurred to me that he could be tired. He seemed so unearthly to me most of the time, so obviously a supernatural creature, that I hadn't thought that he could ever be weary. But now that I looked closely, I could see the dark shadows underneath his closed lids, and the pallor in his cheeks. It was more than just the play of light and shadow in a darkened room. He looked exhausted and ill.

And healing me time after time probably isn't helping, I thought guiltily. I sat up, pulled my knees to my chest and watched the rise and fall of his chest for a few moments, wondering if I would be able to push his significantly taller form onto the bed without my waking him. He clearly needed to rest, and sleeping in a kitchen chair wasn't going to do the trick. I wasn't going to sleep any longer. Now that I was awake I felt jittery and slightly nauseous, like I'd had too much caffeine.

I eased my legs out from under the blankets and started to scoot down the bed. Gabriel's eyes snapped open immediately and his head came up. He pinned me with a glare.

"Where do you think you are going?" he asked.

I felt guilty, like I'd been caught doing something wrong. "I'm getting out of bed."

"You need to rest," he said. He stood and grasped my shoulders, trying to push me back to the pillows. "You have been through an ordeal."

"You're the one who needs to rest," I snapped back, feeling a little annoyed at his peremptory attitude. I swiped at his hands and he released me. "You look like the walking dead."

"My health is no concern of yours. However, your health is of utmost concern to me. If you had suffered lasting

harm today because of my inability to protect you . . ." He
trailed off, looking grim.

"What?" I asked.

"Lord Azazel's rage would be a terrible thing to behold."

"And wouldn't his rage be a terrible thing to behold if
you managed to get yourself killed because you didn't take
proper care of yourself?" I asked.

"No," he said, and smiled briefly. "My life is nothing
to him."

"Why?" I asked.

"Because of who I am," Gabriel said.

There was something in his eyes, and I knew that if I
asked the question now, I would finally get my answer.

I took a deep breath. "Who are you?"

The words hung in the air between us like wisps of
smoke. I could feel tension radiating from his body.

"You promised me that you would tell me," I reminded him.

"I did."

"Are you a fallen angel, like Azazel?"

He looked wary. "Why is it relevant?"

"Because I want to know," I said. "Because you've
saved my life."

"I am . . . not exactly like your father," Gabriel said.

"Are you half-and-half, like me?" I pressed. "You've got
starshine in your eyes, like I had when you showed me in
the mirror."

"Madeline, you must understand. I want to tell you. But
I fear what you will do when you have the information.
You need to trust me. I cannot fulfill the charge that Lord
Azazel has placed on me if you do not trust me."

"And I do." I didn't think that there was anything
Gabriel could say that would make me trust him less.

"Before I tell you this, you must understand that Lord Azazel, your father, trusts me absolutely. He would not have put you in my care if he did not. There is nothing in all eternity that is more precious to him than you, his daughter."

I nodded slowly, and I was ashamed to feel tears prick at the backs of my eyes. I had never known my father. If I was so precious to him, why had he left me here all alone? Why had he chosen to leave rather than stay with my mother? If he had been with her, would she have been protected from Ramuell?

"I understand," I said.

"My mother," Gabriel said, "was an angel. Not fallen. She was still a child of paradise when she came to Earth to deliver a visitation upon a human. While she was here, a nephilim found her."

I could read between the lines without any further coaching. "She was raped."

"Yes," he said without inflection. "Violently. Even as a divine being with divine powers, she barely survived. When it was discovered that she had gotten a child from the nephilim, she was cast out of Heaven. By this time the Grigori had also fallen, for the sin of coupling with human women. My lord Azazel sheltered my mother until I was born."

Why? I wondered. From everything I had heard about fallen angels so far, they weren't exactly models of altruism. Azazel must have had some ulterior motive for sheltering Gabriel's mother.

"After my birth, my mother left. She wanted no truck with a thing born of such a monster. The Grigori would have had me destroyed—it is forbidden for the nephilim to reproduce—but Lord Azazel argued on my behalf. He swore that if I ever became a danger, he would destroy me himself. So Lucifer consented, and I was allowed to live as Lord Azazel's thrall."

"My father kept you as a servant?" I said, a little offended. Why hadn't he raised this lost half angel as his own?

"Of course," Gabriel said, surprised. "What else would I be? And I am grateful to him. He taught me to understand my powers. And now he has sent me to you, so that I could use those powers to protect you from Ramuell."

His face was braced, expectant. He thought that I was going to explode now that I knew he was part nephilim. But instead of being angry that he'd deceived me and hidden his identity from me, I could feel only pity. Pity for his mother, who lost Heaven through no fault of her own. Pity for this lost child, who was abandoned to death by his mother and lived as an outcast because his father's magic was inside him.

"So Ramuell is . . . what? Your cousin?" I asked.

Gabriel's face was very white in the darkness, and he seemed almost unable to speak. "He is my father."

The ground beneath me shifted a little. "Ah," I said, feeling lame. "Your father."

I wasn't really sure what else to say to that. This beautiful half angel sitting before me, this man who had already tangled up my feelings every which way from lust to fury since the moment I'd met him, was the son of the creature that had murdered my mother. But it did explain why Beezle insisted on calling him "the devil." He was the grandson of the one and only Morningstar himself.

"My lord Azazel sent me to you because my father's magic lives inside me, and only I have hope of containing him alone. When the Grigori first bound the nephilim to the Valley of Sorrows, it took the combined might of all of their magic to contain them. But now that I have reached maturity, my magic is enough to disable Ramuell until he can be bound again."

I remembered something then, something that I'd nearly forgotten in the revelations of the last day. "That first night, when I faced Ramuell at the overpass . . . I remember that I was half-conscious after I bolted him with nightfire. Somebody chased Ramuell from me, and then picked me up and carried me home."

Gabriel nodded his head in acknowledgment.

"You also bathed me, and dressed me, and braided my hair, just like tonight," I said thoughtfully. "That's the part that I think I'm annoyed about."

He looked stunned for a moment, then let out a sharp bark of laughter. He seemed surprised that the noise had come out of his mouth. "I tell you that I am a monster, that I am kith and kin to the creature that wants to destroy you, and you are worried that I kept you from sleeping in the stench and filth of that overpass?"

"See, when you put it that way, it sounds unreasonable. I'm just not sure how I feel about the fact that you performed such an intimate service when I don't know you that well," I said, and the air suddenly seemed charged with another kind of tension.

I couldn't read the expression on his face clearly. I was a little confused by his revelation, but there was something that I wanted him to know, and something that I had wanted to do from the moment I first saw him.

I stood and approached him, stopping in front of where he sat in the chair. He looked up at me, his face revealed in the moonlight.

He didn't back away from me, but he watched me cautiously, unsure of what I would do. I wasn't really sure what I would do, either.

I stopped when there were just a few inches between us, close enough that I could feel the heat coming off his body. I laid my hands very gently on his cheeks, and looked into his starlit eyes. "But what I do know, what I can see, is that you are no monster."

He said nothing, but the muscles beneath my fingers jumped. His skin was hot, like he was running a temperature.

"Why are you always so warm?" I wondered aloud.

"Because angels, even fallen ones, are born of the sun, and we carry a tiny piece of it inside us. You do, too, but it is tempered by your humanity and your inexperience. When you come to the full maturity of your magic, you will not be as aware of the differences between us."

I had leaned closer to him without realizing it, mesmerized by his eyes and his voice. His breath was sweet, like cinnamon and cloves, and it brushed across my face, featherlight.

My lips touched his, for an instant, and then I stepped away and smiled down at him. I wasn't ready yet for whatever else might come, not ready to answer the tension I'd felt thrumming through his body. He watched me warily as I stepped away.

I sat on the bed again, and we just watched each other for a few moments. I considered what Gabriel had said about being born of the sun, and it reminded me of my dream.

The magic inside me surged up, warning me not to tell Gabriel. I wondered why my magic was so vociferously arguing against sharing the dreams with anyone else. It was almost like the power inside me was its own being.

"Gabriel, do you remember when the nuvem attacked me?"

He raised an eyebrow. "How could I possibly forget such a thing?"

"Well, you asked me what happened when the nuvem was inside me."

"And you never answered me."

I gave him a dirty look. "I wasn't the only one around here keeping secrets."

He lifted his shoulder in acknowledgment and indicated that I should continue.

"It was weird. I had a kind of vision, or a dream, about a girl named Evangeline," I said. "It was like I was there, in her body. I saw her in love with a fallen angel, and she was pregnant."

"Evangeline," Gabriel whispered, and he said it like her name was holy.

"What about her? Is this something else I should know about before another demon shows up to kick my ass?"

"She is the Lost Mother," Gabriel said.

"Refresh my memory?" I said, giving him an exasperated look. "Just because you've decided to let me into the club doesn't mean I know all the secret passwords."

"She was Lucifer Morningstar's bride," Gabriel said. "Evangeline carried his children, the first he had successfully gotten upon a human woman.

"But the Morningstar's enemies stole her from him before the children were born, and he never found her again. It was as if her existence had never been," Gabriel finished, and he looked troubled.

"And the children?" I asked, and I thought I felt the fluttering of tiny wings inside my own body.

"Also lost. How the Morningstar raged when she was taken from him," Gabriel said. His eyes looked haunted. "The nuvem is just a minor demon. It should have tried to bind your magic or suffocate the life from you."

"Well, to be fair, I think it was probably doing that, too."

"I am disturbed by this vision of the Lost Mother," Gabriel said.

"As far as I'm concerned, it's the least disturbing thing that's happened to me all week."

"Tell me what you have seen, exactly, down to the last detail," he demanded, and there was an urgency in his voice that hadn't been there before.

So I told him of Evangeline, and how she had loved Lucifer, and how she had escaped the house of her enemies and destroyed them, and given birth to her children.

"Are they nephilim?" I asked. "Is that why I'm seeing these visions? Is Ramuell trying to manipulate me?"

"I do not believe Ramuell has this kind of power. In any case, the children of Evangeline were not nephilim. That is why Lucifer cherished her above all others."

"Not nephilim? But how?"

Gabriel shrugged. "We do not know. I do not believe Lucifer himself knows. But there is this, Madeline—there has been no trace of the Lost Mother since she disappeared. There have been no dreams or visions, no evidence of any kind. If there had been, the Morningstar would have heard of it and used it to try to discover her."

"So you're saying . . ."

"That your vision has endangered you further. Once the Morningstar discovers that you have had this vision of

Evangeline, you will become as valued to him as she once was."

"And that will mean his enemies will find me just as interesting."

Gabriel nodded. "Yes."

As if I didn't have enough on my plate, I was now Lucifer's most wanted. Hooray.

11

"I CAN'T SLEEP ANYMORE," I SAID, PUSHING OFF THE bed and going to my dresser. I yanked a pair of raggedy gray sweatpants from the bottom drawer and pulled them on underneath the nightgown. I felt exposed in my virgin-sacrifice garb. I didn't want to be caught wearing nothing but a cotton nightgown when the demonic hordes came for me.

I found a heavy blue Cubs sweatshirt and pulled it over my head. Gabriel watched all this with a bemused expression on his face.

"Are you cold?" he asked.

"Yes," I said shortly, and headed into the kitchen, flipping on lights as I went. The overhead glare nearly blinded me but I plowed forward. I sensed rather than heard Gabriel following me, a dark shadow in his omnipresent overcoat.

"What are you doing?"

"Making cocoa," I said, pulling out two cups and a pan.

I grabbed the milk out of the fridge and poured it in the pan, and then set the pan on the stove.

"Madeline, you need to sleep. Your body needs to rebuild itself. You used too much magic on Ramuell. When I awoke I found you nearly dead. Your life force had dwindled to nothing. When I tried to heal you, it was like touching the fluttering wings of a moth," he said, and I thought his voice trembled a little. I turned to look at him, but his face was as impassive as ever.

"Thank you," I said, looking at him steadily. "Thank you for saving my life, again. But I don't want to sleep anymore. I feel like I want to get out and run a few laps, actually."

He frowned at that. "My healing should not have restored you so quickly. You have only been sleeping a few hours."

I held my hands up in an I-don't-know gesture. "And I feel a little nauseous."

"That is a common side effect of overuse of magic. You have thrown your body out of balance and you may feel a little sick until the balance is restored. But you should not feel so energetic."

I stirred the milk on the stove, watching the heat carefully so that the milk didn't curdle or boil. I voiced a concern that had been troubling me for some time. "Gabriel, I don't understand the magic that's inside me. When I have tried to use it in the past as an Agent, I felt like my magic came only reluctantly and with great exertion on my part. But now it seems like it wants to leap out of me. Earlier today, with Ramuell, it came pouring out of me and I couldn't control it. I don't understand what happened at the end at all."

"At the end?"

I tested the milk with my finger. It was hot enough for cocoa but not so hot that it would scald. I poured two packets of instant mix into the cups and added the milk. I opened a cabinet and began rooting around for the mini-marshmallows.

"After you were knocked out, Ramuell got ahold of me. My magic was pretty tapped out at that point, and he was doing his evil villain thing, telling me horrible things to make me even more upset before he ate me." I found the bag of marshmallows and added generous amounts to both cups.

"One does not generally refer to the threats of a nephilim as an 'evil villain thing,' " Gabriel said dryly as I handed him one of the cups.

I waved my hand at him to indicate that he should follow as I went into the living room, turning on more lights. I curled up in my favorite chair and pulled a crocheted blanket over my legs. I wasn't tired, but I was very cold, cold in my core, like I'd been out running in freezing rain.

"Anyway," I said, dismissing his commentary, "Ramuell was threatening me, and I thought I was going to die. And then all of a sudden, some kind of force came out of me."

"A . . . force? What kind of force?"

It sounded really goofy when Gabriel repeated it in that dry-as-dust tone. "I had no magic, and then all of a sudden I felt something enormous surge out of me, like a bomb going off. There was this burst of white light that sort of burned through me and out through my skin. Ramuell dropped me, and when I looked up at him I saw that whatever had come out of me had melted away his skin."

The look of astonishment on Gabriel's face would have been hilarious if it wasn't so terrifying. Whatever I had done, it was clearly something Gabriel had never seen before, and that frightened me. I did not want to be any freakier than I already was.

"This is not good, is it?" I asked. My hands trembled and a little cocoa spilled from my cup onto the blanket.

"It is unexpected," Gabriel said.

"A very careful answer."

"I am not sure what to say to you. From the beginning, there have been events surrounding you that I did not expect."

"Such as my vision of Evangeline?"

"Yes. And now this power that can harm the nephilim. As I have told you before, it took the power of every one of the fallen to bind the nephilim. The strength and invulnerability of these creatures is legendary. For you to manifest a power that can do such damage to them is unheard of, especially since you are part human. I wonder . . ." Gabriel trailed off, looking thoughtful.

"You wonder what?" I asked.

"Perhaps your mother was not simply an Agent," Gabriel said. "Perhaps she had some other supernatural lineage in her blood that she passed to you, and that mixed with your father's power in a way that we have not seen before."

The idea disturbed me, not least because it would mean that my mother had kept yet another secret from me. But there was one creature living who would know the truth. I pushed the blanket off my lap and went to the front window. Sure enough, Beezle was crouched just below the sill, listening to my conversation with Gabriel. He gave a guilty little start when I appeared at the window. I lifted the screen and crooked my finger at him. He flew into the room, scowling at both of us, and perched on the arm of my chair.

"I didn't know of any magic in Katherine's blood other than her powers as an Agent," he said immediately. Then his face took on a hangdog expression. "You made hot chocolate without me?"

Wordlessly I passed my cup to him and he downed the remains in one long gulp.

"Can I get back to my job now, please?" he said.

"Only if you promise not to lurk under the sill like a creepy stalker. Otherwise you may as well stay in here where you can contribute something useful," I said.

In response he settled more comfortably on the chair.

"I thought so," I said dryly. "Do you have any theories about this strange power of mine?"

"Perhaps it is simply Azazel's power and Katherine's mixing inside you. I do not know of any other Agents who are also the children of fallen angels," Beezle said, and he looked questioningly at Gabriel.

"No, I do not believe that there are any others," Gabriel said. "But I would have to confirm this with Lord Azazel. Additionally, this power is significantly greater than that of a mere Agent, or even Lord Azazel's. I have never heard of this . . . What would you call it?"

"It was almost like a star bursting inside me, like a sun," I said slowly. "A tremendous buildup of heat that happened all at once, and then exploded out of me without focus."

Beezle looked disturbed. "We have to start teaching you how to control your powers. This starburst didn't harm you—this time. But who knows what may happen next time? The power may be so great that the force of it could hurt you, or even kill you."

"I'm all for the controlling of the powers," I said. "I'm getting more than a little tired of feeling like my magic is jerking me around on a chain."

"Tomorrow, when you are more rested . . ." Gabriel said.

He wasn't able to finish his thought. The doorbell rang, and we all looked at one another in confusion.

"Who could that be?" I asked, as I glanced at the clock and stood up. Gabriel followed suit, coming to stand at my side. "It's nearly four in the morning."

"I'm going to see," Beezle said, alighting from his perch.

"Be careful," I hissed after him. "Remember what happened when Antares came by for a visit."

He flapped his claws at me in a don't-remind-me-I've-got-it-covered gesture.

The few moments that Beezle was gone seemed interminable. Gabriel quietly took my hand and I laced his fingers tightly in mine. We said nothing and waited for Beezle's return.

Beezle fluttered back in the window and grimaced at the handholding. I gave him a look that warned him not to bring it up right now.

"It's J.B.," he announced.

I let go of Gabriel's hand and let out an exasperated breath. "Does that idiot Antares think that I'll fall for this a second time?"

"I think it really is J.B.," Beezle said. "If he is using magic to disguise himself, then it is a very powerful spell. I looked at him through all five layers of reality and it appears to be J.B. down to the bone."

"Well, swell," I said. "It's not my demon half brother, but if J.B.'s here at this hour, then that means that I'm in trouble for something."

I hurried down the stairs as the bell rang again a few more times. Swinging open the door at the bottom of the stairs, I saw that J.B. stood inside the foyer, and that reminded me that both Gabriel and Antares had been unable to cross inside from the porch without my permission. The last bit of tension in my gut unknotted. I didn't really want to see J.B. right now, but at least he wasn't some horror show coming to take me back to his master in pieces.

"I need to talk to you—now," he said grimly as soon as he saw me. His face was drawn, his cheeks were stubbled and his hair stuck up all over his head like he'd been pulling on it for several hours—or maybe it was just bedhead. Either way, J.B. looked a mess.

"You look a mess," I said tactfully. "And it's a bit early—or a bit late, depending on your point of view—for a social call, don't you think?"

"I've been up all night and I don't need any of your crap right now, Black," he said, pushing past me onto the stairs.

"Not bedhead, then," I mumbled, and closed the door. As I turned to follow him I bumped into his back. "Get going if you have to be here, Jake. Otherwise, I can think of things I would rather be doing right now than standing on the stairs looking at your ass." *No matter how fine it is,* I added mentally.

"Who are you?" J.B. demanded.

I peeked around him and saw Gabriel standing at the top of the stairs. He gave J.B. a menacing look.

"That's my neighbor," I said, squeezing around J.B. and marching up the stairs. "Stop intimidating J.B., Gabriel."

Gabriel nodded. "As you wish."

He disappeared into my apartment. I sighed and beckoned for J.B. to follow.

"What's he doing here in the middle of the night?" J.B. asked crossly.

"That's a question that I could ask you," I said, leading

the way into my living room. Beezle had disappeared, although he was probably eavesdropping under the windowsill again. Gabriel had resumed his position in the chair opposite mine.

I didn't offer J.B. a chair or a drink, but he dropped onto the couch anyway. I closed the front door. Before I could make it to my chair, J.B. launched into his usual speaking mode—attack, attack, attack.

"Just what in the hell happened at Clark and Belmont tonight, Black? Twenty-six souls disappear without a trace or a record of their choice, and you're the only Agent on scene. The whole intersection looks like it's been destroyed by flamethrowers. I want some answers and I want them now."

As usual, J.B.'s presence made my back teeth grind and brought all my worst instincts to the fore. "Well, J.B., I'm sure you're distressed over the lack of properly filed reports, but I was very busy in that intersection fighting for my life. You see, this completely horrific creature called a nephilim showed up, munched on a few souls, melted a few people into taffy, and tried to take me out, too. And oh, by the way, it's the same creature that I warned you about yesterday when I was in your office, and you ignored me completely. So, as far as I'm concerned, this mess is on your head, not mine."

"What the fuck is a nephilim?" J.B. exploded, his face red. "Is this another one of your fairy tales about soul-eating monsters?"

"It's not a fairy tale," I said, rising to my feet. "It's a nightmare the likes of which you have never known. We are on the verge of a real biblical-style apocalypse here. I don't need you giving me crap about paperwork right now. I have to find this thing before it finds me, or else I'm going to end up just like my mother, my soul trapped inside its body forever."

J.B. stared at me. "You've cracked. You've finally lost it. I always wondered if your mother's death would do it, and it finally has. You're imagining some nonexistent monster ate her up, and now you've killed twenty-six people in an effort to prove your wacko theories."

"What?" I said, unreasonably hurt by his assumption. He'd known me for years. We didn't always like each other—okay, we didn't like each other at all—but how could J.B. think I was a murderer? "You think that I killed those people? How the hell would I be able to do that?"

"I don't know, and the truth is, I don't want to know. Those people died horrible deaths," J.B. said grimly.

"I was trying to help them!"

"Right. Help them by melting their faces off."

"If I am a murderer," I said through gritted teeth, "don't you think that you should be running out the door right now instead of standing in my living room making ridiculous accusations?"

From the look on J.B.'s face, I would say that the thought hadn't occurred to him. Gabriel coughed into his fist. The cough sounded suspiciously like laughter.

J.B. visibly tried to pull himself together. "You are suspended until further notice. Any pending collections will be reassigned to other Agents."

"You can't suspend me solely on the merit of your asinine conclusions," I shouted.

"I can and I will," he said, standing up and approaching me so that we were nearly nose to nose.

"I don't have time for this. Why can't I make you understand that there is something horrible out there that is going to eat its way through the city until it's stopped?"

"The only 'something horrible' that needs to be stopped is you," he said.

I had actually pulled my fist back to deck him right in that smug mouth, but Gabriel's hand closed over mine.

"Why not?" I said to him through gritted teeth.

"Because it will cause unnecessary complications," Gabriel said softly.

I breathed hard through my nose and glared at J.B., who watched this little interchange with widened eyes.

"You have no sense of self-preservation whatsoever, do you?" I asked.

"What do you mean?" J.B. said, his eyes darting from me to Gabriel and back again.

"I don't think you fully grasp how angry I am at you right now, and you're standing very, very close to me."

12

I SMILED, AND I KNEW THAT IT WAS NOT A PLEASANT smile. Somewhere deep inside, I felt a little flicker of magic, as faint as a match flame.

He finally seemed to understand, and he stepped back a few inches. As he did, I saw his expression change. He stared at me like he'd never seen me before.

"What now?" I asked.

"Your eyes," he said, his voice half-strangled. "What happened to your eyes?"

Worried that I had manifested some new freakiness since my altercation with Ramuell, I looked at Gabriel, who said, "You have starshine in your eyes."

"Oh, that," I said, waving my hand in a dismissive motion.

J.B. backed away slowly, his hands up in the air like he was surrendering to the cops. "I don't know what the hell is going on here, but you stay away from me, Black. You're some kind of freak."

I watched him, content to let him go and deal with the suspension later. He continued his careful path backward out of the room until something behind me made his face turn paler and he let out a yelp of surprise.

"What the hell is that thing?" he shouted, pointing at Beezle.

"Great timing, Beezle," I said as he landed on my shoulder.

"Umm, you might not want to let J.B. leave right now," he said in an undertone close to my ear.

"And why is that?"

"Antares and a few of his buddies are hanging out on the front lawn. They asked for, and I quote, 'Azazel's half-breed bitch to come forth and engage in mortal combat.' Then they mentioned taking your entrails back to Focalor or something else of that nature."

"You didn't think the details were important enough to remember?" I asked. I was a little concerned for my entrails even if Beezle wasn't.

"Frankly, demonic threats get a little boring after a while. It's always 'I'll pull your beating heart out of your chest' or 'I'll suck your eyeballs out of your skull.' They haven't had any new material in a couple of millennia," Beezle said.

"He is absolutely right. Demons do have an unfortunate tendency of repeating themselves," Gabriel added, straight-faced.

"I gather from your jocular attitudes that neither of you are taking Antares very seriously?" Even though I was loaded with enough energy to clean the house five times over, I could feel that the strength of my magic was still very low. I didn't think I was up to taking on Antares right now, especially since our last meeting had involved a lot of punching and kicking of my vulnerable human parts.

"The devil here can manage your measly half brother," Beezle said, jerking a claw in Gabriel's direction. "The other two will run once Antares has learned his lesson."

I frowned. "Doesn't that make it look like I can't fight my own battles?"

"No," Gabriel said. "It shows Antares—and, more important, Focalor—that you are not a weak link to be exploited. It shows that Lord Azazel cares enough for you to come to your aid. After tonight, they will think twice about attempting to threaten you simply because you are Azazel's human daughter."

"What are you going to do?" I asked as Gabriel strode past me toward the door.

"As the gargoyle says." Gabriel nodded at Beezle briefly. "Teach Antares a lesson he will not soon forget."

"I love it when you talk sexy like that," I said, and then my heart dropped into my stomach. "Wait a second— where the hell is J.B.?"

"Gods above and below," Beezle swore, launching from my shoulder to fly out the window.

I raced to the door. Gabriel had already disappeared down the stairs ahead of me. I took the stairs two at a time, almost tumbling down in my haste. J.B. drove me crazy, and yes, he thought I was a murderer, but I did not want his death on my conscience. I wanted him alive so I could kick his ass tomorrow for suspending me.

"Please, please, please let him be all right," I said as I rushed out the open door and onto the front porch. I crashed into Gabriel, who stood stock-still on the peeling red boards, his hands fisted beside him.

I stepped around him and saw Antares in all of his black-horned, red-skinned glory. He held J.B. loosely around the shoulders, almost as if he was showing us that the two of them were pals. But the black sickle claws of Antares's right hand hovered dangerously close to J.B.'s jugular.

J.B. looked like he wanted to throw up. I was surprised he hadn't already—the stink of sulfur was overwhelming. I cupped my hand over my nose.

"Let him go, Antares," I said in the most commanding voice that I could. It wasn't very commanding since my hand was over my nose. I ended up sounding like I had a cold.

Antares smiled and showed his mouthful of sharp teeth. He pulled J.B. a little closer and stroked one claw down J.B.'s neck. J.B. was pale but to his credit he made no sound.

"But your friend and I are having so much fun," Antares said. "Isn't that right, Jacob?"

"A laugh a minute," J.B. said, his voice hoarse.

Antares threw his head back and guffawed. "You are quite brave for a man about to have his throat slit."

I dropped my hand from my face and stepped forward. The little match flame inside me roared to about the size of a candle and then sank back. I had no magic. But Antares didn't need to know that.

"Let him go," I said again, this time putting the force of my will behind the command. I saw Antares's face flicker for a moment—confusion? fear?—then return to a smug expression.

"And what," Antares said silkily, "will you give me in return, little virgin?"

Antares's compatriots snorted and leered suggestively at me. The sight of them nauseated me more. Antares looked like a Hollywood stereotype of a demon—the red skin, the bat wings, the black claws and horns. His friends, however, looked more like the Thing in the Carpenter movie. One demon was a mass of loose, rubbery gray flesh that oozed from side to side as it paced—I assumed it paced; I couldn't see anything resembling feet—behind Antares. Underneath the flesh something moved, like millions of maggots were crawling beneath the demon's skin.

The second demon had a more humanoid form, but it was squat and grossly fat. Its skin was pale and its eyes were a slitted purple. When it opened its mouth to smile at me, I saw blood caking its teeth.

"How about you give me J.B. and I keep Gabriel here from kicking your ass from here to next Tuesday?" I said sweetly.

Antares had been steadfastly avoiding Gabriel's gaze up to this point, but now he was forced to acknowledge Gabriel's silent presence beside me. The angel seemed content to let me handle the talking while he did the menacing bodyguard thing.

My demon half brother said nothing for a moment, clearly unsure how to proceed. If he handed over J.B., he might not be humiliated in front of his little buddies. If he didn't hand over J.B., he would *definitely* be humiliated in front of his little buddies. He apparently decided to continue the show for his audience.

"I do not fear Azazel's thrall. He cannot lay a finger on me without endangering his own life or the life of his master," Antares sneered.

I wondered if that was true. Gabriel had said that my father had sworn an oath in order to save Gabriel's life, an oath that said Azazel would keep Gabriel from becoming a monster like his father. But did that mean that Gabriel couldn't physically defend himself from another demon? I didn't want to appear uncertain or ignorant, so I mustered up my own bravado to match Antares's.

"So if Gabriel defeats you in combat, you'll run and tattle?" I tutted. "Not exactly the most demonic response ever."

If Antares's face hadn't already been red, I'm sure that a blush would have risen on his cheeks. His eyes narrowed into slits as he yanked J.B. closer and opened his palm threateningly over J.B.'s neck. I watched, mesmerized by the sharpness of the claws that hovered over J.B.'s pulse.

"I would not have to tattle, as you put it," Antares hissed. "I would return to my master with the thrall's entrails as my necklace as well as those of this foolish human."

"See," Gabriel murmured for my ears alone. "Same material as always."

Then he took a step forward, motioning with his hand that I should stay back.

"Regardless of what you believe the outcome might be were we to engage in combat, you know as well as I do that the Accords forbid the spilling of innocent human blood," Gabriel said. "I do not believe Focalor would welcome the punishment our lord Lucifer would mete out if one of Focalor's subjects violated the agreement in his name."

Behind Antares the other demons shifted nervously. The fat one spoke to Antares in a language I didn't understand. It had an ugly, harsh sound, made worse by the demon's wet, slurping voice.

Antares barked back at the demon in the same language and it shrank away from his vehemence. He turned back to Gabriel, who had a smug little smile on his face.

"Your friend is smarter than you," Gabriel said. "Or at least, he has a stronger sense of self-preservation."

The second demon now joined in the protests of the

first. Antares shouted at this one, too, but it didn't seem to be as easily cowed as its companion. There were a few moments of heated exchange while J.B.'s life hung in the balance.

I clenched my fists at my side and cursed my own powerlessness. If I could summon up another of those starbursts, I could blast Antares into oblivion and that would be the end of it. Of course, having zero control over my power, I would probably blast J.B. into oblivion, too.

"Just wait," Gabriel murmured, sensing my frustration. "I do not think that bloodshed will be necessary this day."

The second demon's voice rose, and then it turned away from Antares. Antares shouted after it, but the second demon ignored him. It moved a few feet away from Antares and called to the fat demon, who hesitated for a moment, clearly unsure what side his bread was buttered on. Antares said something threatening to the fat demon, but it shook its head and ran to the side of the oozing demon.

The oozing demon said a single word in that ugly language, and for the second time that day I saw a rent in the fabric of reality. A dark hole opened out of thin air in front of the oozing demon. All I could see inside it was a swirling vortex of smoke. Then the oozing demon disappeared inside the vortex and the fat demon followed.

Antares wavered for a moment, long enough that the hole began to close a bit. Then he abruptly dropped J.B. to the ground and dove after his companions. The hole closed just as Antares's barbed tail flicked inside.

"Well, that was anticlimactic," Gabriel said.

"What the hell was that thing they used to get away?" I asked as I hurried down the steps to J.B. He attempted to stand but his legs buckled under him. I tried to put my arm under his shoulder to help him up, but he waved me away. I was hurt for a moment by his rejection, until he rolled over and puked on my lawn. Then I was just grateful.

"A portal. Demons and angels use them for ease of travel over long distances," Gabriel said as we waited for J.B. to pull himself together.

"I saw Ramuell disappear into one of those before I blacked out," I said.

"Really?" Gabriel asked, intrigued. "A nephilim has no power to open a portal. This certainly lends credence to the notion that Ramuell's puppet master is one of the fallen, most probably an enemy of Lord Azazel's. It also explains why Ramuell did not destroy you when you were vulnerable."

"His master called him home at the wrong moment," I said.

"Precisely."

J.B. struggled to his feet, waving off my attempts to help him. "Water," he croaked.

I crooked a finger at him and bade him follow me inside. Gabriel went ahead of us. Beezle fluttered down from his perch on the roof to land on my shoulder.

"Did you enjoy the show?" I asked mildly.

"The denouement kind of sucked, but up until that point I had high hopes," Beezle said. He glanced around at J.B., who was staring. "What are you looking at, ape?"

"An ugly little what-the-fuck-are-you?" J.B. answered, following me up the stairs.

I covered my mouth so that Beezle wouldn't be offended by my snort of laughter, but his stony stare indicated that I hadn't been very subtle.

"Beezle is a gargoyle. He's the protector of this house," I said, when Beezle didn't deign to answer.

"And the stinky horror-movie monsters? What were

those?" he asked as we entered the kitchen. I got a glass of water from the sink faucet and handed it to him. He drank deeply until the glass was empty, and then handed it back to me and said, "More, please."

I took the glass and refilled it. "Those things on the front lawn were demons, and I don't think I've ever heard you say 'please' before."

"If you could have heard my thoughts while that thing was holding on to my jugular, you would have heard a lot of 'pleases,'" he said, and smiled.

I smiled back, and was reminded of how handsome he was. He was always such a flaming jerk it was easy to over-look his positive points.

Gabriel cleared his throat, and I was suddenly reminded that he was in the room, and that Beezle was still perched on my shoulder, following this little exchange with avid interest.

"So tell me again," J.B. said. "What exactly is going on around here, Black? Was one of those demons the thing that you've been complaining about for the last couple of days?"

"No," I said, irritated at his dismissal of the nephilim as "that thing you've been complaining about." "If it had been Ramuell, he wouldn't have let you go. In fact, he wouldn't have waited for me to watch—he would have just devoured you and told me about it later."

"Fine, then fill me in about this Ramuell so we can take care of him," J.B. said, his natural arrogance reasserting itself now that he was out of danger.

I shook my head. "First of all, you can't just 'take care of' Ramuell. He's nothing like you've ever imagined. And second—now you believe me? Now you've decided I'm not a crazy murderer?"

He looked abashed. "Well, what the hell was I supposed to think?"

"You were supposed to think better of me. You've known me for years." I glared at J.B. and he glared back. It was almost as if the incident on the lawn had never happened. We had returned to status quo with barely a ripple.

"Madeline," Gabriel interrupted. "May I speak with you a moment?"

I glanced over at Gabriel. He leaned against the counter, his arms crossed, his face impassive. If I didn't know him, I would have thought that he was as calm as Lake Michigan on a clear day. But I could see stars burning deep in his eyes.

"His eyes are like yours were," J.B. said wonderingly. "Just what is going on here? Are you in some kind of cult?"

"Cult? No, it's . . ." I said, and Beezle gave me a warning squeeze of his claws. I realized quickly that he was right. J.B. would have to be on a need-to-know basis, and I wasn't sure yet what he needed to know. ". . . a really long story. Listen, J.B., why don't you go home? There is nothing else we can do tonight."

"That's it?" he said. "You're just going to shuffle me out the door without an explanation?"

"Yes," I said firmly, taking him by the elbow and leading him to the door. "I'll meet you tomorrow morning at ten in your office, and explain everything. In the meantime, go home and get some sleep."

"I have a meeting with McConnell and Baroja tomorrow at ten A.M. to review some procedures," he said.

Now, that was the J.B. I knew. Never mind the demon attack; procedures needed reviewing. "Ten thirty, then. I promise to explain everything. And don't mention this to anyone else, all right?"

I unceremoniously pushed him out the door and shut it behind him.

Beezle lifted off my shoulder and said, "I'm ready for a nap." He flew out the front window without another word, leaving me alone with Gabriel. And being alone with Gabriel suddenly made me nervous. There was something very predatory in his eyes at that moment, something that made the match flame of power inside me flutter.

"You wanted to talk to me?" I said.

He said nothing, merely continued to stand with his arms crossed, leaning against the counter, stars firing in his eyes.

"You know, I have had a very stressful few days, and if you have nothing important to say, then I think that you should head on down to your own apartment," I snapped.

Still he said nothing, and he didn't move. I walked to the front door and pointedly opened it, standing beside it with an expectant look on my face.

He moved then, and if I had a better sense of self-preservation, I would have gotten the hell out of the way. But I knew he was coming for me, and my heart sang out in welcome. He stopped in front of me, close enough for our thighs to brush together, and he closed the door with a flick of magic.

I watched him, not speaking, hardly daring to breathe. Though I didn't often think about the complete and utter lack of romance in my life, I felt terribly *virginal* at that moment. I didn't really know what to do, or how to make sure that he did what I wanted him to do.

And as he had done so often, Gabriel seemed to understand all of this without my saying a word. He put his hands on my shoulders, gently but firmly, and pulled me closer so that I could feel the heat of him pressing against me. It felt natural to put my arms around his neck, to turn my face up to his like a flower seeking the sun.

He hesitated an instant, his mouth a whisper away from mine, and then he kissed me, a kiss so sweet and gentle that it brought tears to my eyes. I pressed closer to him, and his arms came around my back and his kiss deepened, and I heard a little moan escape my mouth. The sound seemed to break the spell, and he pulled back from me, his eyes fierce and blazing.

"This is madness," he said. "I cannot do this."

I wanted to ask why, to ask questions, to force him to come back to me. But I realized in an instant that I had other powers of persuasion. I stood on my tiptoes and brushed my mouth across his lips, his jaw, his neck below the ear. His breath was harsh and he gripped me tighter. He kissed me then with a bruising ferocity, like he wanted to devour me, and I kissed him back and held on tight.

He pushed me against the door, his mouth on my face, my neck, my breasts, his hands moving underneath my clothes. I gasped for air, and in the midst of the storm of sensation, I felt something growing inside me, something like that starburst of light that had blasted out of me when Ramuell was on the verge of victory.

And as before, I couldn't stop it; I couldn't control it. My body filled up with heat and light and it exploded out of me in a supernova, and I had no time to think or to worry about Gabriel because I fell away into the darkness.

13

"MADELINE. MADELINE."

Someone was calling me. I floated in water and darkness, and I was tired, and I wanted to sleep, and someone kept calling me, telling me to wake up. There were hands on my shoulders, strong hands that held tight, tight enough to hurt. I feebly tried to push them off, but they only shook more insistently.

"Madeline, open your eyes and look at me," he said.

"Go 'way," I mumbled. "Sleep."

"No, do not sleep," he said, and his voice was a command, and the command pissed me off. I opened my eyes to tell him so, and saw Gabriel's anxious face.

"Stop looming," I said crossly, and he released me instantly, the relief in his eyes palpable.

"Thank the gods you are all right," he said.

"What happened?" I asked. "How come I've been knocked out *again*?"

"You do not remember?" he asked carefully.

Images started to filter back—Gabriel's hands, Gabriel's mouth—and I felt my face redden. I sat up, and immediately felt dizzy. Black spots danced in front of my eyes.

"What do you need?" he asked immediately.

The question was entirely innocent, but our recent activities made it seem very suggestive to me. I wondered vaguely if everyone felt this stupid and awkward after they made out for the first time.

"Umm, some water," I said.

He got up and went into the kitchen, and more memories trickled back, and then I remembered the explosion. I shot to my feet, then swayed and grabbed the doorknob so I didn't slide to the floor again.

Gabriel came back in with a glass of water and saw me hanging on to the wall for dear life. "Gods above and below. You are as white as chalk."

He placed the glass on the table and rushed to my side, lifting me easily. He laid me on the couch and would have pulled away, but I grasped his hand and pressed it.

"You aren't hurt?" I asked urgently. My eyes roamed all over him, looking for signs that his skin had been blasted off like Ramuell's. But he looked as perfect as ever.

"I am unhurt," he said, and to my surprise the tips of his ears turned pink.

I looked at him questioningly. "What happened? How come the starburst didn't mince you up the way it did Ramuell?"

"I do not know why your power behaved that way, or why it harmed Ramuell and not myself," he said. "I have never seen a manifestation like that before."

"But something happened to you," I guessed.

"Yes, well, I imagine it was due to the nature of our activities at the time," he said, turning his face away.

I had never seen him less than perfectly composed, and that in itself was so distracting that it took me a minute to put two and two together.

"It felt *good*, didn't it?" I guessed.

"Yes," he said, barely opening his lips.

"How good?" I pressed.

"Very good," he almost whispered. I was surprised to see a bit of red creep up his cheeks.

I gave out a bark of laughter. "So Ramuell gets roasted alive, I get a hangover, and you get a happy. There is something very unfair in this equation, and I'm pretty sure it's unfair to me."

Gabriel stiffened for a moment, and then some of the tension went out of him and he laughed. He kissed my forehead gently. "I think the issue to address is the source of this power. It seems to manifest itself at unexpected moments."

"And, apparently, it has varied effects," I said.

"Most important, it appears to exhaust you completely afterward, which is dangerous. If this power burst out of you while you were in combat with Ramuell or Antares, you would be left vulnerable to an attack."

"Assuming that the power didn't blast them off the face of the Earth," I pointed out.

"I am not certain that we can count on that happening," he said. "Obviously, your power affected me differently from Ramuell. The next time, it may do something else entirely."

A sudden thought occurred to me. "Just tell me that Beezle slept through this."

"I have not seen the gargoyle," Gabriel said.

"Good," I said. "Because I don't want to hear any lectures right now."

"Lectures?" His right eyebrow quirked up.

"Beezle thinks that it's dangerous for me to . . . involve myself with you." I watched his face carefully as I said this, and my heart sank when he turned grim.

"The gargoyle is correct," he said. "It is very dangerous for you, which is why this must never happen again."

"I don't understand," I said, and I cursed the plaintive note in my voice. Why did he make me feel this way?

"For us to be involved, as you put it, would threaten your life and mine. Lord Azazel would not thank me for putting his beloved daughter's life in peril."

"But you haven't explained why," I said. I wanted to cry out in frustration or to beg him not to say these things, and I thought that attraction was a terrible thing if it made you so vulnerable.

"Maddy, no matter how much I may want you," he said steadily, "it cannot be. *We* cannot be."

I turned my head away, embarrassed by my longing for him, by the way I had thrown myself at him.

"Don't," he said, putting his finger under my chin and turning my face back. "Do not turn from me in shame. The fault is not with you, but with me. I allowed myself to be overcome by my own jealousy."

"Jealousy? Of what?" I asked.

"Of that puling human Bennett," he said, and his vehemence startled me.

"Bennett? J.B.?" I asked incredulously.

"You do not see the way that he looks at you," Gabriel said. "And you think he is attractive."

"Well, yeah," I said. "Because I'm not blind."

The pouty expression on his face made me laugh. "Gabriel, there are many, many attractive men in the world, but not one of them holds a candle to you. You're an angel, for Pete's sake."

"Half angel," he said.

"Yeah, well, you seem to have gotten your looks from your mom. Ramuell got beat hard with the ugly stick. And besides, J.B. is a pain in my ass at the best of times and a total flaming jerk otherwise. It doesn't matter how cute he is. I don't think too much of his personality."

"You did not think too much of my personality recently, either," he said. "You were quite furious with me for entering your mind."

I colored in embarrassment. "Well, yes. And I'm still annoyed about that, to tell you the truth. It was wrong of you."

He nodded.

"But you saved my life a few times, so I've decided to forgive you. Besides, I'm sure that you were acting on my father's orders."

"Yes."

"So he's the one I need to yell at." I sobered, remembering why we were having this conversation. "But I still don't understand why you're breaking up with me before we've even gone on a date."

Gabriel exhaled heavily and pushed off the sofa, pacing the room like a restless lion. "The nephilim's lives were preserved because the Grigori did not want to murder their own children, however monstrous. But neither did the Grigori want further generations of nephilim. So the nephilim were forbidden to reproduce, and since I am half nephilim, this edict also falls on me."

I stared at him. "So, you can't have babies. Does that mean that we can't be together? Hello, birth control?"

Gabriel's mouth twisted. "Human methods of preventing conception would be unable to stop you from getting pregnant. We are supernatural beings. There has never been a case where an angelic being has not impregnated his human partner. I have every reason to believe that if I made love to you, you would conceive my child. And for that sin, we would both be brought before Lucifer and punished."

"By 'punished,' you mean killed?"

Gabriel nodded.

I stared at him. "So, you're saying you've basically been condemned to a loveless existence because you can't reproduce, and if you do, you and your lover and your child will be slaughtered?"

He nodded again.

I pushed myself up to my elbows and felt another wave of dizziness. I was furious, but I felt too tired and sick to move any farther. "You're being punished for all eternity because your mother was raped by a nephilim? That's ridiculous. That's cruel."

"That is Lord Lucifer," Gabriel said. "His word is law, and his law is binding. These are the terms of my existence. Should I attempt to appeal them, I am certain he would remind me that I could have been struck down while still an infant."

I wanted to go on, to argue some more, to find a way for us to make it work. It was beyond unfair that I had finally found someone to be with and he had a sword of Damocles hanging over him that would come down the second we knocked boots.

But there were, as always, more important things to worry about. I decided to revert to professional mode and worry about my tangled feelings later.

"Gabriel, I had wanted to go to the Hall of Records today. And now that J.B. has seen Antares, he's more likely to cooperate."

Gabriel looked a little surprised at my sudden shift in topic but seemed to realize it was best not to spend any more time talking about the whole forbidden-lust thing.

I continued. "I was planning on going there so that I could look for other people like my mother and Patrick—people whose records don't show their choice after death. I thought it could help me find Ramuell."

"And it still may," Gabriel said thoughtfully. "Ramuell's victims may help us define his purpose here if there is a pattern to his choices. It also may help us identify his puppeteer. Whoever loosed this creature did so for their own foul purpose."

There was something not quite right here. I frowned. "One thing I don't get about this puppet master theory, though—if my father sent you here to protect me because only you can contain Ramuell long enough for him to be re-bound, then how could a puppet master control the nephilim? I mean, you said it took all the magic of the fallen to bind the nephilim before, right?"

"Yes," Gabriel said, and a crease appeared between his brows.

"So who, besides you, could possibly have the power to contain it in between rampages?" I asked.

"There could be more than one master," Gabriel said. "It would make sense. Only the combined magic of many powerful creatures could contain even one nephilim."

"Unless you are a descendant of one," I said, and I felt a little tickle in the back of my brain.

Gabriel looked at me with the same dawning comprehension in his eyes. "You think Ramuell has another child."

"It makes more sense than a confederacy of the fallen, doesn't it? I mean, how would that many masters hide what they were doing from Lucifer?" I asked.

"I think you are underestimating the number of enemies Lucifer has," Gabriel said with a half smile.

"But are there that many enemies who share the same purpose?" I persisted.

"Another child of the nephilim," Gabriel mused. "How could one be unknown to us? My birth was so unusual, so unwanted by above and below, that I was sentenced to death virtually at the moment of conception. How could Ramuell's other offspring be hidden?"

"I don't know," I said, feeling suddenly tired. It seemed that every answer I found brought new questions. "There is something else . . ."

"And what is that?"

It was hard to say this without sounding like a child. Every time someone mentioned my father, I felt confused. On the one hand, to be the object of his apparent adoration was a heady thing for a fatherless little girl. On the other hand, I was angry at his desertion of myself and my mother, and even angrier that he still didn't see fit to be present when my life was obviously in danger.

"I want to see my father. Can you take me to him?"

Gabriel looked shocked. "Madeline, you cannot simply appear in Azazel's court. There are protocols to follow."

"Am I his daughter, or aren't I?" I said angrily. I had been attacked by demons and nephilim, been overwhelmed by visions and new powers and assorted revelations, and the being responsible for the whole mess was two states away. I wanted to look him in the eye, to at least see the man who had conceived me and left me with a giant target on my back.

"You are his daughter, yes, but . . ." Gabriel looked more uncertain than I had ever seen him. "You cannot demand to see him. He is a lord, and if you do not follow the correct protocol, you could endanger my life and your own."

I felt a little tremble at the thought that Gabriel might be hurt. I didn't want to subject him to any more harm than he had already obviously suffered at Azazel's hands, but at the same time I didn't want to back off. I wasn't going to wait for Azazel to decide he felt like being a father. By the time that happened, I might be carved into tiny, bite-sized pieces by Ramuell.

"Then tell me the protocol. I want to see him."

"But . . ."

"Make it happen, Gabriel," I said. I was uncomfortably aware of the fact that I had just given him an order, and that he must follow it. I was Lord Azazel's daughter, and he was a thrall. The gap between us loomed up, dark and sudden, and I realized that even without his unfortunate bloodline it would be nearly impossible for us be together.

His body stiffened. He hadn't missed the command in my voice, either.

"As you wish, my lady," he said, and I shivered at the coldness in his voice.

He pulled his cell phone from his pocket and went into the kitchen. I heard the murmur of his voice, too low for me to make out the words.

I went to the front window and looked out. The black field of night was turning blue, and some early risers were already out walking their dogs. It was another day, the fourth since I had stood at this window and waved good-bye to Patrick for the last time.

It was hard to remember that he was gone. So much had happened in the last few days that the girl who lost Patrick was like a dream. We had sat in this room and gorged on pizza and bitched about J.B.'s predilection for paperwork and that had seemed like the most important thing in the world. Would Patrick even know the person who stood here now, the person who had just behaved not like Madeline Black, but like the daughter of Lord Azazel?

I heard Gabriel reenter the room behind me and I carefully wiped my face of tears before I turned. His face was like stone.

"Lord Azazel would be happy to receive you in his court later this morning, my lady," Gabriel said.

"Not that crap, again," I said. "Listen, I'm sorry I acted so high-handed before . . ."

He lowered his eyes from mine. "But you were correct. In Lord Azazel's realm you are akin to a princess, and I no better than a peasant. I should not show undue familiarity with my betters."

"I had no right to talk to you that way, no matter what I am in Lord Azazel's realm."

He looked up at me again, and some of the ice had melted. "The court is a very different place, and we must get into the practice of behaving correctly."

"I hope you won't let me make some stupid blunder that will get us both killed," I said.

"That all depends on if you will actually listen to my advice," he murmured.

"Are you trying to imply that I don't listen well?" I asked.

His lips quirked, but he wisely chose not to respond to my question. "Since you are akin to a princess, perhaps you should change into something a little more presentable?"

I looked down at myself and realized I was still wearing

my baggy sweats over my nightgown. My feet had been bare when I ran outside after J.B., and now they were covered with dirt and grass.

"And when I looked like this, you couldn't resist me?" I asked incredulously.

"My lady, I would find you irresistible in any costume," he said.

"Watch out, buddy, or some might think that you are getting familiar with your betters," I said, my cheeks reddening. I headed to my room to change into something "more presentable."

"I would like to be a great deal more familiar with you," he murmured.

I gave him no sign that I heard him, but I could not stop the smile that spread across my face.

14

TWENTY MINUTES LATER I STOOD NERVOUSLY NEXT TO Gabriel in my postage stamp of a backyard. Beezle perched on the railing of the back porch, arms crossed and looking desperately unhappy. He had spent several minutes telling me that my father was, essentially, an untrustworthy scumbag. I'd patted and comforted him as best I could and assured him that I was too smart to be fooled by Azazel. But he was still distressed and most definitely did not want me in Azazel's territory.

Beezle's attitude had done nothing to reduce my worry. For all of my bravado, I was scared stiff at the prospect of meeting my father. I had no idea what kind of reception I'd get.

Gabriel spoke. "When I open the portal, we will have but a few moments to take advantage. It requires a great deal of magical energy to open and direct the portal to our location, so it is urgent that you step into the portal immediately. I will follow once I am certain you are safely inside, and then I will close the door behind me."

"What's going to happen once I'm in the portal?" I asked.

"It will not be comfortable," Gabriel averred.

Beezle let out a little caw of laughter. "That's the understatement of the century. You're going to feel like your head is being squeezed between two cast-iron pans wielded by a sumo wrestler."

"Beezle, I don't know where you get your similes but that is definitely conjuring up some weird imagery," I said.

"It is not quite that bad," Gabriel said.

"It will be for her," Beezle snapped. "She's half human; you're not. Your body is designed to withstand this kind of rigor."

For the first time Gabriel looked uncertain. "Surely my lord Azazel would have thought of this. He would not risk Madeline's well-being."

"I'm not certain that he wouldn't," Beezle said darkly.

I held both of my hands up in a "stop" motion. "All right, all right. Look, the more we stand here talking about it, the worse I feel. Let's just get it over with. If my head gets squashed, then at least Ramuell won't have a chance to eat me."

"And that's going to be a real comfort to me," Beezle said, his face twisted up in unhappiness and anger.

"Beezle," I said, and I crooked my finger at him. He flew to me and wrapped his little arms around my neck, and tears pricked in my eyes. He was the only creature in the world whom I had loved and who had loved me all those long years without my mother. "I will come back to you in one piece."

"You'd better," he sniffed. Then he pulled away and

turned to Gabriel, pointing a claw in the half angel's face. "If one hair of her head is harmed, I am holding you accountable."

Gabriel swept into a bow. "I give you my word that I will keep her safe."

Beezle looked as though he didn't think too much of Gabriel's word, but he nodded anyway and returned to his perch.

"My lady?" Gabriel said.

My heart was in my mouth so I just gave a frozen nod.

Gabriel said a few words in another language. It wasn't the harsh syllables of the demons' tongue, but something lovelier and more ethereal. As I listened, I felt that I could almost understand it, like the translation was just out of reach, tickling the back of my brain.

A moment later an opening appeared in the air before me, growing longer and wider quickly. The hole was filled with swirling white mist.

"Step inside," Gabriel said.

Two cast-iron pans wielded by a sumo wrestler, I thought, and then said, "What the hell."

I stepped inside.

Immediately my body was sucked forward as if into a vacuum tube. The skin of my face was pushed back until my teeth were bared. My lungs gasped for air. And yes, the pressure between my ears was so intense that it did feel like my head had been clamped between iron. All around me was wind and white mist, like I was caught inside a tornado.

All I wanted was for the pain to end. And abruptly it did. I tumbled out of the tornado and crashed onto a cold marble floor. Half a second later, Gabriel appeared beside me, stepping coolly out of the portal just before it closed.

"How come you didn't crash?" I asked sulkily as he helped me to my feet.

"I have done this a few times," he said, looking around as he spoke.

I followed suit. We had landed in some kind of ante-chamber, a small room with double doors at the east and west ends. The floor was black marble, the walls a stark white. There were no paintings, sculptures or decorations of any kind except on the doors. The doors were a heavy dark wood, polished to a high gloss. In the center of each set of doors was carved a large five-pointed star, and crossed over the star was a sword with a rose wrapped around its hilt. Outside the eastern set of doors was a small bench, with cherry legs and a red velvet cushion.

There was no one to greet us, and no movement from behind the doors. I felt a little tremor of nerves in my stomach. I was about to meet my father.

"I know it is not in your nature, but *please* hold your tongue and let me speak when we enter your father's court," Gabriel said as we approached the eastern set of doors.

"Afraid I'll start a civil war?" I asked dryly.

"Something of that nature," he said. "And you must not mention Evangeline unless you are alone with Lord Azazel. My lord has not revealed your visions to Lord Lucifer as of yet."

"Why not?" I asked. "Isn't that a little . . . seditious?"

"Quite probably," Gabriel replied. "But Lord Azazel knows what he is about. He is understandably wary of drawing Lord Lucifer's attention to you. Finally, you must not be too familiar with me when we enter the court."

"Why not?"

"I am your inferior. It would be seen as an insult both

to Lord Azazel and to yourself were I to behave as your equal."

He sounded so matter-of-fact that it pissed me off. "You are not my inferior in any way."

"To the Grigori, the fallen, the demonic, I am. This is a very different world you are about to enter, Madeline. Be careful where you tread."

Just as he reached for the silver doorknob, the handle turned on its own. The door opened inward and a surprisingly familiar figure stepped out.

"You!" I cried. "What are you doing here?"

Ms. Greenwitch narrowed her eerie gray eyes at me. "I could ask the same of you, cursed one."

I heard Gabriel's sharp intake of breath beside me. "Whatever. I don't really care why you're here. You just keep the hell away from me."

"Madeline," Gabriel said in an undertone. "You must not be so disrespectful. She is . . ."

"Disrespectful?" I said, my voice rising. "This crazy bitch blasted me for no apparent reason the last time I saw her."

The door was slightly ajar behind Ms. Greenwitch and I heard a rustle of movement from inside.

"She did what?" Gabriel asked, looking from my furious face to Ms. Greenwitch's stony one.

"She blasted me. I tried to shake her hand and she lost her mind. Those bruises I had on me the last time you healed me weren't just from Ramuell."

"Obviously I didn't use enough power on you," Ms. Greenwitch said icily. "I will take care to remedy that the next time."

"Cease at once," Gabriel hissed. "Both of you. Your lives are in danger if you continue this quarrel. Lady Greenwitch, this is Lord Azazel's daughter."

Greenwitch blanched. "What? *She* is his daughter?"

"I'm guessing you didn't check my references thoroughly enough," I said snidely.

"And Lady Greenwitch," Gabriel said, turning to me, "is the mother of Lord Azazel's only son, Antares."

I was confused. How could this woman, witch or otherwise, be the mother of that monster? But anger overrode my curiosity.

"You're Antares's mother? You? You need to keep that jackass on a shorter leash," I said, furious.

"Now do you see the danger?" Gabriel said to Greenwitch.

"I did not . . . I did not know," Greenwitch said, her hand over her heart. "I had the vision . . . The vision I had did not show her origins, only her curse. Lord Azazel has always been careful to disguise her identity—I could not know!"

"Nevertheless," a voice said behind her, a voice so melodic and beautiful that it made me dizzy to hear it. "You have broken the word of Lord Azazel, and so must be punished."

The double doors swung open and revealed a crowd of about twenty people, all avidly listening to our conversation. At the forefront was a man so blindingly beautiful that I had to close my eyes and turn my head away for a moment. When I reopened them and turned back, his shine seemed to have dulled a bit, enough that I could look at him and the assemblage gathered behind him.

There were no demons in this crowd. Each figure was clearly one of the fallen. Every one, male and female, had soft golden hair and dark blue eyes filled with a deep canvas of stars. Every one was surrounded by a soft aura of light and warmth. They were dressed in modern clothing—very expensive and chic modern clothing that looked incongruous next to the enormous white wings folded at their backs. I felt bereft without my wings, like the only one without a gun at a gunfight. Especially when I realized that Gabriel's wings, usually hidden beneath his omnipresent black coat, had appeared sometime after we had arrived in the antechamber.

The leader of the group was very tall, even taller than Gabriel, who outstripped me by at least a foot. Every feature was perfect, but there was no warmth in his face, only the coldness of stone. It diminished the effect of his beauty somewhat.

"Lady Greenwitch," he said, and reached out to grip her by the elbow. She looked like she was about to faint. He handed her off to someone standing behind her and the crowd moved farther into the room, the murmuring of their voices like the tinkling of silver bells.

"What's happening?" I hissed to Gabriel.

He shook his head at me, as if to say, "Not now."

"Yes, now," I whispered.

He gave another little headshake as the leader turned back to me. The fallen angel gave me an embarrassingly deep bow.

"My lady Madeline. It is my greatest honor to welcome you to your father's court." He reached for my hand and I sidled out of reach, put off by his obsequious manner. Annoyance flared in his eyes but he banked it quickly, so quickly I almost thought I imagined it.

"And you are?" I asked.

"Forgive me, my lady. You are correct. I am Nathaniel, Lord Azazel's most trusted advisor, and he has asked me to escort you to his presence." He looked at Gabriel and his mouth twisted into a sneer. "You are also to report to Lord Azazel, thrall."

Nathaniel held out his hand for me to take. I stared at him until his hand dropped to his side. Two bright spots of color appeared on Nathaniel's cheekbones and I heard Gabriel sigh softly next to me.

I didn't care if I offended Nathaniel. Something about him struck me as shifty. And I didn't like the way he talked to Gabriel at all. I didn't want that creep touching me. What I did want was to take Gabriel's hand and hold on tight, because at that moment I was terrified and unsure. What was happening to Ms. Greenwitch? What would my father think of me?

"If you will follow me," Nathaniel said abruptly and turned on his heel. I noted his pricey black leather boots as they rang out on the marble floor.

We crossed into the room, which seemed to be a kind of parlor. I didn't think much of the decorations, which leaned toward the Baroque. Gold leaf and heavy velvets everywhere, dark carved woods, silk wallpaper. There was a doorway at the far end of the room that led to a hallway, and at the end of the hallway was a wide marble staircase that swept upward in a long curl, so that the top of the stairs faced the direction opposite the bottom step.

Nathaniel said nothing further. He led us past several more carved doors in the hallway, all closed, and I wondered what was behind them. Kitchen, dining room, guest room? Torture chambers? My father's harem? Armies of the undead?

We followed Nathaniel up the stairs in silence, my trepidation growing with every moment. The stairs opened to an enormous room flanked by white columns. The ceiling was at least thirty feet high and the room was about a hundred yards long. It was like entering a cathedral.

Jewel-toned rugs were scattered all over the floor, and

there were more pieces of uncomfortable-looking Baroque furniture artfully arranged throughout the room. Several dozen more of the fallen were here, and I got the impression that they had artfully arranged themselves as well. Whether this show was for my viewing pleasure or Azazel's, I didn't know.

At the far end of the room a small crowd was gathered, blocking my view. Nathaniel walked forward, and as he walked every person in the room turned to look at us, and there were whispers as we passed.

"That's her."

"Who?"

"Lord Azazel's daughter."

"*That's* Madeline?"

"Awfully small, isn't she?"

"Where are her wings?"

"That can't be her. She's too puny."

"She's supposed to be half human."

I ignored the whispers, which were surely meant to reach my ears. So what if this bunch of beautiful poseurs didn't think I looked like much? I knew the content of my own character, and I didn't need their approval.

But they, I thought with sudden amusement, *probably need mine. After all, Gabriel said I was something like a princess here.*

The thought brought a mischievous smile. Gabriel, ever attuned to my changes of mood, looked at me with a question in his eyes.

Later, I mouthed.

The crowd around us parted as quietly as water, and the tableau before me wiped the smile from my face.

Ms. Greenwitch knelt on the floor, her back to me, her hands clasped in front of her. A guard stood beside her, also turned away from me. Facing Ms. Greenwitch was the man who could only be my father. I had a little start when I realized he didn't look that much older than I did. I supposed I had forgotten he was an angel and, though he'd lived thousands of millennia, would not have aged. I guess I had always kept a vision of him as looking, well, fatherly.

Instead, he looked like a well-heeled businessman in his thirties, but I could see muscles bulging beneath his tailored blue shirt. He was the first person at the court that I had seen with dark hair besides Gabriel and myself. It was jet-black and cut short on the sides, longer on the top. I saw with a jolt of recognition that his nose was the same as mine, straight and defined, and his ears were also the same shape as my own. He did not have the same sunshiny aura as the rest of the angels, but there was a sense of controlled power around him that the others did not have. He frowned thunderously down at Ms. Greenwitch, and his anger was so palpable that I shuddered.

Then my father looked up, and I had another shock when I saw my eyes, my own dark eyes, burning with the fury of the stars.

I might have run to him, embraced him. I might have had a moment of embarrassed tears, overwhelmed by my feelings for this man who had fathered me, this man whom I had never seen before this moment. But none of those things happened.

Lord Azazel looked at me, and he said, "Daughter, is it true that this woman harmed you?"

Every eye was on me with laser intensity, including Ms. Greenwitch's. There was blood on her mouth and a scrape across her cheek. Her strange gray eyes overflowed with tears.

I realized that her well-being depended on my answer.

She had already admitted to harming me in front of witnesses, but perhaps I could downplay what had happened.

"It was a misunderstanding," I said firmly. "No harm done."

"Did she physically harm you? Did she draw your blood?" Azazel demanded.

I thought about smashing against her living room wall, being shocked by bolts of power. "It was really nothing."

I felt stupid, pinned by the intensity of his eyes and the lash of power in his voice. I should be doing more to help her.

"But you were harmed at her hand?" Azazel pressed.

"Um . . ."

"Yes or no?" he said, and the command in his voice put my back up.

"No harm done," I said again, meeting his eyes boldly.

Azazel narrowed his eyes at me. "A truth of a kind, but not all of it. Gabriel?"

"Don't you dare," I hissed under my breath.

"I cannot refuse my lord, Madeline," he said in a whisper so low that I barely heard him. "I am sorry."

Then he stepped forward and said, "By her own word and before a witness, Lady Greenwitch physically harmed your daughter, the Lady Madeline."

Ms. Greenwitch dropped her head to her chest and let out a sob. I looked at Gabriel, whose face was white.

My father nodded at the guard standing beside Ms. Greenwitch. Before I could speak, he pulled a sword that looked like it was made of lightning from a sheath at his side. The sword swung to her neck as I stood frozen in horror, and her head rolled and came to a stop at my feet.

15

AZAZEL LOOKED IMPASSIVELY AT THE BODY OF HIS lover, now slumped and headless on the ground. The lightning sword had cauterized the wound immediately, so there was no blood leaking on the fancy rug.

Pretty handy. You know, for when you've just got to have that execution in your living room, I thought a little hysterically.

Despite all of Gabriel's warnings, somehow I had never really considered that it would come to this. I hadn't believed that a person could be killed so easily, so blithely, for nothing at all.

And it was my fault. I hadn't done enough, said enough, to prevent Greenwitch's death. My own fear was not an excuse. Her murder was on my soul, even if I hadn't been the one holding the sword.

"Your forgiveness, my lady," the guard said as he bent before me to scoop up Greenwitch's head. I noticed, in a distant part of my brain, that he looked completely human save for the large fangs that jutted over his lower lip.

Azazel raised his eyes to the assemblage. I turned my head slightly to look at them, and I noted that not one of them seemed shocked by the suddenness of death in their midst. I also realized that I hadn't seen an Agent come to take Greenwitch's soul. What did that mean?

"Lady Greenwitch has been tried and executed according to the law. Let this be a warning to all those who would doubt my word. If you harm my daughter, you will pay the same price." My father turned his burning gaze upon me and held out his hand.

Something inside me froze, like a small mammal hiding from a predator. But I knew what was expected of me. I walked to him, coolly stepping around the body that lay between us, and placed my icy hand in his outstretched one. His skin was hot, hotter than Gabriel's, so hot that it hurt me a little to touch him.

Spontaneous applause broke out as Azazel kissed my hand.

"Daughter," he murmured, and his eyes surveyed me keenly, as if assessing my value.

"Father," I said, and gave him a little nod of acknowledgment.

"Walk with me," he commanded, and I didn't dare disobey.

The assembled crowd fell back, breaking into small groups. Cocktails and hors d'oeuvres appeared on trays that floated around the room. Murmured conversation filled the air.

Azazel tucked my arm through his and walked toward

the front of the room, away from the crowd. The proximity was uncomfortable. The power that radiated from him was much more potent up close, strong enough to make me feel a tinge of nausea. The heat coming off him was also too much in close quarters. Finally, I didn't know him, for all that he was my father. I have never been comfortable touching strangers.

Nathaniel and Gabriel followed us, hanging back far enough not to eavesdrop. My father led me to one of the many windows that ran along each side of the chamber. Each one started at the ceiling and fell to about three feet above the floor. On a sunny day, with all the windows open, the angels would have sparkled like jewels in the light. But the day that we faced as we came to the window was overcast and gray. I wondered what it was like at home, and what Beezle was doing while I was gone. Eating popcorn and pacing, probably.

Azazel released my arm and turned to me. I was relieved that he had let me go and hoped that it didn't show on my face.

His eyes flicked over me again, penetrating. I said nothing. Gone was all of the bravado that I had spat at Gabriel in my living room only an hour earlier. I was afraid of this man. I had seen his ruthlessness, and I had no doubt that he would kill me as easily as he had killed Greenwitch if I displeased him.

After several discomfiting moments he spoke. "You look very like me."

"You could have found that out anytime in the last thirty-two years," I said, and immediately regretted it. What had happened to my caution, my self-preservation?

I expected him to hit me, or blast me with magic, but instead he threw his head back and laughed.

"Gabriel told me that you had spirit. I am glad. It will aid you in the future."

"Aid me in what?" I asked, my usual truculent personality emerging despite my best efforts. "My snappy wit hasn't prevented Ramuell from trying to kill me several times over."

Azazel sobered immediately. "Yes, Ramuell. I am sorry, Daughter, that I have not done a better job of protecting you."

"Are you sorry that you weren't there, or that you didn't send Gabriel sooner?" I watched him carefully. This answer was important to me.

He seemed to know what I was asking. "I could not live with you and your mother, Madeline. I swore fealty to Lord Lucifer long ago, long before you or Katherine were a glint in the universe. If your mother could have lived here, perhaps it would have been possible. But she had her own master to serve, and chose to stay in Chicago."

"Did that mean you couldn't visit? Those portals are faster than the commuter jet," I said, and felt the familiar little sparks of anger rising. "And, you know, it might have made a difference when I was thirteen and alone except for Beezle."

"Who do you think ensured your safety and independence until adulthood? Who made sure that you had funds for food, and that the authorities did not examine you too closely?"

That made me pause for a moment, but I was too wound up to stop now. "You couldn't just come and get me? Why the cloak-and-dagger routine?"

"I do not have to explain my actions to you, Daughter," Azazel said icily.

I heard a little voice in the back of my head, and it sounded like Gabriel. *Careful,* it whispered.

The air around us smelled like cinnamon rolls in the

oven. How come every creature that came from an angelic bloodline smelled like they just came out of a bakery? Even Ramuell smelled like burnt cinnamon and sulfur. I wondered if I smelled cinnamony when my power manifested. I would have to ask Gabriel.

I saw that thunderclouds had risen in Azazel's eyes. He was, consciously or not, responding to my hostility. I realized that any display of power would be interpreted as a threat, whether it was intended that way or not.

I tamped down my anger. I'd seen ample proof to know it wasn't wise to provoke him. "Whatever. You couldn't visit. I don't really want to talk about the past now, anyway. What I want to discuss is how Gabriel and I can find Ramuell and destroy him."

Sensing I had backed down, Azazel relaxed visibly. I vowed again to be more cautious.

"Gabriel has told you of his history with Ramuell?" he asked.

I nodded, and he went on.

"I believe that Gabriel could hold Ramuell with his powers, long enough to call the chiefs of the Grigori to his aid. We could re-bind the nephilim in the Valley of Sorrows. But I do not believe that you could destroy Ramuell."

So Gabriel hadn't told Azazel about my little starburst. I spoke carefully, so that he wouldn't think that Gabriel had deliberately withheld information. The last thing I wanted was for Gabriel to be hurt.

"Something new has happened since yesterday. Perhaps Gabriel hasn't been able to tell you about it. He was very busy caring for me after Ramuell's attack," I said.

Azazel's expression did not alter, but I could sense a metaphorical pricking of his ears.

I described my battle with Ramuell, the draining of my

magic, and the sudden manifestation of the starburst. I did not mention the second episode, since Gabriel had already warned me that it would be his death if anyone knew he had touched me.

Azazel's brows drew closer together as I told my tale. "And you say that this power harmed the nephilim? Do you believe that you mortally wounded him?"

I thought of the missing skin, the gaping sores. "I don't know if he was mortally wounded but I definitely messed him up. He ought to be out of action for a little while."

"Madeline," Azazel said, and he took me by the elbow to draw me closer. We both turned to look out the window as he whispered to me. "You must be very careful. I do not have a child among the nephilim, but most of the Grigori do. They did not want their offspring destroyed; that is why the nephilim are bound. Lord Lucifer would not thank you for murdering his firstborn."

"And if it's a choice between my life and his?" I said.

Azazel looked troubled. "I cannot guarantee, even under that circumstance, that Lord Lucifer would permit you to live."

Somehow I had expected that answer. I sighed in resignation. "Well, at least I could take Ramuell out. And set Mom free."

"Of all the things that I regret, and there are many, I regret most of all that your mother came to this fate. You do not know how it has tormented me that her soul is trapped in the body of that monstrosity," Azazel said fiercely.

A fist squeezed my heart. "So you did love her," I said.

"Of course I did. I will never know another love like that of your mother."

"And still you got it on with Greenwitch, and had that jerk Antares—who, by the way, has a real attitude problem."

"And again I will remind you that I do not answer to you, my daughter."

I was already sick to death of bowing and scraping. "I apologize, Father," I said stiffly.

Azazel seemed content with my reluctant fealty. "Gabriel has told me of Antares's attacks on you. He has always been jealous of your place in court, a place that he felt was rightfully his. But the court would never accept a half demon as my heir."

"Wait a second. Wait," I said, my thoughts whirling. "I'm your heir? And Greenwitch was a demon?"

"Of course," Azazel said.

"Of course which?" I asked.

"Of course you are my heir, and of course Lady Greenwitch was a demon."

"Why didn't she look demonic?" I asked. "I thought she was an ordinary human."

Azazel shrugged. "Some demons, such as Greenwitch, possess sufficient power to disguise their aspect. She was particularly adept at masking her true nature. In any case, you did not see a soul leave her body at her death, did you?"

I was very distracted by this "of course you are my heir" business, but I had been curious about the lack of an Agent at Greenwitch's death. "Are you saying that demons don't have souls?"

"You have been an Agent for many years, Madeline. Have you ever taken the soul of a demon?"

"Well, no," I admitted. "But I never knew that demons existed until a couple of days ago. I have taken the souls of other supernatural beings, though—vampires and werewolves and faeries."

"All of those creatures are part human, even if the

humanity is very far back in the bloodline, as with faeries. Only humans have souls."

"And why is that?" I asked, and for the second time in the last day I felt that I skated very close to the origin of the Universe, to the secret behind the Door.

"That is not for humans to know," Azazel chided. "Do not think me a foolish child that can be cozened by an innocent face."

I felt the blood rising in my cheeks. "Right, well, on to that other thing. This heir business."

"On the day that you were born, you were named my heir. This means that in the event of my death you are to take over the duties of this court."

"And those duties are . . . ?" I asked, rotating my wrist to indicate that he should explain.

"To swear fealty to Lord Lucifer and protect the sanctity of his kingdom."

"And that's it? No tempting humans to the dark side?"

Azazel smiled mysteriously. "That is all you need to know for now."

I felt the acid sloshing in my stomach. I didn't want to be the heiress to a piece of Lucifer's kingdom. I wanted to get married, and have a baby or two, and grow old and die like an ordinary human. I didn't want to be a part of this.

"I thought you said that Katherine couldn't be with you because she had her own master to serve—because she was an Agent," I said. "How could I inherit your place in court if I have the same responsibilities?"

"Those responsibilities could be passed to your child," Azazel said. "Death is not the only circumstance under which that could happen. You could voluntarily relinquish your soul-collecting powers to your offspring."

I could not disguise a shudder. I would never do that to

my child. Voluntarily condemn them to a life of loneliness, like mine? I would only pass my inheritance when I had no other choice—when another Agent was taking me to the Door. And since as far as I knew there were no long-lost cousins hiding in the closet, it was very likely that the blood-line would die with me and no one would get my suck job.

But I did not say any of this to Azazel. "Well, I probably won't have to worry about it. You look like you've been around for a while. And besides, marriage and babies are not in my future right now."

Azazel's eyes twinkled as he turned and beckoned to someone behind me. "I wouldn't be so sure about that."

My heart sank. What now?

Nathaniel appeared beside Azazel. The smug expression on his face made me want to punch him. "Yes, my lord?"

"Madeline, meet your betrothed. Nathaniel, you may take her hand," Azazel said.

I stepped back and bumped into the windowsill, keeping my hands at my sides so that Nathaniel couldn't touch me. My eyes searched frantically until I found Gabriel. He stood ten feet away, watching the proceedings with a stony face. I felt heartsick. Had he known about this? Why hadn't he warned me?

"What is the matter, Madeline?" Azazel asked. "Nathaniel is my chief advisor and a very powerful angel in his own right. This is a good match for you."

"Him?" I asked, pointing at Nathaniel. "Captain Condescension? I don't think so."

"Be careful, Madeline," Azazel said, and there was an undercurrent of warning in his voice. "In this court, my word is law. And it is my word and my wish that you marry Nathaniel today."

"Today?" I thought that I would faint. I also felt a powerful surge of regret. I could have made love to Gabriel. I could have at least been tied to this angel with the knowledge that I had sown some wild oats. But instead I was going to be handed off to this unknown for the sake of political expediency, and a creature that I had hated on sight would take my carefully preserved virginity. "Today? I don't even know him, and you want me to marry him today? You have no right to marry me to someone I don't love. I just met you!"

"I have every right. I am your father, and I am the right hand of Lord Lucifer. If you disobey me in this, Madeline, you will be punished."

Azazel's voice had gone icy cold, and the room had gone still. We spoke so softly that I doubted anyone could hear us, but all were attuned to the vibrations of power in our little corner.

I felt a surge of fear, and caught Gabriel's eye again. His eyes implored me to take care. I didn't need the warning. I could sense that I walked a very fine line. I backpedaled quickly.

"May I speak with my father alone, Nathaniel?" I asked, taking care to modulate my voice.

Azazel nodded, and Nathaniel moved away. His confident grin had slipped a little.

"Father," I said urgently. I took his hand, although it repulsed me to touch him, and to grovel to him. I didn't think very much of a man who would hand me off to a stranger without a word of assent from me. "Forgive me. I am still new to this world. A couple days ago, I didn't know that you were my father, or that the Grigori existed. I am still learning about my own magical gifts. And now you've told me that I am to marry a creature that I have never seen before, and to give up responsibilities that I have carried my whole life. Forgive me if I am overwhelmed and unsure. This is so new to me."

Azazel's face softened, and he covered my hand so that it was clasped between both of his. "Daughter. There is nothing in this world that is more precious to me than you. You are right; I had forgotten that you have lived the life of a human, ignorant of the ways of our people. You need time. Very well. You shall have time."

He snapped his fingers and Nathaniel immediately appeared at his side.

Like a dog to its master, I thought sourly.

Azazel placed my hand in Nathaniel's, giving me no opportunity to pull away. Nathaniel closed his fingers around mine possessively. His skin was very warm, like Azazel's, to the point of discomfort. I wanted to yank my hand back, grab Gabriel and go anywhere in the universe, somewhere far away from angelic power plays and soul-eating nephilim. I stood still and waited to see what Azazel would do.

"Nathaniel, my daughter has wisely reminded me that she is a stranger to our world. I have decided to give her an opportunity to grow accustomed to life at court before her marriage.

"Madeline," he continued. "I will give you one year's grace. During that time you will visit the court twice a month for a period of three days each trip."

Three days? I thought. What the hell was I supposed to do with the souls on my list while I was trapped in Azazel's court for six days each month?

"Additionally, you and Nathaniel will have an opportunity to get to know each other. Nathaniel will formally court you, both here and in the human world, and twelve months from today you shall marry."

The air crackled a little at this pronouncement, and I realized with horror that Azazel's words were like a magical binding. If I didn't follow his edicts, appear in court and marry Nathaniel one year from that day, I would suffer the consequences of breaking the binding. I didn't know what those consequences might be, but after witnessing Greenwitch's fate, I didn't want to find out.

Nathaniel lifted my hand to his lips. I kept my face composed even though my heart rabbited away in my chest. There was a tinkling of glass. We all looked toward the sound, which came from near Gabriel. He looked blandly back at us. I think I was the only one who noticed his left hand was stuffed in his pocket.

My betrothed muttered some words about my beauty, and I made the appropriate noises, but my mind was far away, frantically trying to think of a way out of this marriage, this court, this ridiculous notion of myself as a royal heir. Conversation ebbed and flowed all around us. Azazel moved among his people, leaving Nathaniel and me alone. There was a trill of laughter from one of the assembled crowd.

My heart stopped. I knew that laugh. I yanked my hand away from Nathaniel, whose look turned glacial, and frantically scanned the crowd for its source. Gabriel was at my side in an instant.

"What is it, my lady?" he asked in a low voice.

"That laugh . . . I've heard it before," I said, so that Nathaniel couldn't hear me. "Help me find her."

Nathaniel glared down at Gabriel. "The Lady Madeline has no need of you, thrall. Return to your post."

Gabriel nodded his head respectfully. "I beg your pardon, Lord Nathaniel. But Lady Madeline has requested my assistance."

Nathaniel puffed up his chest. "If my lady needs assistance, then I will provide it. I am her betrothed."

"Of course, my lord. But Lord Azazel has charged me with serving Lady Madeline, and I must do as she wishes." Gabriel said this in a way that sounded polite on the surface but was undercut with steel. He wasn't about to cede territory to Nathaniel.

I took note of this little exchange with half an ear. I was still trying to place the angel who had sounded so familiar to me.

"Enough with the testosterone," I snapped. "Nathaniel, Gabriel stays; you go."

Nathaniel gave me a look that could have frozen molten lava. "Very well, my lady. We will speak again before you depart."

He bowed low and then moved away.

"Don't count on it, buster," I said in an undertone, and Gabriel's mouth quirked into a half smile. "And don't think I appreciate your fighting over me like a couple of dogs with a package of bacon."

"Madeline, I think much, much more of you than bacon," Gabriel said.

I laughed at his solemn face and then sobered. "What did you do to your hand?"

"Shattered a wineglass," Gabriel said shortly.

I raised an eyebrow at him.

"Do you really think it enjoyable for me to watch that dog touch you?"

"About as enjoyable as it is for me to be touched by him, I imagine."

The laughter sang out again, and I shuddered.

"There!" I said. "Who is that?"

Gabriel could see more of the crowd than I could with his advantage of height. "It is the Lady Ariell."

"Ariell? Who is she?"

"She is not one of the Grigori. She is of a group of angels that came later, to join Lucifer's kingdom. But why would you know the sound of her laughter, unless . . ." Gabriel looked at me, and the word was unspoken between us.

Evangeline.

As if the very thought of her name was a summoning, I immediately felt dizzy. Black spots danced in front of my eyes. I felt myself slipping downward into darkness, and I fought it. I would not faint in front of all these angels. I could not show such weakness. I gripped Gabriel's arm.

"Get me away from here," I whispered. "I think . . . I think I'm going to have another vision."

He immediately swept me toward a door that I hadn't noticed before, only a few feet away in the corner of the room. The door led to another, smaller chamber. I hoped that our disappearance would go unnoticed.

This room appeared a great deal more comfortable than any of the others I had seen in Azazel's palace. There were two large leather sofas and a thick woolen rug underfoot that muffled our footsteps, and the walls were painted a comforting pale blue. There was a stone fireplace with a fire crackling merrily away. In the corner was a cherry bookcase filled with paperbacks, and a rocking chair next to a reading lamp.

"This is Lord Azazel's private receiving room," Gabriel said as he led me to one of the sofas. His voice sounded very far away. "Only a very few are permitted to come here. You will be safe."

Something about the room made me like Azazel a little better. It made him seem more human, more like me.

That was my last thought before Evangeline took me again.

Evangeline felt the first child slide from her belly. She heard it cry out for her but the next one was already coming, hurrying behind the first. She gave a tooth-scraping, belly-folding push, and the second child came forth.

They wailed in time together and Evangeline reached for them, drawing them to her, two perfect little boys with black wings. The Morningstar's sons.

She cleaned them gently, even as the afterbirth pulsed from her body, and used the Morningstar's power to sever the cords that bound them to her body. Then she gave them her milk, shading them from the burning sun in the shelter of the smoking ruin that had been her prison.

After a time, the children slept, and Evangeline felt her weariness overcome her. She did not know why Lucifer had not come for her already. She knew that if he was able, he would have been at her side. He should have felt the life force of the children as they were born. He should have been there to bless them with his grace, to mark them as his for all time.

So their enemies must have him, as they had imprisoned Evangeline. And she knew the Morningstar would not want his sons endangered, so she must stay far from him. But she also knew that the one who had escaped her wrath, the green-eyed one, would return for her and the little boys who slept so sweetly now in her arms. She was very weak from the escape, and the birthing, and she did not know if she could call forth the Morningstar's power again.

Her grief and fear threatened to overwhelm her. She

was just a lost and helpless girl, a girl who had wandered out in the night and seen a being so terrible and beautiful that she could not help but be ensnared by love for him.

Now her love was gone and she was alone with his sons, two boys who would need guidance and care from one who would understand their power. Evangeline could not give them this. Her powers were a borrowed gift; she did not understand their source nor how to teach her children.

She cried, and her tears fell on the faces of her sleeping boys, and they shifted and fussed in their sleep. She held them tight to her chest and sobbed out her grief and fear, and she whispered, "Help me."

Her eyes were closed and her sons were warm against her chest but it seemed that suddenly the sun had grown brighter, and her eyelids burned in the light. She opened her eyes and then turned her face away, for before her was a being of such purity that it shone with a light far brighter than the sun.

He was as lovely as her Morningstar, but his wings were whiter than the snow on the capped peaks of the mountains. His eyes were as blue as the jewels that studded the walls of the Morningstar's palace. And his hair was fairer than the yellow sand that sifted beneath her feet.

"Who are you?" she asked, and she trembled in her heart, for she was a little afraid of the answer.

He did not speak aloud, but into her mind. He told her that he was called Michael, and that long ago, he and Lucifer had been almost as one, as close as the two boys that she snuggled in her arms. Then Lucifer and his Grigori fell, and Michael grieved at their separation. So he kept watch, always. He was not permitted by law to aid Lucifer, but he could help Evangeline and her children.

"How?" she asked.

Lucifer's enemies will always hunt you, *he said. He told her that he could disguise the children from those who desired the death of the Morningstar, that he could infuse them with his grace so that no one would recognize them as coming from Lucifer's line. He could raise them as his own, and teach them the ways of their powers. They would be safe, and grow in goodness and light, but they would never be able to return to Lucifer again.*

Evangeline bowed her head and held her children tightly, and felt a piece of her heart fall away.

You must choose, *Michael said, and his eyes were gentle and knowing.*

Evangeline stood, and looked to the east, where the first star of the morning would rise.

"Good-bye, my love," *she said. She must protect his sons. That was her duty now.*

Michael reached for her, and she placed her frozen hand in his burning one. A tear slipped from her cheek and melted in the sand.

As Michael bore them away from her life and her love, Evangeline saw something golden moving on the mountaintop, and she knew that a pair of blazing green eyes followed her with hate.

16

I OPENED MY EYES, AND FOUND THAT GABRIEL HAD covered me with one of the blankets, a very warm, red fleece one. Azazel stood with his back to me, looking into the fireplace. So much for my sneaking away from the court unnoticed.

Gabriel sat on a hassock beside me, as I expected he would be, his brows knit together in a frown. He relaxed visibly when I looked at him.

"You are well?" he asked. He made no move to touch me, and I felt bereft. But I understood why he didn't.

"I know I've mentioned this before, but I am getting really sick of passing out. I'm starting to feel like Giles on *Buffy the Vampire Slayer*," I said, and sat up. "And I'm getting a very bad suspicion about why I'm having these visions of Evangeline."

Azazel turned at that, and his eyes were unreadable. Was

he relieved that I was safe and healthy? Was he plotting the next move with his very valuable pawn—me? And why hadn't he told Lucifer about my visions of Evangeline yet?

"I am glad that you are well, Daughter," he said.

The question was on my lips, so I asked him. "Why haven't you told Lucifer of my visions of Evangeline?"

Azazel paused, and I could see him weighing and discarding information in an instant. Apparently I was on a need-to-know basis. There seemed to be a lot of that going around.

"The Lost Mother is a very sensitive issue for Lord Lucifer. It is imperative that we not bring him this information until we are certain what it means."

"I've got an idea what it means," I said grimly. "I think Lucifer is my great-great-great-how-ever-many-freakin-greats-it-is-granddad."

I could see that I had shocked both of them. Azazel shook his head decisively, and I could read his face easily—*No, it is impossible.*

Gabriel said it. "That is impossible."

"Why? Nobody knows what happened to Evangeline, right? And I've had a vision of her giving birth to Lucifer's children, and those children were hidden by another angel."

"Another angel?" Azazel asked. "Who?"

"Michael."

"Michael. Of course. They were as brothers, once upon a time," Azazel said, and there was wonder in his voice. "But Lord Lucifer would know if you were of his bloodline. You would be marked by his power, and he would be able to trace you and every other member of his line by this mark."

"That's the thing. I think I am marked by his power," I said, and threw off the blanket so that I could pace restlessly around the room. I was less than thrilled by the idea that I might be related to Lucifer. I had more than my share of problems already. "In my vision, Evangeline destroyed her captors and the place where they held her with a starburst."

Gabriel's mouth fell open at that. It was comical to see him lose his ever-steady composure. "The same power that you used on Ramuell?"

I nodded.

Azazel moved toward me, and I could see he was thinking fast. Meteors streamed in rapid succession across the blackness of space in his eyes. He gripped my shoulders and held my gaze with his own burning one.

"Daughter, it is imperative, *imperative*, that you share this information with no one. If there is even a hint, a whisper, that you might be the descendant of Lucifer, then his enemies would fall upon you like the plagues of Egypt."

"You mean the way *your* enemies have already descended on me?" I said, and knew that my eyes reflected his own. I was already sick to death of Azazel's world.

Azazel's eyes hardened. "Antares will be punished for harming you. He has broken the law of my court and he is an outcast."

"But, my lord," Gabriel said. "How could it be that she carries Lucifer's power and yet is still unknown to him? This would mean that Katherine Black also came of his bloodline, and all her ancestry."

This thought had clearly not occurred to Azazel yet, and it visibly disturbed him. I don't know if it was the idea that my mother might have deliberately kept information from him, or simply that he had been the lover of Lucifer's descendant. Either way, he didn't look happy about it. I was going to tell about the infused-with-Michael's-grace thing, but I suddenly recalled that I had other tasks to do that day.

"Wait a second," I said. "What time is it?"

Gabriel glanced at the face of his cell phone. "Nine forty-two."

"Holy crap! We have to go. I have an appointment with J.B. in an hour. And I'm supposed to get some souls today, but I can't remember what time I was supposed to do it," I said, rushing to Gabriel's side. "Make that portal thing happen."

"Wait a moment, Daughter." Azazel's eyes were narrowed. "I have not given you leave to depart."

The hierarchy and formality of this court already made me insane, and I had been there for only a few hours. I didn't have time to massage Azazel's ego. I had things to do.

"I apologize, Father," I said stiffly, resisting the nearly overwhelming urge to roll my eyes. "I have my responsibilities to attend."

His face softened. "How like your mother you are. She, too, was always leaving me to tend to human souls. I wonder how Nathaniel will take it."

He chuckled at this thought and I was very careful not to look at Gabriel.

"Do I have your permission to leave?" I asked, impatient to be off.

"Of course, my daughter. And I will see you fourteen days hence in this court. Although I am sure that you will be seeing Nathaniel much sooner."

Azazel came to stand in front of me and he kissed both of my cheeks. "Go with the grace of the Morningstar."

"See you in a couple of weeks," I said awkwardly. "Can we make the portal here?"

"I think it is better, yes, that you do not return through the court. But first, I need to have a word with Gabriel."

He drew Gabriel toward the corner of the room near the rocking chair and he whispered some instructions in such a low tone that I could barely tell he was speaking. Gabriel nodded and then came back to stand at my side.

"You are ready?" Gabriel asked.

I grinned at him, eager to be away. "There's no place like home."

Beezle was on me the second I landed in the backyard. And I do mean "on me." He fluttered to my shoulder, dug in his claws and started firing off questions about what had happened and what had Azazel said and had anybody been rude to me and so on and so on and so on.

Gabriel emerged from the portal and helped me up.

"Beezle, calm down. I'll tell you all about it later. Right now I've got to find my list." As we mounted the porch and went up the inside back stairs to the door that led into my kitchen, I asked Gabriel, "What did Azazel say to you?"

"He said that I was not to leave your side under any circumstance until Ramuell is re-bound in the Valley of Sorrows. If you come to harm, it will be on my head."

"Or off with your head, as the case may be. He's got quite a Red Queen streak, does dear old Dad," I said dryly.

"Red Queen?"

"From *Alice in Wonderland*? The Red Queen was always coming up with excuses to have people's heads chopped off." I started rummaging in the pile of mail on the sideboard. I knew I had left my list there somewhere.

"I did warn you that you needed to be careful."

"What happened?" asked Beezle, who had been sulking because I'd put off describing the trip.

"Azazel had Greenwitch's head cut off for no apparent

reason," I said, distracted. That was all I needed—to miss a pickup and have J.B. on my ass.

"Greenwitch? The crazy lady who sold you the charm last night? The one who tried to blast you into oblivion?"

"That's the one," I said. "Oh, and did you know that she was Antares's mother?"

Beezle flew off my shoulder and fluttered around, looking anxious. "No, I didn't know that. That means that she was a demon."

"Yeah, that's what Azazel said." Where was that list?

"But I didn't see that when we went to her house." He sounded so distressed that I stopped searching for the list and glanced up at him.

"What's the problem?"

"I should have been able to see that she was demonic. I should have been able to see through every layer of reality to her core essence. That is my gift as a gargoyle. But I couldn't see her."

"So Greenwitch has discovered a way to disguise her true essence, not simply her physical appearance," Gabriel said slowly, meeting Beezle's frightened eyes. "If this is true, then others could have discovered her trick as well, or borrowed the way of it from Greenwitch."

I was tired and distracted, and had difficulty grasping the import of this discussion. "So what?"

"So if what you believe is true—that Ramuell has another half-nephilim child—then that child or his mother could have disguised his essence and his presence from Lucifer. It would mean that your theory is correct, and that there is only one puppet master for Ramuell—his own child. My half sibling."

"So if we can find the master, then we can find Ramuell,

and shut down the whole operation," I said. "And I still think the key to finding Ramuell is tracing his victims."

"I agree," Gabriel said.

"I'll get J.B. to let us into the Hall of Records. He should be a little more amenable to it now that he's had a close encounter of the demon kind."

I glanced down and realized I held my list in my hand. I had to pick up three souls at two thirty-seven on Lake Shore Drive. All the souls had the same last name. That meant it was probably a car accident, and that I would be picking up a family. On the one hand, families tended to like to stay together, so they usually all chose the Door and made my job as an Agent a lot easier. On the other hand, the human in me was always a little upset by these deaths. It was difficult to take kids to the Door, knowing all their promise had been snuffed out and it was the last choice they would ever make.

Beezle still hovered anxiously, his eyes huge and worried.

"Hey, Beezle, hey, it's all right. You're still the best guardian a girl could ever have," I said, and held out my hand so that he could land on it.

He was heavier than he used to be. He needed to lay off the popcorn and chocolate or his wings weren't going to be able to hold him anymore.

"What if I can't protect you?" he whispered. "What would Katherine say?"

"Beezle," I said. "Greenwitch was an exceptionally powerful demon—Azazel told me himself. I'm certain that there are very few creatures who could disguise their essence the way that she could."

"But what if there is another nephilim out there, hidden

from us? That nephilim is not included in Katherine's circle of protection. It could walk up to the front door and I would never know it wasn't human."

I thought of Ramuell's burnt cinnamon smell and how the smell had warned me in the alley of his presence just in time. "Would you be able to smell it?"

Both Gabriel and Beezle did the blank-stare thing.

"You know, that cinnamony smell that anything angelic seems to have."

"Madeline, what are you talking about?" Gabriel said.

"Azazel smells like cinnamon, and so did Nathaniel. Ramuell smells like burnt cinnamon and sulfur. Antares smells mostly like sulfur with an undertone of cinnamon. You haven't noticed this?"

Gabriel looked intrigued. "And myself?"

I felt blood heating my cheeks. "Apple pie, more or less. Cinnamon and sugar and cloves."

"I have never noticed a particular smell of angelic beings before," Gabriel said. "Gargoyle?"

"Me neither. Are you sure it's not in your head?" Beezle patted my forehead. I wasn't sure if he was checking for a fever or for signs of the crazies.

I pushed his hand away, annoyed. "It's not in my head."

They both looked doubtful.

A thought occurred to me. "Gabriel, if there is another nephilim child, and that child's essence is disguised, isn't it likely that Greenwitch helped hide the child from Lucifer?" I asked. "Like I said, there can't be that many creatures that could disguise their essence the way she could."

"I suppose it is probably so. But what would be her motive for doing such a thing? She was Antares's mother, and as such held a place of status in your father's court."

"I don't know why she would do it. I just want to know if it's likely."

Gabriel nodded. "Very likely, I would think."

"Then would we be able to trace the mark of Green-witch's magic? Couldn't we find this disguised nephilim that way? Since my cinnamon-scent test appears to have gained no votes," I said, sticking my tongue out at Beezle.

Gabriel smiled at me. "Yes. Yes, we could. It would take some doing, but if I had the sense of her magic, then I could use it to trace anyone she had hidden. Madeline, that is brilliant."

I shrugged, all false modesty. "I know. Now I've got to go. Beezle, it's going to be okay. Guard the domicile, and I will see you in a little while."

Beezle said nothing, just flew down the hall and out the front window with a frown on his face. It wasn't like Beezle to send me off without a word, and I stared after him.

"The gargoyle is taking the truth of Greenwitch very hard," Gabriel observed. "This has cut him to the core of his existence. If he cannot see through the layers of magic, then his life is meaningless."

"His life is *not* meaningless," I said heatedly. "He's my best friend, and he'll always be that, even if he isn't my guardian. Let's go."

I thought of the office downtown and felt my wings expand on my back. I flew from the kitchen without another word. I didn't need to see him to know that Gabriel was right behind me.

The office was busier than usual when we arrived. It seemed that while I was at Azazel's court, there had been a train accident that left several souls to take. Several souls equaled more paperwork, so it took J.B. a while before he could see us. When we finally managed to get into his office, I told J.B. what I thought he needed to know—that Ramuell was a nephilim, that nephilim were the children of the Grigori and human women, that my father was a Grigori, and that it was my job to track down Ramuell. He expressed a lot of disbelief, and more than a little annoyance, when I explained that I was going to need six days off each month, and that I couldn't tell him exactly why but that it was a family matter. I was subjected to a little rant about the importance of my responsibilities as an Agent.

"Why is it your job to track down this monster?" J.B. asked. He leaned forward in his office chair and fiddled with some papers on his desk, making marks here and there with a pencil.

"You know, that's a very good question. I started to track Ramuell myself because I wanted vengeance for Patrick and my mother. But Azazel could probably take care of this problem more efficiently than I could." I looked questioningly at Gabriel.

"Ramuell's freedom appears to be largely unknown in Lucifer's kingdom. Lord Azazel is not certain why this is so, but he feels that Ramuell's puppet master wants to maintain secrecy regarding the nephilim's status, perhaps to use Ramuell as a surprise weapon during a gambit for power. Because of this, Lord Azazel is watching and waiting. He feels that Ramuell's puppet master will be more easily discovered if the truth of the nephilim is not widely known. Additionally, hunting the nephilim presents a delicate problem for Lord Azazel."

I thought of something that Azazel had told me in his

receiving room. "Because if he harms Ramuell, it could be interpreted as a move against Lucifer."

"Precisely. So Lord Azazel has entrusted you with this task, and I am to assist you, in hopes that we can quietly discover the traitor and return Ramuell to the Valley of Sorrows."

"And what is it that *you* can do?" J.B. asked Gabriel, a sneer in his voice.

Gabriel got that steely look that told me there was going to be another stupid testosterone-fueled argument, so I quickly cut in.

"His powers are beyond your understanding. Listen, J.B., can you get us a pass into the Hall of Records? I want to see if I can trace Ramuell's victims."

J.B. and Gabriel shared a manly if-she-wasn't-here-I'd-kick-your-ass look. I rolled my eyes.

"J.B.?"

"Yes, yes," he said. "But I'm coming with you. Until you catch this soul-sucking thing, I'm glue and you're . . . something that needs to be glued."

"A construction-paper turkey?" I said, thinking of a second-grade art project. "Look, J.B., I appreciate your offer to help, but you really don't know what your dealing with here. Your powers as an Agent mean nothing to a creature like Ramuell."

"What do you know about my powers? I could have unsuspected depth."

"Right. You've never seen Ramuell. There's no way your depths are that unsuspected."

"I'm with you or you get nothing from me," he said. "I could have you barred from the building if I wanted."

He would do it, too, just to be a pain in the ass. I thought that Gabriel and I could probably let J.B. feel like he was involved and still keep him from the worst of it.

"Fine, let's just get to it," I said.

A couple of hours later the three of us were dusty and irritated and not a bit closer to finding Ramuell. We'd decided to narrow our search to the year that Katherine had died and the last six months. Gabriel and J.B. had split the files of the general populace and I had taken the Agents, which were in a different section. The records of each death were kept on typed index cards. The index cards were sorted by date and kept in long thin drawers, like the cards for the Dewey decimal system at the library—before libraries had gone digital. We each pulled several drawers from a cabinet and sat down at a table that would seat eight, and began the laborious process of flipping through each card.

We'd discovered that twelve Agents had died without showing a record of their choice, and there was no discernable pattern or link between them. None of the Agents was directly related. Ten of the deaths had occurred the year that Katherine had died. Patrick and one other Agent had died in the last six months.

"I don't understand," J.B. said. "If ten Agents in the Chicago area died without showing their choices, wouldn't their supervisor have noticed?"

"Not every supervisor is as anal as you are," I muttered.

"You know, Black, I am really sick of your attitude. You may think that paperwork is just a chore, but it is necessary to the functioning of this business," J.B. snapped.

"Yes, because soul-collecting just couldn't happen unless paperwork was filed afterward," I said sweetly.

J.B.'s face turned red and he opened his mouth—no

doubt to remind me of my place—when the building suddenly shook, like an earthquake had struck. The lamps swung crazily from side to side, the drawers of index cards shook from the table and plaster dust fell from the ceiling.

My chair tipped to one side and I landed heavily on my elbow, crying out in pain.

Gabriel was at my side in an instant, J.B. right behind him. They both manhandled me to my feet, Gabriel on the left side and J.B. on the right. Both of them patted me all over, looking for injuries.

"Get off, get off!" I shouted, and flapped my arms at them. They both stepped away.

"Are you all right?" Gabriel asked.

"Are you hurt?" J.B. asked.

"I'm fine," I said, and wobbled a little as the ground shuddered again. Gabriel put his hand just above my elbow to steady me. I waved him away. "What the hell is going on?"

That was when the screaming started. We could hear it through the vents.

J.B. dashed into the hallway, Gabriel and I following. The Hall of Records was in the subbasement, two floors below ground level. The hall was filled with confused-looking Agents, the ones who worked on the thankless task of moving the Agency into the twenty-first century. These were the data processors who spent their working hours entering information from the file cards into a database. They looked like naked mole rats seeing the sun for the first time.

"What's happening?" a woman asked as J.B. shot past her and into the stairwell.

The sounds of screams and snarls filled the air. Heating/cooling vents lined the hallway, and they broadcast human agony as clearly as if it had been a P.A. system.

"Stay here," I shouted, slowing long enough to make sure they understood. "All of you stay together and go into the Hall."

The Hall had a steel-reinforced door and a coded entry system. It was one of the few rooms in the building with anything that resembled security. The Agency took the records of the dead very seriously.

Gabriel ran past me and followed J.B. The stairwell door banged into the wall as he threw it open, and then slammed shut with tremendous force.

"But what's happening?" a man asked.

"I don't know, but the important thing is that you stay safe and you stay together. Go into the Hall and lock the door, and don't open it until I or J.B. Bennett comes back."

"What if you don't come back?" another woman asked.

"Then wait until the screaming stops," I said, and ran to the stairwell.

17

THERE WAS NO SIGN OF GABRIEL OR J.B. THE STAIR-well was eerily quiet—there were no vents. My boots echoed as I pounded up the two flights of steps and threw the door open at the first-floor lobby.

Hell awaited me.

The carnage was nearly too much to process. Everywhere I looked there were bodies of Agents, dozens of them, most of them in pieces. Blood had been spattered on the floor, on the walls and on the ceiling—the air was filled with the tang of it. This was death at its ugliest, its most undignified. I covered my mouth and nose with my sleeve so that I wouldn't throw up.

The bodies of the receptionist and security guard were slumped over the front desk. There was nothing left of the guard but his torso and a few dangling entrails. His uniform appeared to be torn by the teeth of something very large.

The receptionist had fared a little better. Only her head was missing.

I shivered and realized that there was a big gaping crater where the front door and part of the exterior wall used to be. Chunks of glass and cement appeared to have been thrown inside the lobby from some kind of explosive impact. That must have been what shook the building when we were in the basement.

There were several rubberneckers standing outside on the sidewalk, most of them looking in and then backing away to scream or vomit. The sounds of screams still echoed through the vents, and I realized that whatever was in the building had moved upstairs. And that J.B. and Gabriel had gone after it.

Nobody at the Agency seemed to have been aware that many of their colleagues would be dying today. That meant that these deaths were not planned, not part of the natural order.

Ramuell.

I bolted across the lobby, trying not to think about what squished beneath my boots. I mumbled an apology to the dead. There was no way for me to get to the elevators without stepping on the bodies of my colleagues.

Like many downtown buildings, floors one through three were accessible only by elevator. The stairwell to those floors was locked and could be opened only by a security guard or in the event of an emergency, such as a fire. I figured that the current situation probably qualified as an emergency, but the only person who knew how to open the stairwell was currently in pieces scattered all over the lobby.

There were three elevators. One of the elevator doors was propped open by a human leg. The interior looked like a charnel house. The Agents inside had been trapped. I felt sick when I thought of their dying moments—confused, terrified, helpless.

This is not helping, I told myself. *You have to worry about the living now, not the dead.*

The other two elevators were closed. I pressed the button and crossed my fingers, hoping that they still worked.

The middle elevator doors opened with the familiar ding of the bell, and the interior was miraculously free of either Ramuell or mutilated Agents. I climbed in and stabbed the button for the fourth floor. I was sure that the nephilim had already moved past the second and third floors, and I didn't need to see the bodies of any more people that I couldn't help. If the battle had already moved on, then I could access the stairwell from the fourth floor and go up from there.

My stomach was knotted with anxiety as I watched the numbers change for each floor. *2 . . . 3 . . . 4.* Just before the doors swished open, I felt a little twinge of magic flare up. I hadn't felt more than a whisper since I'd set that starburst on Gabriel. It still didn't feel like my magic was anything close to full power, but there was more than a match flame. Hopefully it would be enough to keep me from getting eaten alive.

The elevator doors opened and a screaming Agent, who must have been leaning against the closed exterior doors, fell backward into the car. I jammed the OPEN DOOR button so that I could check on the Agent, whose face was covered in blood.

"Are you all right?" I asked. "Are you hurt?"

The guy kept screaming, eyes widened, obviously in total shock. I patted him all over and couldn't find anything obvious—no gaping wounds or limbs gnawed off—so I hit the button for 1, stepped off the elevator and let the doors close. Hopefully he would have the sense to get out and run as soon as he hit the bottom floor.

There were more bodies strewn in the hallway just in front of the elevators, and the sounds of screaming, snarling and yelling to the left. I darted past some open office doors and to the conference room at the end of the hall. Just as I reached the doorway someone's arms came flying through and I had to duck to avoid getting hit. Hot blood spattered on my face.

The stink of sulfur filled the air. Six Agents had been cornered by a horror that they would never understand.

Ramuell looked even more disgusting than he had before. The skin on his arms was shredded and burnt, some of it still hanging in pieces from his hands where the starburst had caused the most damage. His head scraped the ceiling and knocked the tiles out of place. I wondered briefly where J.B. and Gabriel were if they weren't fighting Ramuell.

Oh, please don't let them have been eaten.

Before I could think of or do anything, a clawed hand shot from the red mass of Ramuell's body, wrapped around a skinny male Agent who looked like Buddy Holly, and snapped back to the creature's mouth. I couldn't actually see his mouth as his back was to me, but I heard the crunching of blood and bone and the terrified screams of the Agent as he was eaten alive.

The magic that had lay dormant inside me roared to life in protest. This was not to be borne. I would not allow anybody else to suffer. I just had to lure Ramuell away so I could get a safe shot at him with my nightfire, and allow the Agents time to escape.

"Hey, Big 'n' Ugly!" I called.

The crunching paused, and several of the Agents in

the corner looked panicked when they noticed me. One of them made a shooing motion at me, trying to tell me to get away. For some reason the gesture made me a little teary-eyed. He was about to get eaten and he wanted me—a total stranger—to escape.

The nephilim turned toward me. Ramuell's eyes lit up with glee. A jean-clad leg hung between its large teeth like a macabre toothpick. Each tooth was fang-sharp and his breath stank like a butcher's floor.

"I have been looking for you, little girl." The leg fell out of his mouth as he spoke. "You owe me a debt for this." He held up his burnt arms.

I launched a quick, short blast of nightfire at him, just enough to sting. The magic flowed easily from my finger-tips.

"Catch me if you can."

I smiled and crooked my finger at him, then dashed into the hallway. I heard Ramuell roar behind me and hoped that he couldn't move very fast in the close confines of the building. I had no clear idea of where to go. I just wanted to limit casualties. If I led him into another office, I would be cornered myself, but if I kept him in the hallway, then the other Agents would be unable to make their way to the elevator and freedom.

I had only a few moments to decide. Since most Agents were not the children of fallen angels, I figured I had a leg up in the magic department. That meant that I would have to deliberately corner myself and trust my magic to see me through.

"Well, you were looking for Ramuell. You found him," I muttered to myself.

My stomach jittered as I raced into an office a few doors away. It is not easy to make a decision that might lead to your horrible death at the hands of a people-eating monster. I checked to make sure Ramuell followed me. He was only a few feet behind me, closer than I thought he would be, and he smiled at me as he came.

Sulfur flowed off the creature in waves. My eyes stung and my nostrils burned. I skidded into the office and behind the office door, hoping Ramuell would be distracted for a moment by my Tom-and-Jerry trick while I figured out a game plan.

I guess Ramuell wasn't a big fan of Chuck Jones. He grabbed the door and tore it off its hinges, advancing on me.

"Boo," I said, as I gave him a full-on blast of nightfire. At least, that was what I meant to do.

Instead my magic roared up, uncontrollable, eager for the fight. White flames seared through my palms and arrowed to the nephilim like bolts of lightning. The monster had only a moment of wild-eyed shock before the flames touched its skin.

This was different from both nightfire and the starburst, which had come forth in one huge pulse. This was a continuous flow of power that I couldn't stop, and I wasn't sure that I wanted to. I was beating him. This could end now, and there would be no more innocent deaths.

Ramuell screamed in agony, and so did I. The power was painful, burning inside me even as it burned the monster. I could feel my palms cracking and blistering from the force of the magic. The nephilim backed away from me, knocking over furniture as it lashed out in fury. The desk was set alight at Ramuell's touch. The heat of the flames scorched my face.

"I can end this. I can end this," I said as I moved closer. The power was consuming me. It was more than I could handle. But I didn't want to let go. I wanted vengeance for all the deaths that this monster had caused.

I was so focused on Ramuell that I didn't see the portal opening behind him until it was too late. He fell into the portal and it snapped closed behind him.

"No. No!" I screamed. The power pouring out of me shut off abruptly and I fell to the floor, panting, my face pressed against the carpet. The air was filled with the smell of charred flesh, and the burning desk had ignited the curtains. I had to get out of this room before I burned alive.

The sudden manifestation of yet another new power that I could not control had exhausted me. If my life ever calmed down for a few moments, Gabriel and I were definitely going to have some words about controlling my magic. I could not allow this kind of power to run roughshod over my will. I pushed to my knees and crawled toward the door, crying out in pain as my burned hands pressed into the carpet.

I heard a rustle of movement, and felt hands underneath my arms drag me out of the room. I closed my eyes as someone turned me over and rested me against a wall. There were several voices, and the smell of a fire extinguisher.

"Whoa," said a voice next to me. I felt someone's fingers take my wrist and assess the damage the new power had done to my hands.

I opened my eyes and saw that it was the Agent from the conference room, the one who had tried to wave me away to safety. He and the remaining Agents crowded in the hallway, several of them rushing forward to put out the fire.

"You need medical attention. Right away," he said. "Your hands are a mess."

I flapped my hands at him. I needed to get up, to find Gabriel and J.B. I didn't have time to be fussed over.

"What did you do to that thing?" the Agent asked, his eyes curious. "I've never seen power like that before. And it . . . knew you."

I really didn't have time for answering questions about my freaky new magical abilities, even if I was inclined to explain everything to this guy I'd never met before.

"I nuked it," I said shortly. It seemed like as good an explanation as any. "Tell me what happened here. I was in the basement."

"I don't know. I was in my office when the building started to shake, and then I heard the screaming coming through the vents. I went into the hallway just as a bunch of other monsters came out of the elevators."

"There are more of them?" I asked, my magical senses on high alert.

"At least a dozen. I don't even know how they all crammed into the elevator, to tell you the truth."

"What happened to them?"

"J.B. Bennett and some other guy I've never seen before—he must be another Agent from somewhere; he had the biggest wings I've ever seen—anyway, they came busting out of the second elevator right after the monsters and started blasting them with magic I've never seen before. Kind of like yours. They managed to divert most of the creatures into the stairwell," he said. "Then a few minutes later that big thing came out of another elevator and came after us."

There was an unnerving combination of gratitude and suspicion in his eyes, and I thought it prudent to get away before he started asking more questions about my abilities. These people were on edge and they might decide that a burning stake was just the thing for the weirdo Agent with creepy powers.

"Listen, I'm not sure if the building is completely secure, but if you can get an elevator to the first floor, you should be able to get out. I was in the lobby before I came up here and there were no creatures down there. But," I said, holding up a warning hand as they started to move past me. "Whatever you saw up here, it's a hundred times worse down there. So be prepared."

The first Agent nodded and the others bobbed their heads in time.

"Be careful," I said, and ran to the stairwell. Now that the shock of the dead bodies and Ramuell was over, I was petrified with fear for J.B. and Gabriel. I thought that Gabriel could probably handle himself—he was half nephilim, after all—but he would have to watch after J.B., who was just a puny human with an Agent's magic.

The stairs were coated in blood and there were unidentifiable organic bits everywhere. It looked like one of the monsters had exploded. The air was a strange mixture of sulfur, ozone, apple pie—*ah, there's Gabriel*—and pine tar. I hurried up the steps as quickly as I could, tracing the path of the battle by following the trail of blood and gore.

As I climbed I had time to calm down and think. I was confused by the smell of sulfur since Ramuell hadn't made it any farther than the last floor. The smell could mean only one other thing—demons. How had they managed to get inside? The building was warded against magical intruders. There are a lot of supernatural creatures—witches, faeries and the like—that would love to have foreknowledge of certain deaths, and it was in our interest to keep them out.

Of course, I thought, *the existence of demons isn't exactly common knowledge. J.B. hadn't believed they existed until one of them nearly filleted him. Maybe the wards hadn't stipulated the repellence of demons.*

And had Ramuell purposely brought the demons with him, or had they simply hitched a ride when they saw him busting into the building? Ramuell had obviously been looking for me, but why would demons attack one of death's regional offices?

The carnage grew worse as I climbed, until my boots were ankle deep in monster bits, and I clung to the railing so that I wouldn't fall flat on my face.

"This is stupid," I said, and let my wings out.

I rose through the well between the winding staircase until I reached the rooftop. My wings tucked neatly behind my back, I kicked open the door and rushed out, prepared for an attack.

I did not expect to see J.B. blasting magic at a demon with some kind of wooden rod. I also didn't expect to find him winning. As with the staircase, there were demon parts everywhere.

As I watched, J.B. seemed to focus his power and gave one last strong blast from the rod. It hit the demon squarely in the chest and the thing burst into monster confetti. J.B. panted, wiping blood from his face with his sleeve. I ran to his side and identified the pine-tar smell from the hallway. He reeked of it.

"What happened? Where the hell is Gabriel? And what's that thing you're playing with?" I asked.

"I told you that you don't know everything about my powers."

"Fine. I was wrong. So what's up with your powers, then?"

"Let's just say that my mother is about as interesting as your father. I'll tell you a story about her sometime. And I'm perfectly well, thanks for asking, Black," he said, his face pale and drawn and dotted with small burn marks.

From the demonic blood, no doubt. "I've just taken out a platoon of demons by myself, but why should you care?"

"Are you hurt?" I asked.

"No, but . . ."

"Then I need to find Gabriel. Where did he go?" I was worried. Gabriel had sworn to my father that he wouldn't leave my side, and I knew that Gabriel took his vows very seriously. He wouldn't have left me behind unless he had to.

"He was chasing that asshole from your front lawn, the one who tried to kill me," J.B. said.

"Antares? He was here?"

That was worrisome. That was more than worrisome. It meant that Antares had tracked either J.B. or myself here, and likely for reasons of demonic vengeance. That meant that all those Agents had been slaughtered on our account. I already had Greenwitch's death on my soul. How many more people would be killed because they had been caught in the cross fire of a war they could never understand?

"Tell me exactly where they went."

"Black, you can't be thinking of going after them. That Gabriel guy looked like he had things pretty well under control. What is he, anyway? He isn't any Agent, not with powers like that."

"Just tell me where the hell they went, Jake!" I shouted, and J.B. backed away from me a little.

"You've got that freaky star-eye thing going again," he said.

"Now!" Even in times of crisis, J.B. Bennett was the one person in the world who could push my buttons and make me act like a toddler.

"Antares took off flying and Gabriel followed him. They went toward the lake."

"Right. I'm after them, and I'll check in with you later," I said, and then remembered something. "J.B., have you seen the lobby?"

"Yes," he said grimly. "If there is anyone left in the building, I'll coordinate cleanup and . . . disposal."

"I told some people to stay in the Hall of Records until you came for them. They should still be there, waiting."

He nodded, his eyes far away, probably already thinking about the Agent pieces that needed to be collected and returned to their families, if possible. I hated to leave him to deal with this alone, but I had to find Gabriel. I launched from the roof and flew toward the lake, my eyes searching for any sign of Gabriel or Antares.

I crossed Michigan and then over Millennium Park, and just as I was about to fly over the yacht club at Monroe I looked down and noticed that traffic was backed up on Lake Shore Drive. It was unusual for traffic to be that bad in the middle of the day. I panicked, thinking that Gabriel and Antares had taken their battle to the street and that collateral damage was piling up even as I searched for them.

Then I noticed the two cars snarled together in the right lane, and the ambulance, and the blue police lights flashing. And I remembered that I had a pickup on Lake Shore Drive at two thirty-seven. I glanced at my watch. It was already two forty-five.

"Fuck!" I shouted. I am not inclined toward regular use of expletives, but when I do use them I put my whole heart into it. "Fuck! Fuck! Fuck!"

I hesitated for a moment, hovering above the scene of the accident. *Should I perform my sacred duty or go after Gabriel?* I could almost hear the conversation that I would have with J.B. if I told him I hadn't collected three souls.

Sacred duty won out. I could find Gabriel and Antares afterward.

I flapped slowly down to the accident scene, looking for the souls I was to take to the Door. I circled around a few times, checked the ambulance and the cars, but there was no one. Just like with James Takahashi, the souls had broken loose and were condemned to wander the Earth because I had screwed up.

I thought of my promise to Takahashi that I would keep him safe. I thought of Greenwitch's head rolling to my feet. I thought of the Agents whose families had nothing left of their loved ones except bits that hadn't been chewed on by monsters. I thought of a limbless torso and blood spattered on the wall. I thought of Patrick's body underneath the Metra overpass, and holding my mother's lifeless form in my arms.

The grief rose up so suddenly and completely that I couldn't control it. Tears filled my eyes. My throat was choked with sobs, great heaving sobs that seemed to have no end. From the time I'd discovered Patrick I had been careening around, completely useless, leaving a string of bodies and lost souls behind me. It didn't matter if I wasn't the one who had killed them. My incompetence had contributed to their deaths. And my very existence had caused the carnage at the Agency; Ramuell and Antares would never have been in that building if not for me.

I cried so hard I couldn't see. I lowered myself to a park bench that faced the bike path so I wouldn't fall to the ground and get smashed by a car. Just because nobody could see me when I had my wings out didn't mean that the laws of physics stopped applying. If I was hit by a car while I was invisible, it would still hurt.

Joggers trotted past me with their iPods blasting. Cyclists zipped by dressed in brightly colored spandex. Wealthy retirees walked tiny little dogs that yipped. Mothers in yoga pants pushed jogging strollers and dispensed goldfish crackers to their restless children.

All of them were completely unaware of my presence, unaware of the other world that butted up against their normal, everyday existence. Demons. Angels. Faeries. Werewolves. Witches. Vampires. Agents of death. Creatures that were fun to read about in books or see in movies, but could never have a place in their comfortable, ordinary, everyday lives.

I put my head in my hands and let the sobs come. I had never felt so helpless, so much like a failure, as I did in that moment.

"Excuse me?" A woman's voice, light and soft.

I ignored it. Nobody was talking to me. Nobody could see me.

"Excuse me? Miss? Are you here for us?" I felt a hand brush my shoulder, featherlight, and I looked up.

A young woman in her twenties stood there, fashionable without being too chic. A man about the same age with stubbled cheeks and a shaggy haircut had his hand on her shoulder. The woman held a wide-eyed little boy of about four in her arms.

These were my lost souls.

I felt a pang as I looked into the little boy's eyes. Another lost life, so much promise snuffed out. But death has its own rhythms and reasons, and I comforted myself with the thought that they would all be together when they faced the Door.

"Yes," I said, wiping the tears from my face. I stood up

and let my wings out, trying to present myself with a little dignity. "Yes, I am here for you."

I held out my hand. The little boy smiled and put his fingers in mine.

The Door closed, and my sight returned. The souls had entered together and there was no trace of them left on Earth.

I felt drained as I flew from the Door. I needed to find Gabriel, but it occurred to me that I didn't even have his cell phone number—or my father's, for that matter. I had no way to get in touch with either of them.

I thought briefly about returning to the office building downtown, but—coward that I am—I couldn't face the thought of sifting through the bodies. I knew that I should, that since their deaths were my responsibility I should be there. But I couldn't. I was exhausted; I was frightened; I was alone and unsure about my next move.

Gabriel was gone, presumably off fighting Antares and hopefully not lying dead or injured in a ditch somewhere. I didn't know what I would do if he didn't return to me. The search through the Hall of Records had yielded no usable information for finding Ramuell unless he decided to attack me. I needed Gabriel to help me try to trace Greenwitch's magic so that we could find Ramuell's master. I was paralyzed without him.

And it wasn't just that I needed him to find and fight Ramuell. I had barely had time to think over the past couple of days, much less sift through my feelings, but I knew one thing for sure—there was no way in hell that I was marrying Nathaniel, and I was going to do everything I could to find some way for Gabriel and me to be together. I had a year's grace from my father and I was going to use it.

I headed toward home on autopilot, worried about Gabriel and about my newest power. I followed the lake shore since my house was north and just a little west. Just as I was about to fly over Addison I noticed a flashing light out of the corner of my eye. I turned more fully, hovering in the air, and saw what looked like a geographically isolated lightning storm high above Hollywood Beach.

A lightning storm. In the middle of a clear blue autumn sky.

"Gabriel," I breathed, and shot toward the light.

I flew as fast as I could, my wings beating against the air, my breath coming in harsh pants. As I got closer I saw Gabriel lay a blast of nightfire at Antares, and Antares fly upward, avoiding it. He held a silver charm in his fist and he pointed it in Gabriel's direction. A blast of magic emitted from it, strongly scented with sage. This must be Greenwitch's magic, then.

Gabriel neatly avoided the blast just as I reached him. Antares narrowed his eyes at me in hatred.

"You!" he spat, and tried to blast me with the same magic he'd just launched at Gabriel.

As it had before, my magic seemed to know what to do even if I did not. I held up my hand and a blue pulse emitted from my palm. It captured Antares's magic and deadened it, almost like an electromagnetic pulse will knock out anything technological.

Gabriel looked at me with respect. "Impressive. Where did you learn to do that?"

"I haven't the faintest idea," I said. I was starting to worry that my magic and my body were not my own, that some other force was working through me, and I had a strong suspicion about the name of that force. But I was wary of mentioning Evangeline. The last time I'd thought of her I'd blacked out. I really didn't want to do that now and fall in the lake.

"So what's the deal with the charm? I figured you'd have taken Antares by now, being half nephilim and all," I said to Gabriel, as Antares watched us with narrowed eyes, plotting his next move.

Gabriel made a *pfff*ing noise. "The demon cheats. He has no magic of his own other than simple spells, so he borrows his dead mother's power."

That seemed unusual—not that I was an authority on demon magic. But Antares came from two exceptionally powerful parents—Greenwitch and Azazel. Shouldn't he have had some magic of his own? Then again, perhaps his lack of power was the reason why he'd been passed over as heir to Azazel's court.

Antares had settled on the long-held tactic of talking your opponent to death. "Little virgin, I will have your eyes for your part in my mother's death."

"First it was my heart; then it was my entrails; now it's my eyes," I complained. "Can't you just pick a body part and get to it, *little brother*?"

"Ah, so the outcast has told you who I am." Antares's eyes flickered to Gabriel. "It will be doubly precious to dismember you, knowing that Azazel's grief will be legendary."

"That's assuming you can get near me in the first place. You can't even fight without borrowed magic—or a gang of cronies to back you up," I sneered.

If Antares hadn't already been red, I'm sure I would have seen him blush. He gritted his teeth. "Make no mistake, sister. You have the blood of my mother on your hands and I will have vengeance. You will not be able to sleep or wake without looking over your shoulder for me. I will not rest until I have destroyed you and our father utterly."

"Right," I said, and inside me my magic sang out for Antares's destruction. I realized that if I didn't destroy him, he would dog me until I made a mistake, and then he would kill me. So I didn't stop to think. I let the magic have its way.

The same white flames that had scorched Ramuell in the office downtown burst from my fingertips. Antares's mouth fell open in shock, and then a moment later he was gone, with no time to even cry out.

Gabriel moved away from me a little, as if he were afraid. "Madeline, what did you do?"

"Nuked him," I said, breathing hard, unable to believe it had been that easy. "Neat trick, huh?"

"These unexpected manifestations of your power aside, you have now endangered yourself yet again," Gabriel said angrily.

"What *now*?" I shouted. "What violation of protocol did I commit by killing a demon who swore up and down that he was going to hunt me to the ends of the Earth? Why the hell can't I just smash the guy who was responsible for the deaths of dozens of my colleagues?"

"I know you do not understand," Gabriel said. "But the system of loyalty and protocol within Lucifer's kingdom is absolute. Antares was Azazel's son and Focalor's thrall. The law of the kingdom forbids blood combat between siblings in order to preserve peace and prevent unnecessary grasping of the throne within each court."

"So it was okay for Antares to show up at my house and kick the snot out of me?"

"No," Gabriel said patiently. "It was not 'okay.' Azazel was planning to capture and punish Antares."

" 'Punish' meaning 'kill,' right? So I saved Azazel a step."

"No. Azazel would not have been able to kill Antares because he was Focalor's thrall, and there are also laws about harming the subjects of another Grigori. Lucifer does not want constant bloodshed in his kingdom. The laws are designed to prevent the courts from going to war over minor slights."

"So what now?" I said, still angry. "Do I get punished for taking out Antares?"

"Yes," Gabriel said. "But not by Azazel, who would likely simply torture you briefly and release you."

I felt queasy. "Just a little torture before breakfast? No problem."

"Yes, there is a problem. Because Antares owed allegiance to Focalor and you owe allegiance to Azazel, there are two possible outcomes. The first is that Azazel and Focalor will engage in combat to the death, in Lucifer's court, before witnesses."

"And the other option?" I said.

"Azazel can give you to Focalor as an apology."

My stomach lurched. I could imagine what my fate would be.

"That's not good," I said.

"No. It is not."

18

GABRIEL DIDN'T SPEAK TO ME ALL THE WAY HOME. I felt that the silent treatment was a little unfair, considering that I was the one who was going to get handed over to an unknown Grigori court to be used as a plaything. It never crossed my mind that Azazel might engage in blood combat for me. Gabriel had indicated to me time and again that Azazel would do nothing to risk his court or the sanctity of Lucifer's kingdom.

Beezle was in the kitchen when we returned. He was watching a bag of popcorn go around on the microwave plate. I could see three torn and discarded bags at the top of the garbage can.

"What happened?" he asked, yanking the bag of cooked popcorn from the microwave and shoving fistfuls in his mouth. "Why were you gone so long? Did you find out anything in the Hall of Records?"

Gabriel crossed to the cabinet where I kept the hot chocolate and pulled out three packets, and then he filled the kettle with water and placed it on the stove. Apparently he was in need of some therapeutic chocolate. He crossed his arms and leaned against the counter next to the stove, stony-eyed and silent.

Between Beezle's nervous popcorn binge and all of the extra hot chocolate being consumed, there was a trip to the warehouse store in my future. I wondered if I would have time to do something as ordinary as shop for groceries ever again. And if I did have time, what were the chances that I would be able to get through a trip without being attacked by something freaky?

"We didn't find anything in the Hall of Records. Ramuell, Antares and a bunch of demons attacked the field office. Dozens of Agents are dead. J.B. has powers that I have never seen before, and I didn't have any time to really ask him about them. I tried burning Ramuell to death and he escaped into a portal. Gabriel chased Antares away from the building and I caught up with them. And then I nuked Antares. Oh, yeah, that's a new power of mine."

My dispassionate summary hardly seemed to convey the difficulty and horror of the last few hours, but Beezle appeared suitably shocked.

"You did *what* to Antares?" Beezle shouted, dropping the bag of popcorn to the floor. Kernels spilled everywhere. What I had done must have been pretty bad if it caused Beezle to waste perfectly good popcorn.

"I didn't know," I said. I felt strangely numb inside. I didn't want to think too hard about the consequences of killing Antares or I might break down again. "It wasn't my fault."

"No," Beezle said furiously, pointing a claw at Gabriel. "It is his fault. You were supposed to protect her. You swore to me that you would. How could you allow this to happen?"

"It appears that our little Madeline has—how do you put it?—'powers beyond our understanding.' She manifested yet another ability that I have never seen before. Additionally, she manifested this ability so quickly, and without prior warning, that I had no opportunity to stop her."

He said all these things in a monotone. His coldness hurt almost as much as the fact that he was talking about me like I wasn't in the room.

"I didn't *know*, okay?" I shouted, furious and hurt and scared. The tears I had wanted to hide rose to the surface, filling my eyes and falling down my cheeks, unbidden. "I thought I was supposed to be smiting the bad guys! Every time I turn around you're telling me that I've violated some rule that I don't even know about. Four days ago I was happily making a fucking pear tart and worrying about money and the stupid paperwork I would have to file for J.B., and now I have to worry about my own damned father turning me over to a fallen angel so that I can be tortured for the rest of my life! *I didn't know!*"

My voice got louder and louder as I spoke, and the flames of magic inside me rose higher and higher. The air around me crackled with energy. I turned my burning gaze on Gabriel, who had gone very still.

"Uh, I'm going to go outside, okay? Just in case . . ." Beezle said, and flew out the kitchen window.

I barely heard him. I struggled to control my magic, to not let it control me. I didn't know what would happen if I allowed it loose when I was in such a high emotional state. I didn't want to do something else I would have to regret.

Gabriel pushed away from the counter and moved toward me slowly and deliberately. I panted from the effort to control my magic, to keep it inside me. It felt like a million pins and needles under my skin, pushing, testing, searching for signs of weakness. My hands were fisted at my sides and I felt my hair rise around my face in a halo. Sweat beaded on my temples and the air suddenly smelled like cinnamon and nutmeg.

The kettle began to whistle on the stovetop and I looked at it and said, "Be quiet." The gas flame underneath the kettle abruptly snapped off and steam stopped pouring from the spout. Something else I could do that I had never done before.

Gabriel put his hands on my shoulders.

"Be careful," I said, breathing hard. "Be careful. I don't know what I might do."

He said nothing, only leaned forward until his forehead pressed against mine and we stared into each other's eyes. The stars in his were quiet, bright little jewels in the vastness of space. His hands rubbed up and down my arms, gentling me. My breath unconsciously fell into the rhythm of his, slowing down, becoming less harsh and more steady.

The magic inside me eased down to a flicker and the crackle of electricity disappeared. I closed my eyes, felt myself returning to normal again.

Gabriel brushed his lips against mine, once, twice. Just enough to comfort, but not enough to lead to more dangerous thoughts. He pulled away and I opened my eyes.

He nodded, and the only hint that I had that the kiss had affected him was the shower of meteors deep in his eyes. Then he took my hands, my poor burned and abused hands, and I felt the light of the sun flowing through me as he healed them.

"I think I need that hot chocolate now," I murmured.

Gabriel stayed quiet for a few moments while he fixed

the chocolate and then handed me a cup. In silent understanding we went into the living room and took our usual chairs. As I settled myself under a blanket I realized something.

"You're going to be punished, too, aren't you? Because I killed Antares?" I asked.

"Yes," he said simply.

"I don't understand why you are responsible for my stupidity," I said.

"Because the gargoyle is correct. I should have told you that to harm Antares would endanger your well-being. Lord Azazel will most certainly blame me for your actions."

"Azazel should be thanking you and me for getting rid of Antares. Anyway, when Antares attacked J.B. you said that if Antares drew human blood, he would be in violation of some kind of accords. Doesn't that mean he forfeited his rights in Lucifer's kingdom when he broke the law?"

"Yes," Gabriel said slowly. "But he would have been brought to trial and judged by one of the chiefs of the Grigori or perhaps, because of the magnitude of his crime, by Lord Lucifer himself. You have not yet taken your father's place; therefore, you have no right to judge or punish Antares. You will be treated like a common citizen who has broken the law."

"How do you live like this? Bound to this complex web of strictures and dictates, punished when you violate the smallest of rules? Why would any of the fallen choose to conform to such ridiculous laws?"

"Presumably because they believe that Lord Lucifer's way is better than what they left behind. And don't ask what that was. You know I could not tell you, even if I knew.

"And besides," he continued, sipping from his cup. "Not all of the fallen wish to serve Lord Lucifer. My lord is constantly dealing with any number of minor rebellions and struggles for power. It is why his word must be followed absolutely and all traitors punished swiftly. Lord Lucifer must maintain his base of power and ensure that the majority of his subjects are loyal to him."

"But their loyalty is based on fear, not respect."

"To one of the fallen, it is the same thing. They respect Lord Lucifer's power and will not violate his laws because they fear the repercussions of that power."

I felt myself grow frustrated again with the ludicrous dictates by which I was now forced to live. And thinking of that reminded me that an unpleasant fate awaited me whenever Azazel and Lucifer realized I had smoked Antares. There had to be a way out, but I was too tired and confused to think it through. I decided to focus on the more immediate problem—my out-of-control magic.

"Let's not worry about Lucifer's stupid laws right now," I said. "I need you to help me get my magic under control before I blast the entire city of Chicago off the map."

"Yes," Gabriel said, frowning. "It would be easier if I thought that we had seen the full extent of your powers. But it appears that you have spent many years suppressing your true nature, and now that your magic has been loosed, it is manifesting itself in unforeseen ways.

"Be that as it may, at a minimum I can help you learn to control your emotions and thereby the flow of power, if not the exact type. Your emotional state seems to increase the likelihood that a buildup of power will occur inside you and explode out with dangerous consequences."

"Like that little nuclear blast thing. Or the starburst."

"Yes. However, the shield defense that you used against Antares should be quite useful—"

"I thought the nuclear blast was pretty useful, myself."

"—and if you had better control over your emotions and powers"—Gabriel ignored my comment—"you would likely be able to call up the shield at will."

"Let's be fair here. My emotions have been careening in every direction because every time I turn around another curveball is thrown at me.

"It's difficult to feel in control when, in the last four days, my best friend has died; a nephilim keeps trying to eat me; my new tenant turns out to be a half angel as, I should mention, do I; my long-lost father tries to gift my virginity to his lieutenant; I discover I have a demon half brother who I *finally* manage to kill, after he attempts to murder me and everyone I know, only to find out I've totally broken some rule I didn't even know existed, which means I am going to suffer horribly for the rest of my natural-born life. Oh, and I almost forgot—Lucifer's long-lost lover decides to use me as a megaphone for her life story every time I pass out, an event that has occurred with astonishing regularity from the moment I met you. I think I deserve a little slack here."

I was out of breath and dizzy at the end of this pronouncement. Somehow the act of speaking aloud the ordeal of the past few days made me realize just how exhausted I was.

"I'm tired," I said, my eyes drooping.

"Perhaps now is not the best time for magical lessons," Gabriel said, putting his cup on the end table and standing up.

I stared up at him stupidly and shook my head to try to jolt some blood back into my brain. "If not now, when? If I go to sleep, I'm just going to get woken up because there's another crisis, and there won't be time to teach me anything before the next unknown power manifests itself."

"You cannot learn anything if you are so tired you can hardly keep your head up." He put his arms under my body and lifted me easily.

I swatted at him ineffectually. It was too easy to rest my head against his shoulder and close my eyes, especially when he radiated heat like a furnace. He carried me down the hall and into my bedroom and placed me on the bed. The bedcovers were still rumpled and thrown back from the night before.

Gabriel tried to pull away but I grasped his sleeve. "Stay," I mumbled.

He moved toward the chair that he had used to watch over me the night before.

"No," I said, my eyes barely slit open. I patted the space next to me. "Stay with me."

He shook his head. "It is too dangerous for me to be near you."

"Just stay," I insisted. "And take off your coat, for crying out loud. I know you've got wings under there, so you don't need to hide them when we're in the house."

He smiled at that, and I could see indecision warring in his eyes.

"I just want you to hold me," I whispered, my eyes fully closed now. I felt myself drifting. "Before they take me away from you forever."

My eyelids were too heavy to open again, but I heard the soft rustling of cloth, and the thunk of his shoes on the floor. A moment later the bed shifted as he settled his weight behind me.

"Closer," I demanded sleepily.

"Yes, my lady," he said, and his body pressed against my back. His right arm hugged me and his face was buried in my hair. There was more rustling and then I felt something fold over my body, soft as down and as warm as the sun.

I fell asleep like that, wrapped in his wings.

When I opened my eyes the digital clock on my nightstand read 11:36 P.M. I didn't know what time it was when I conked out—I'd stopped looking at my watch after I'd delivered my souls to the Door—but I felt rested and refreshed. And hungry.

I tried to sit up and realized that I was cocooned in Gabriel's wings, and that I was very, very warm.

"There is no crisis," Gabriel murmured sleepily. "You can relax."

I turned in his arms so that I faced him. His eyes were at half-mast, still drowsy with sleep. The last four days had been hard on him, too. He'd been chasing around after me and expending nearly as much magical energy as I had. I stroked my hand down his cheek and felt soft stubble beneath my fingers.

"You need to shave," I said. "I didn't think angels would have to worry about hair growth."

"I am not perfectly immortal, as Lord Azazel is," he said, his hand coming up to close around mine. "I do age, but very slowly—so slowly that you would not notice the passing of years on me. There is a small strain of human blood in me, from the line of the nephilim."

His fingers rubbed against mine, and our faces were so close together that I could feel the puff of his warm breath on my skin.

It was easy and natural to move closer, to let our mouths brush together, to pull away and smile, to be happy for this quiet moment together.

Then my stomach rumbled, and Gabriel burst out laughing.

I watched him in delight. He almost never smiled, and when he did it never really seemed like a happy smile. I had heard him laugh only once or twice, but it was magical to hear, a bright and shimmering thing that danced in the air.

His laughter trickled out but he still had a huge grin pasted on his face.

"Pizza," I said, giving him a quick kiss and climbing out of bed. He shifted his wings so that I could move. "Someone around here must do late-night delivery. And you're buying. I haven't actually gotten any rent money from you yet."

"Ah. That," Gabriel said, sitting up and letting his wings stretch out. His wingspan was about twelve feet and I had to scurry to the foot of the bed to allow him room.

" 'Ah, that' what?" I said, pushing my feet into my fuzzy slippers.

It had been hours since I'd thought about my clothes, but I looked down and realized I still wore the black skirt, purple button-down shirt and black blazer that I'd put on that morning to appear in my father's court. The sharp-heeled, knee-high boots that I had worn were crumpled on the floor next to the bed, and they were caked with gore. I didn't even want to think about cleaning the leather, so I picked them up and tossed them in the kitchen trash. I found the Cubs sweatshirt that I had thrown aside in haste that morning, pulled off the blazer and replaced it with the sweatshirt.

"The rent money."

"Don't even tell me that there is no rent money," I said,

panicked. "Because that's going to be a problem. My income has not been too stable for the last few months."

He finished stretching and folded his wings behind him again. The chilliness of the room didn't seem to affect him. He padded around the bed in bare feet, black trousers and a white shirt with the sleeves rolled up and followed me into the kitchen as I began searching through the stack of take-out menus that I had clipped to the refrigerator.

"There is no rent money . . ." he began.

"What?" I shouted, turning to him.

He held his hands up. "Peace. There is no rent money, because now that Azazel has acknowledged you as his daughter he is able to give you the legacy he has been saving for the last thirty-two years."

I narrowed my eyes. "What legacy?"

"Lord Azazel is a very wealthy man. And also a prompt one. If you check your bank balance, I am sure that you will see he has given some of the legacy to you already."

I couldn't let that pass without investigation. I marched to my laptop, booted up and logged on to my Internet banking website. When I saw the figures for my checking and savings accounts, all the blood rushed out of my face.

"I've never seen that much money in one place in my whole life," I said. "Well, maybe in news items about government spending."

"And I am certain that it is only part of what you will receive. There are bound to be investments in various forms, scattered here and there. Lord Azazel will no doubt apprise you of these soon." He smiled at my look of shock.

My heart did a little jig. No more worries, no more scraping to get by. Then I sobered, remembering what else had happened that day.

"I don't think he'll have to apprise me of anything," I said, "seeing as I'm going to be given to Focalor."

The smile faded from Gabriel's face. "Yes. Of course. I had forgotten."

"Me, too," I said. My appetite was suddenly gone. At this rate I'd lose the extra fifteen pounds I was carrying in no time. It's the My Daddy Was a Fallen Angel diet!

Antares. I couldn't believe that I had ever thought I wanted a brother when I was kid. My only sibling had been a giant pain in the behind from the moment he kicked me down the front porch stairs until I snuffed his life out.

My stomach rumbled. Okay, maybe my appetite wasn't completely gone.

"Let's have pizza." I thought that there was a strong possibility that this could be my last good meal on Earth. "And wings. And maybe cheesecake. I'm buying."

19

AS WE ATE, GABRIEL AND I DISCUSSED MY LAST VISION of Evangeline, the one that I'd had while at Azazel's court. Beezle smelled pizza and fluttered in from outside, wordlessly thrusting an extra plate at me to fill for him. Gabriel still seemed astounded by what I had learned.

"I cannot believe the Archangel would take Lucifer's children as his own," Gabriel said wonderingly. "How did he manage it? He could not pass them off as his own blood, even if they were infused with his grace. Mating with a mortal woman would have resulted in his expulsion from paradise."

"He did it somehow." I shrugged. "Anyway, the important thing here is that Evangeline has filled in a lot of holes for us."

"Such as?" Beezle said through a mouthful of cheese and dough.

I put down my slice of pizza to tick off points on my

fingers. "Number one, I am definitely from Evangeline's bloodline. You said yourself, Beezle, that Lucifer's power was that of collecting souls. That's what I do. That's what every Agent does."

Beezle's eyes widened. "And the Morningstar's power was disguised when Michael infused the children with his grace. How could I have been so stupid?"

"I do not believe that anyone could have predicted this. We have long suspected that Evangeline and the children were lost or killed, and that Agents were created by the light for the purpose of replacing Lord Lucifer," Gabriel said.

"Agents probably were created for that reason," I said. "But we weren't created out of thin air. We came from Lucifer's line. Anyway, point number two. There was one survivor of Evangeline's scorched-earth policy, and that being is probably the one controlling Ramuell's puppet strings."

"That's an awfully big leap," Beezle said. "How do you come to that conclusion?"

"Because I seem to be targeted specifically. Because Evangeline heard an angel speaking of her death and the deaths of her children as a way to destroy Lucifer. Because if Ramuell's puppet master wanted to kill Lucifer, what better way than to destroy the last direct descendant of Evangeline?"

"And how do you know you're her last direct descendant?" Beezle asked.

"She's spending an awful lot of time sending me visions," I said. "You think she'd bother if I was just some yahoo? Obviously she thinks I need this information now. Evangeline wanted me to see her escaped captor, so that I will recognize Ramuell's master when I see her."

"Or perhaps she just wanted you to know that one of

her captors survived so that you can turn over that angel to Lord Lucifer's justice," Gabriel pointed out. "It could have nothing to do with Ramuell at all. But I agree that it is likely you are her last direct descendant. It is doubtless the only reason that she was able to awaken these memories in your blood."

I lifted my eyebrows at Beezle, as if to say, "See?"

"Whether she wanted me to see the face of her captor so that I could tell Lucifer about it or capture Ramuell, it doesn't matter. The point is that she's leading me toward this angel for some reason and I should probably find out what that reason is."

"But if it is not related to Ramuell, we cannot afford to waste valuable time on what is, essentially, a matter of old justice," Gabriel said.

"Do you really think that Lucifer would view the fate of his lover and her children as 'old justice'?" I said.

Gabriel looked uncomfortable. "Of course not. But it is essential that we capture Ramuell and his puppet master. That is the task that Lord Azazel has left to us. And besides, how would Evangeline's captor know that you were her last descendant?"

"Because she saw Michael take Evangeline and the children. She witnessed the whole thing from a mountaintop. That means that she alone besides the involved parties knew the fate of Evangeline and the children. I'm telling you," I said, "that I think that my visions are related to our problem with Ramuell."

"And you believe this angel bided her time for thousands of years, waiting for an opportunity to kill Evangeline's descendants? Why not kill the children when they began acting in their father's stead as soul collectors?" Gabriel asked, his tone doubtful.

I threw my hands up in frustration. "I can't fill in all the blanks here. I just know what Evangeline has showed me, and what I feel in my gut. Evangeline could have sent these visions to me anytime in the last thirty-two years. I have to believe that she is sending them to me now to help me capture Ramuell and whoever is controlling him. Evangeline loved Lucifer. She sacrificed her life with him to protect him and his children.

"And besides, I don't care how much money he's given me—I am not at Azazel's beck and call. If I want to trace the angel instead of following Ramuell's path directly, then that's my business."

Beezle threw his hands up in the air. "Here we go again."

"No, I'm serious," I said. "After what I did to Ramuell today, I don't think that Azazel could make me do anything I didn't want to do."

"What makes you think you will be able to summon that ability—or any ability—again at will?" Gabriel said reasonably.

"Oh, sure, now I get a lecture about my magical deficiencies," I said, crossing my arms and glaring at him.

"You do not know how to control your power or your abilities. You admitted as much yourself. And in any case, it is not simply your own life that you risk when you defy Azazel."

The reminder that Gabriel's fate was tied to my own was sobering. And he was right. I shouldn't put myself or him in a position where we could be punished by Azazel simply because I made a threat and was unable to follow through when my magic went haywire at the wrong moment.

"So we're back to the same issue I brought up earlier. I need to understand how to control my powers. Before the next big, bad whatever tries to kill me."

"You're not going to be able to learn control in three and a half seconds," Beezle said. "You've got to keep your emotions in check, for one thing."

"Well," I said, holding my arms out. "There's no time like the present, is there?"

Beezle and Gabriel looked at each other and shrugged.

"I'll take that as a 'yes,'" I said. "Let's finish eating so we can get started."

Four hours later I flopped onto the couch with a blazing headache. I had changed out of my semi-fancy clothes and into a white T-shirt and gray sweatpants. We had practiced in the basement so as not to destroy any furniture that I actually liked. My pants were covered in dust—it had been a long while since I'd thought to vacuum the basement. The shirt was drenched in sweat and my hairline was soaked.

Gabriel and Beezle had run me through the wringer. First, Beezle had instructed me to find the source of my power (the little thing in my belly that I thought of as a match flame), then helped me focus my concentration so that I could metaphorically increase or decrease the flame at will. It required me to link my brain and the source of my magic together. I imagined the match flame connected to a knob that I could flick on or off with a thought. It seemed the best way to help me focus.

It took me several tries and a lot of cursing—on my part and Beezle's—before I could focus on the power without falling into a meditative state. As Beezle pointed out, it was not a good idea to need that much concentration in order to tap my powers. Ramuell would have devoured me by the time I got into the proper frame of mind.

Once I could tap the source of power pretty quickly,

Gabriel started testing me. He blasted me with different spells, occasionally taunting me. It was up to me to stay focused and controlled and not let the magic flame up too quickly. I also had to produce the correct abilities at the correct time—offensive blasts, defensive shields and so on.

Gabriel was a patient teacher, but I was not a patient student. About half the time I got so irritated that I blasted a massive, and completely unnecessary, amount of magic back at him and ended up exhausted and tapped out, magically speaking. I'd needed time to recharge in each instance—time enough to get my goose cooked in a real battle, as Beezle so helpfully pointed out.

I never realized just how little self-control I had. My loner lifestyle had left me at a disadvantage. I'd never had to control my temper for the sake of another person, or keep my cool under pressure in a job. For all intents and purposes I had the emotional control of a three-year-old.

And while I learned how to find the magic inside of me, and turn it up or down as needed—if I stayed in control— I didn't know how to call specific abilities. Twice I used the electromagnetic pulse to defend myself without knowing how I'd called it to me. And since neither Gabriel nor Beezle had ever seen abilities like mine, they didn't know how to tell me to do it. Both of them just counseled control, control, control until I was ready to blast them with night-fire just so that they would shut up.

And that, I thought to myself, *is exactly the reason why they told you to stay in control in the first place.*

By the end of the training session I'd broken an old futon that I had been meaning to sell or give away and blasted apart several boxes of accrued junk. All in all I felt lucky not to have nuked Gabriel by accident or had a massive starburst explosion that collapsed the entire building.

Beezle went in the kitchen to make popcorn—again—and Gabriel went downstairs to his apartment to change. I closed my eyes and let myself doze.

I opened my eyes when I heard Gabriel open the front door. His face was troubled.

"What's the problem?" I said.

He hesitated, and I saw an indefinable emotion flicker across his face.

"Lord Azazel has ordered that we do not track Ramuell at this time. After the incident at the Agency he is wary of your drawing too close to Lucifer's enemies."

I wanted to retort that one more enemy wouldn't make much of a difference, but I bit my tongue. Gabriel didn't deserve to be shouted at just because I didn't want my every breath approved by Azazel first. Although I was pretty annoyed that he had talked to Azazel. It made me wonder if I would ever come first in his eyes.

"And he is sending Nathaniel to you to ensure your safety," he said.

"What!" I exploded, coming to my feet in one angry motion. "I don't want that pompous jerk hanging around and annoying me while we have work to do."

"You do not have a choice, Madeline. He is your betrothed," Gabriel said softly.

"We'll just see about that," I muttered. "Look, it's almost daylight. Ramuell attacked me in the alley near Greenwitch's house. You may be able to trace him directly from there. And maybe we can avoid Nathaniel while we're at it."

"He would still be able to trace you," Gabriel said.

"How?"

He held up his cell phone.

"You don't have to answer that, you know."

"Yes," Gabriel sighed, "I do. And you cannot ask me to directly ignore an order of Lord Azazel's."

Which told me everything I needed to know. When push came to shove, Gabriel would choose Azazel over me. It made the feelings between us a little easier to ignore, I supposed. I wanted him but there was a universe of obstacles in our way.

"Fine. You don't have to ignore Azazel's orders, but I can."

Gabriel took a deep breath and closed his eyes, as if he were searching for patience. "It is seditious for you to ignore the will of your father."

"If my father wanted me to respect his will, then he should have hung around. As it is, he missed the key personality-formation years and therefore can stick it."

"Madeline . . ."

"No," I said, growing angry. "I am not going to sit around and wait for Ramuell to come after me again. I am not going to wait for him to tear some innocent bystander to pieces. I am going after him. Are you helping me or not?"

Gabriel looked at me. I gazed steadily back. Beezle rotated his head back and forth between us, trying to see who would break first.

Something shifted in his eyes. "Lord Azazel did not, I suppose, directly order you to stay away from Greenwitch's."

I nodded.

"And I am bound to stay at your side."

I nodded again.

"Then I suppose I must accompany you there, and if we happen to come upon Ramuell's traces, then it would be folly not to follow them."

I smiled. Maybe the obstacles between us weren't so great after all.

"Can nephilim come out in the daytime?" I asked.

"I suppose so," Gabriel answered. "Why?"

"Nothing. It's just that I've only seen Ramuell at night. I was wondering if maybe sunlight . . ."

"Burned the nephilim to ash like a vampire?" Beezle snorted. "Maddy, remember that the nephilim are half-angel, and angels are born of the sun."

"Right." I nodded and went into my room to change.

But I was thinking about the ragged shreds of skin left on Ramuell after I'd blasted him with the starburst. That power seemed to have a lot in common with the sun. Maybe every nephilim wasn't vulnerable to sunlight, but Ramuell could be. His father was the Morningstar, after all, and Beezle had said that the traits of the angels were twisted inside the nephilim. Wouldn't it stand to reason that a father so closely associated with the sun could have a child that couldn't bear the touch of it?

It was something to think about, anyway.

We managed to get out of the house before Nathaniel arrived. Beezle promised to delay the angel as long as possible so that Gabriel and I could work uninterrupted. The sun was just peeking over the horizon when we arrived at Greenwitch's place. It was too early even for the coffee shop on the corner to have opened yet.

The building looked much the same as it had the last time I had been there. Gabriel stepped up to the door. He put his hand over the doorknob and muttered something under his breath. I heard the dead bolt click open inside.

"It can't be that easy," I said, hesitating on the threshold.

Gabriel stepped inside and headed down the staircase. "My magic is not insignificant, Madeline. I, too, am a descendant of Lord Lucifer."

I dithered for a moment in the doorway and finally decided it was better to follow him and close the door. No sense standing on the stoop, yelling after him and waking the neighbors.

The air inside was filled with the scent of herbs, thyme and sage most predominantly. It didn't have that unused smell that living spaces get when the occupants are gone for more than a few hours. Greenwitch hadn't been gone for that long but still, I'd have expected the air to be a little stale.

"I didn't say your magic was insignificant. And I'm not interested in playing a who's-closer-to-Lucifer's-bloodline game," I said as I hurried after him. "I said it can't be that easy. Greenwitch was an extremely powerful demon. She probably had a lot of enemies."

Gabriel had already turned into the workroom where Greenwitch had taken me on my last visit. "And your point is?" he called back, sounding distracted.

"The point is that she should have had some protective wards or something. We shouldn't have been able to walk right in. Something isn't right here." I rounded the corner after Gabriel and plowed into his back. "Hey."

"You're right," he said, stepping aside so that I could see the room. "Something isn't right here."

It looked as though an extremely destructive pack of toddlers had been through the room. The wardrobe where Greenwitch had kept my charm had been broken open and the doors wrenched from their hinges. Charms and herbs were scattered everywhere and the air was redolent with the smell of the crushed leaves. Her worktable had been smashed in half by something very big, very strong, or both.

"Damn," I said, backing up a little to stand in the doorway as Gabriel picked through the mess. "Who could have done this, and why?"

"I am not sure," Gabriel said, picking up a silver locket, examining it and discarding it.

"Someone needs their apple juice and cheese crackers," I said, examining the destruction, and then I smelled it.

The whiff of sulfur came a breath too late. Antares already had his claws around my neck, even as I was turned, even as I tried to tap my magic. He yanked me close to his body and bent his head close to mine.

"Hello again, little sister," he crooned in my ear. His saliva spattered on my neck and my skin burned where it touched.

"Oh, well, that answers that question," I said as his claws pressed into my flesh. Warm rivulets of blood flowed into the neckline of my peacoat. At least my stupid half brother was alive, and I definitely would not be tortured for killing him. Of course, he was probably going to kill *me* momentarily, so it all came out in the wash, I suppose.

"How is it that you managed to survive?" I said calmly. "I was sure I nuked you to bits."

Antares laughed, and I could feel his chest rumbling against my back. I tried not to show how completely and totally I wanted to pee my pants.

"I have a few tricks up my sleeve," he said.

"Tricks your mommy left you," I taunted, and his arm tightened around me. "No tricks of your own."

Gabriel stood motionless in the middle of the room, watching us. I could see the calculation in his eyes.

"Do not even think about it, outcast," Antares hissed. "I will have slit her throat before you can conjure a spell."

"Do it, Gabriel. He's going to kill me anyway," I said. I felt strangely calm. "Of course, he's going to cheat and use one of Mommy's spells because he's too weak to produce one of his own, but still. You might as well take him out, too."

Antares snarled in my ear and then slammed my face against the doorframe—twice. The second time I heard something crack and I felt hot fluid running out of my nose.

The distraction was enough. While Antares was breaking my nose, Gabriel blasted him in the chest with nightfire. Antares screamed and dropped me to the ground, making sure to kick me in the process. Since he was a demon and a hell of a lot stronger than a human, his kick didn't just crack my ribs. It cracked my ribs *and* launched me across the room into the wall. I smashed into a framed Ansel Adams photo and fell heavily to the ground, the whole time thinking, *Wow, Antares's control issues are worse than mine. I wonder if that's a family trait?*

Then I saw stars and birdies for a few minutes. The smell of sulfur, sage and apple pie filled the air. I could hear the sounds of Gabriel and Antares grunting and snarling at each other as they dueled. The occasional bolt of magic careened around the room.

The little match flame inside me flickered. I needed to get up and help Gabriel. He wasn't allowed to kill Antares—the rules about not harming another demon's thrall still applied no matter what Antares's crimes—but Antares would have no compunction about harming Gabriel. Antares was already an outcast of Azazel's court and facing punishment for killing humans. Offing Gabriel would be nothing to the demon.

I wanted to hurry up, to get to my feet, but all the broken things inside me hurt like hell. I pushed myself to a sitting position and hoped that Antares would be too distracted by Gabriel to launch any spells at me.

While I was pulling myself together the battle had moved into the hall. I was amazed that Greenwitch's upstairs neighbors weren't banging on the front door. It sounded like Antares and Gabriel were smashing every piece of glass and wood in the place.

I staggered to my feet, sucking in air spasmodically. Beezle and Gabriel had counseled emotional control for my magical abilities. Now I needed to control the pain so that I could focus on my power.

I let my breathing slow and tried not to think about the pain radiating just above my belly. The little match flame surged up suddenly, and the power pushed me upright like a string pulling a marionette. It helped me forget about the pain.

"Now," I said, fingertips crackling with energy. "You're mine, little brother."

I strode into the hallway just as Gabriel blasted Antares into the kitchen, which was across the hall from the work-room. The demon slammed into the refrigerator, leaving an indentation that looked like a mold of his body, like in the cartoons where the coyote gets hit by a train and smashed into a canyon wall.

Gabriel never took his eyes from the demon as he blasted Antares again with blue flames. Antares howled in fury and stumbled away, swiping his hand across the counter and knocking over several vases of wildflowers. He fell to his knees, his back to us.

"Can we capture him and bring him to Azazel?" I said, coming to Gabriel's side.

"Yes. I can restrain him." He furrowed his brow and blasted Antares again. The demon collapsed to his stomach, panting, seemingly spent.

Gabriel mumbled to himself and conjured what looked like a pair of blue-lightning handcuffs out of the air. The cuffs crackled with electricity. He strode forward and reached for Antares's arm, which was tucked underneath the demon's chest.

Again, I felt something was not right. Again, I was a whisper too late. "Gabriel, wait . . ."

Antares came to his feet with a roar and a maniacal grin filled with razor teeth. He plunged his clawed hand into Gabriel's stomach and then pulled it out again, covered in gore and gripping what looked like a little nugget of the sun. The rock shone like daylight in Antares's blood-covered fist.

Blood bubbled out of the half angel's mouth as he folded up like a paper fan and collapsed to the floor. I screamed in horror and grief, and all the magic came blasting out of me in a wave, all focused on the creature that had harmed Gabriel.

Antares couldn't move quickly enough. Electricity danced over the demon's skin, searing away the red flesh. It smelled like really bad barbecue. He dropped the shining rock and it skidded across the floor, rolling under the refrigerator. Antares clawed at his skin, howling and tearing off shreds of muscle down to the bone, trying to get my magic off and out of him.

I ignored the furious demon and ran to the refrigerator, dropping to my stomach and peering underneath. The rock was just underneath the lip at the bottom of the refrigerator.

I closed my fingers around it and nearly dropped it. It was jagged and small enough to fit inside my closed fist but it was as hot as a coal from a roaring fire. Smoke swirled from my closed fist, and the smell of my own cooking flesh was added to Antares's.

I crawled to Gabriel and knelt beside him, lifting his head to my lap. His face was chalk white but that wasn't what scared me. When I laid my hand on his face, he was colder than stone.

"Oh, no. Oh, no, no, no," I moaned. I covered the hole in his stomach with my hands. I could feel the blood pumping out between my fingers. "Oh, God. Just hold on, Gabriel. Hold on."

"The outcast is dead," Antares hissed.

I looked up at the demon with furious eyes and gave him another blast of magic for good measure. He screamed and fell to the floor, writhing.

"Gabriel," I said, my tears falling on his face. "Gabriel, can you hear me? What can I do?"

He opened his eyes. There were no stars, no meteors, just the empty blackness of deep space. The heart of the universe.

"You . . . have . . . to . . . get . . . me . . . to . . . Lord . . . Azazel," he said, and then closed his eyes again.

"Oh, no, no. You stay awake, Gabriel. Do you hear me? You stay awake!" I screamed.

A snide, cold voice came from the doorway. "What has happened here, Madeline?"

I looked up. Nathaniel stood in the doorway, golden-haired and dressed in a Burberry coat and scarf. Disgust was etched on his features. I realized that Antares was gone—again. He must have done his disappearing act into a portal while I was concentrating on Gabriel. Apparently there was no amount of pain that could kill Antares's instinct for self-preservation.

"Nathaniel, you have to take Gabriel to my father," I said, pulling my hands away from the wound. I realized I was still holding the daylight rock and I opened my palm. There was a jagged circle branded on the skin. "Antares took this out of him. I don't know what it is."

The angel looked revolted. "It is a piece of his heartstone. If the thrall dies, it is none of my concern. Lord Azazel sent me here to protect you, and I find you not at home, but out doing the precise thing he has ordered you not to do."

I could not believe my father wanted me to marry this asshole. I strode across the room and slapped him across the face. He looked shocked, holding his hand to the place where I'd hit him.

"Gabriel's life is slipping away. You are the only one here who can open a portal. Take him to my father *now*," I shouted.

"If you were not Lord Azazel's daughter, I would kill you for that insult. I am not going to touch a half nephilim, and no fiancée of mine should be touching him either," Nathaniel said haughtily.

My magic swirled up, hot and angry, and I knew that my eyes must have changed, because Nathaniel took a half step away from me. "You . . . will . . . bring . . . him . . . to . . . my . . . father. If he dies, or if he even suffers a moment longer than necessary because of you, then believe this— I will ensure that you bleed every single day for the rest of your very, very long existence."

He looked at me for a moment, and I saw the fear flicker across his face. "You wouldn't dare."

"Believe it, scumbag," I said, and as I spoke my power grew and grew, pushing until I felt that my skin was all that was holding it inside me.

Nathaniel seemed to consider; then he held out his hand for the stone. I placed it in his palm without a word and he grasped my hand with his free one.

"Know this, Madeline Black. I only do this as a favor to you, because you are my betrothed. But in the future, you will cleave unto me as your husband, and it is my wishes that will be obeyed." His eyes were frosted with ice.

"We'll see about that," I said, and yanked my hand away.

He strode to Gabriel and lifted the half angel under his shoulders and knees. Gabriel did not stir. I could barely see the rise and fall of his chest.

Nathaniel opened a portal in the kitchen. Mist swirled inside.

"Take him directly to my father," I said.

"As you wish, Madeline. For now," he said, and stepped inside.

The portal closed behind them, and I was alone in Greenwitch's kitchen, my hands soaked in Gabriel's blood.

20

FOR THE SECOND TIME IN TWO DAYS I BROKE DOWN. I fell to my knees and covered my eyes with my bloody hands and sobbed until there were no more tears. Then I crawled out of the kitchen. The floor was coated in Gabriel's blood as well as bits of Antares's skin and muscle, and it smelled like a slaughterhouse. My knees left dragging tracks in the mess.

I hauled myself to my feet, using the doorway as a support. I'd forgotten about my nose and ribs in all the excitement. The pain now returned to pummel me into submission. My head felt like it had been cracked open with a nut hammer and the throbbing in my ribs made every breath a punishment.

I leaned in the doorway and took a quick assessment of my situation. I was severely injured. My most trusted ally was mortally wounded. My enemy had managed to escape yet again, which meant he would be back at the most inconvenient time possible to try to kill me. Not that there was ever a convenient time for my murder, really.

I still had to track Ramuell or Evangeline's captor or both, and I had basically zero control over my magic. It was miraculous that I had managed to blast Antares with something magically useful, like electricity. I could have just as easily launched feathers in his face.

Without Gabriel, without control over my powers and without a clue how to magically track anyone, I felt pretty hopeless about my cause.

"I don't know what to do. Help me. Help me. I'm all alone," I whispered. I didn't even know who I was asking for help. I just knew that I couldn't do this by myself.

You are not alone.

I stood upright and stared around the room wildly. I knew that voice.

"Where are you?" I said. "Show yourself."

Evangeline appeared before me, small and thin with a long tumble of dark hair. She wore a simple white robe that made her look very sweet and very young. She shimmered as she hung in the air, an idea without corporeal presence.

I looked like her. Not in an obvious way, but it was clear there was a family resemblance in the eyes and the mouth and the shape of the face.

"Are you a ghost?" I said. She didn't really look like a ghost. More like a TV signal that kept flickering on and off.

No, she said. *I am a memory that has been locked in the blood of my descendants for many generations.*

Her mouth didn't move but her voice filled the room. It was fairly creepy.

"So why have you been unlocked now?" I asked.

To help you, my granddaughter. To find the nephilim that kills the children of my children.

I narrowed my eyes at her. "Not to find the angel who held you captive? The one that got away?"

Something flickered across her face but I couldn't read the emotion.

The nephilim's master and my captor are one and the same.

I pumped my fist in the air. "I knew it! I told Beezle and Gabriel."

We must leave. The nephilim cannot show his face in daylight . . .

"Ha! Knew that, too. Why is that, anyway?"

Evangeline looked impatient. *Because, as you suspected, the light of the Morningstar has been twisted inside Ramuell. Sunlight will destroy him utterly. This was hidden by Lucifer. All the nephilim were bound deep underground in the Valley of Sorrows to protect his son's secret.*

But we must hurry now. It will not be long before the nephilim's master realizes that your bodyguard has been mortally injured. She will send others after you.

"How come you waited until now to appear to me and give me all this useful information?" I said suspiciously. "What's your angle?"

Only to help you, my granddaughter, she repeated. *I was unable to assist you directly before because you did not call for aid.*

She looked innocent and full of grace, but I wasn't so certain that her motives were pure. I strongly suspected that some of my freakier powers had manifested as a result of her influence. And it seemed that she had waited until pretty late in the day to get around to helping me.

There is no time, she insisted, holding out her ghostly hand to me. *We must go now.*

I'd wanted help, and here it was. If I took Evangeline's hand, I could find Ramuell and his master. I didn't know if I would be able to capture or injure them on my own, but since she was so hot to get me to them I assumed there would be some assistance on that front.

I just wasn't so sure that my darling great-grandmother wouldn't sacrifice me to reach her own ends. Everyone I had encountered over the last few days had an agenda of their own, and that agenda never seemed to include my well-being at the top of the list.

I could choose to trust Evangeline. Or I could choose to trust that I'd have the wit to keep myself alive. I wasn't so sure about the second choice. It seemed that thus far I'd skated by on a combination of luck and Gabriel's healing ability. But this might be my only chance. If I didn't go after Ramuell now, Antares might come back and kill me. Or a horde of demons might come flying out of the oven. Really, with the week I'd had, anything was possible.

I took Evangeline's hand. It wasn't like grasping the hand of a corporeal being. There was no feeling of firmness, of solid flesh beneath my fingers. But there was a definite feeling of pressure, almost like the air had been molded. I was certain once I touched her that I would not be able to loose myself unless she allowed it.

Stay close, my granddaughter, she said, and gripped me tightly. I felt a warmth in my nose and ribs as my injuries healed.

She pointed the index finger of her free hand and made a circle in the air in front of us. A line of flame appeared where her finger brushed the air.

The center of the circle opened, and the opening spread outward until it reached the flames that hung in the air. It looked like a portal, but it was not filled with swirling mist. Instead, there was a long road with a crack running down the center. In the distance were jagged peaks of gray mountains under flashes of silver lightning. I could see the silhouette of a giant leafless tree, white as bone, scraping thin claws to the dark sky.

"I've been here before," I murmured. "This is the place where you found Lucifer, when you first walked to him from your village."

It is the Forbidden Lands, Evangeline said. *Lucifer kept his palace here, once.*

Her face was full of sorrow. I realized that she had been his bride for only a few short months before she was forced to give him up. I felt pity for her, even though there was something monstrous about her, for she had willingly killed anyone who stood in her path to him. I grieved a little for this child who had destroyed everything and everyone in her village for the love of the Morningstar, only to lose him before their life really began.

"What happened to you, after you went to Michael?" I asked.

She hesitated, then said, *Let us go. I will tell you as we walk.*

Evangeline floated through the circle of flame. I stepped through after her. The circle closed behind us with a soft whoosh and she released my hand, beckoning me forward.

My boots scraped against the asphalt road as I walked. On either side of the road there was nothing except very fine, gray sand and the occasional boulder. The air was cold, much colder than an October morning in Chicago. I'd dressed in my usual uniform of jeans, a sweater and boots with a wool peacoat over it, and I was significantly underdressed for the Forbidden Lands.

I could see my breath puff out before me in white clouds. An icy wind kicked up, blowing sand in my eyes, and I narrowed them to slits. I stuffed my hands in my pockets so that my fingers wouldn't freeze and fall off. I was a little worried about my ears, though, and pulled up the collar of my coat and hunched my shoulders. I succeeded only in keeping my earlobes covered and decided not to bother.

My teeth chattering, I called to Evangeline. "Where is this place? We can't be anywhere on the Earth I know."

She floated a few feet ahead of me, completely unaffected by the cold. Her voice drifted back, carried on the wind. *It is a world that is brushed up next to your world, one of many. Is this not what you give to the souls that you bring to the Door? Their choice of all the worlds?*

I grinned fiercely behind the collar of my coat. Score one for the Agent. "I don't think you were supposed to tell me that."

Evangeline looked back at me and shrugged delicately. She waited until I caught up to her and then floated along beside me. *I have never understood why the celestial ones have insisted on keeping man ignorant.*

I remembered something from the first vision she had sent me. "And this place in particular? There was a nuclear war here?"

Nuclear? She frowned. *Yes. I suppose that is the word that you would use. There were once great cities here, and then there were flames and great clouds of ash, and when it was over this was all that remained.*

I glanced around me, struck by another realization. "I'm not going to get radiation poisoning, am I?"

I suppose the Forbidden Lands could make you sick if you were human. But you are not entirely human, my granddaughter. The blood of two Grigori runs in your veins. That should be enough to protect you.

She looked serene and unruffled, but I wasn't convinced. I'd gotten plenty of colds and flu in my time, and the blood of the Grigori hadn't helped me any then.

"I guess there's nothing to be done about it now," I sighed. "You're not going to take me home until we've found Ramuell, are you?"

No, I am not, Evangeline said.

Just as I'd suspected. Evangeline had her own agenda and I was along for the ride. The only thing I could do was make sure that my goals—capturing Ramuell and his puppet master, and freeing the souls inside the nephilim—took precedence over hers, whatever they might be.

We walked in silence for some time. My legs and feet felt like blocks of ice and the tip of my nose grew numb. I started to worry about frostbite. The great tree didn't appear any closer than it had been when we'd started.

"Tell me about Michael," I said.

She hesitated. *He was kind to me. We did not live as man and wife—we could not, without his being cast out as Lucifer had been for mating with a human. But he was kind to me, and he taught my children the ways of their magic.*

"Which served his own ends as well, seeing as he made them soul collectors," I said.

Yes, Evangeline said. *And in a way, they were taken from me because of that. They had no time for a mother who wanted to play with her children. They were taught from a young age that they had a duty to fulfill, and they spent their lives in pursuit of that duty.*

Just like me, I thought. "How did Michael manage to explain you and the children to the other angels? Why was he allowed to keep you, so to speak?"

He said that I was a victim of the Morningstar's, not a willing accomplice. The others saw that the children were not monsters like the nephilim. Then it was agreed upon that the children could take their father's place as collectors of the dead. So they had a purpose in the hierarchy.

It was not easy, especially for me. The children had some magic. They belonged. But I was always looked on with suspicion. Any magic that I had was buried inside when I agreed to go with Michael. I had to give its use up lest Lucifer try to track me. So I was alone, and very human, in a world of perfection. She gave a wry smile. *But I lived, lived until a very old age, and I was able to see my children grow into men, and have children of their own.*

We are here, she said.

I stopped and looked up. The great tree was before me. I had been lulled by the sound of Evangeline's voice and my preoccupation with the cold, and I hadn't noticed our approach.

The tree was so large that it was almost hard to grasp its size. I had seen the forests of redwoods in California; this tree made redwoods look like dwarves. The trunk was nearly as wide as the base of the John Hancock building, and great gnarled roots as large as city buses twisted around it. It stretched high above me, so high that it disappeared into the low-hanging clouds that circled the mountains. The bark was white as starlight, and it gleamed in the dull gray that surrounded it.

"What now?" I asked.

Evangeline approached the base of the tree. I clambered after her, climbing over the roots, pulling myself over them with frozen hands and feet. It took me several minutes to reach her. She floated patiently next to a knot the size of my fist that marred the white face of the tree. I climbed over the last root and stood at her side, panting.

We must enter the tree, she said, and did that twirly thing again with her finger in the air. A circle of flame appeared on the bark of the tree. The inside of the circle opened to darkness.

"Where does this go?" I asked.

To the Valley of Sorrows, on the other side of the mountains, she said, and floated inside. *Come, Granddaughter.*

I stared after her into the darkness and felt all the misgivings I had been pushing aside come surging up. She could be leading me anywhere. Hell, for that matter, she might not be Evangeline at all but some kind of trick sent by Antares or Focalor or Ramuell's master.

This is a great time to realize that, I thought sourly. But I had committed myself to this course of action, and there was no way home without Evangeline.

The circle of flame closed behind me as I stepped inside and plunged into blackness. I could barely make out the glitter of Evangeline's form several feet in front of me. As my eyes adjusted I realized it wasn't completely black. The walls sparkled with a kind of green luminescence, almost like algae on the ocean at night.

Evangeline called for me to follow her again, and I picked my way toward her, cautiously putting one foot in front of the other. The tunnel was narrow enough that I could touch both sides with my arms outstretched. The walls felt like smooth rock beneath my fingers and the air inside the tree was surprisingly warm and humid. I felt all of my frozen parts thawing out rapidly. After several minutes of walking I unbuttoned my coat and folded it over my arm to carry.

The path was some kind of fine silt and felt slippery beneath my feet. It sloped downward for several feet, then leveled out. I didn't encounter any roots or rocks to trip over, and after a while I picked up the pace. I'd lost all sense of time and wondered how long I'd been gone. I wondered if Beezle would be worried. I wondered if my father had saved Gabriel. A fist squeezed my heart when I thought of the half angel lying bloody and still. I wished that he was with me now.

Evangeline stayed several feet in front of me. She did not speak at all. There was a sense of urgency about her now that infected me. I walked more quickly even as I grew more anxious about what awaited me at the end of the tunnel.

After what felt like an hour, the path started to slope upward again. Unlike the beginning of the path, the incline wasn't gradual. The grade steepened abruptly and I was forced to scramble for purchase several times, digging in the silt with my fingers. I fell flat on my face once and slid backward at least ten feet before I managed to dig the toes of my boots into the dirt and halt my progress downhill.

My coat fell from my arms and tumbled down to the bottom of the slope. I'd have to retrieve it on the way back. It was far too cold on the road for me to even consider going outside in nothing but a sweater.

Evangeline turned with an impatient huff. *Granddaughter, hurry, please. We have no time for this.*

I pushed to my knees and glared at her. "I'm not enjoying this, you know. Some of us can't just float along."

No, but you could fly, she snapped.

"Flying. Right," I said, feeling amazingly stupid. I don't know why I hadn't thought of that before. Maybe because I was still unaccustomed to using my wings for any purpose other than in my role as an Agent. I was used to acting like a human, not a supernatural being.

As soon as I thought of it my wings pushed out my back. I brushed the dirt from my face and sweater and then flew to Evangeline. She turned without another word, moving faster now, and I stayed easily at her side.

We continued upward for a few more minutes; then the path abruptly leveled out again. We were in a small, round anteroom, just a few feet across. I realized that as we'd traveled, the luminescence in the walls had increased gradually. The room was not as shadowed as the rest of the path, and I could see a door with an arched top and a squared bottom in front of us.

The door gleamed in the faint light. It looked like heavy metal, warm and yellow like gold. There was no knob, but there was a series of bolts—seven in all. I fluttered to the ground and folded my wings to my back. Evangeline hovered impatiently beside me.

Open it, she said. *What you seek is behind that door.*

"What I seek, or what you seek?" I asked, but I was already pulling the first bolt free. It didn't really matter anymore if it was my wishes or hers that had brought me here. I still had a duty to fulfill, and Evangeline was part of it.

I pulled the last bolt free and felt acid on the back of my tongue. I stepped back so that the door could swing inward. Beyond the door was an empty cavern, high and wide. The rock was gray and white and veined with silver so the walls glittered even in shadow. There was something that looked like firelight flickering around the bend just past the main room.

And there were noises. Horrible noises—squelching, grunting, screeching, metal clanging against metal.

"What is that?" I asked, suddenly afraid.

Evangeline shook her head and drifted forward, beckoning me. I wanted to turn around and run the hell down that hill and out into the desert and take my damn chances with hypothermia and radiation poisoning. Anything would be better than facing whatever was around the corner. Instead, I followed slowly, my heart pounding, sweat trickling down the back of my neck. I rounded the corner, wondering if she was leading me to my death, and stopped dead.

We were in a giant cavern. It was like being inside Soldier Field and looking all the way up to the nosebleed seats. But this place wasn't filled with beer-drinking, brat-chewing football fans. It was filled with nephilim.

The nephilim hung from metal cages in the ceiling and the walls like so many grotesque birds. Even though they were caged, their wrists were shackled and attached to chains that were bolted to the floors of their prisons. As I stood there, gaping, a nephilim brushed against the bars of its cage and shrieked in pain. It seemed that the bars were enchanted with some kind of magic. It also seemed that the cages were just small enough so that the nephilim would be unable to sit, lie down or relax in any way without touching the bars. All of the creatures moved restlessly within their prisons, seeking repose and unable to find it.

Most of the nephilim looked like Ramuell—taller than any man, red and raw-looking skin, black claws. Some of them had wings, and some didn't. Some looked . . . squishier than others. Their forms had less substance, like the glob demon that had visited my front lawn. And two of them had yellow skin covered in green and bulging sores. When one of these nephilim would brush the bars of their cage, the sores would burst, spraying a jet of foul-smelling pus and causing the nephilim to writhe in agony.

"This is the mercy that the Grigori showed their children?" I muttered, sickened. "Why didn't they just kill them rather than force them to suffer like this?"

Evangeline did not answer. I glanced around and realized that she had disappeared.

"Oh, wonderful," I said. "Great-grandma abandons me just when we get to the scary part of the story."

I wasn't sure what else to do so I started across the cavern floor, skirting close to the wall and trying to go unnoticed by the monsters suspended high above me. That didn't really work out. I don't know what gave me away—the scrape of a shoe, my terrified breath, the unusual movement at the bottom of the cave. But I wasn't incognito for long.

The first one that saw me gave a roar that nearly shattered my eardrums. It echoed throughout the cavern and the other nephilim ceased their restless pacing, growing still and silent.

"Meeeeeeaaat," the first one crooned, and it closed its clawed fingers around the bars of the cage. It seemed unaware that its hands were smoking. The air filled with the scent of burning sulfur. Its yellow eyes were fixed on me and I just barely suppressed the urge to cover myself with my arms. I had a feeling that the nephilim was sizing me up for something a lot worse than lunch.

The nephilim directly above me couldn't see me but I could hear them sniffing the air. The ones that had me in their sights followed the example of the first nephilim. They lunged to the bars of the cage, some of them reaching through and clawing their fingers in the air.

"Meat, meat, meat," they chanted, first softly, then louder and louder. "Meat, meat, meat."

"Oh, crap, crap, crap," I said, and started to run. I had no idea how strong those cages were but I was not going to stick around for a test.

The nephilim's chant grew louder and louder. I was soaked in sweat and terrified beyond belief. I couldn't think of anything. I just needed to get away, just get the hell away from the monsters. I passed beneath the last of the cages and rounded another bend. The nephilim's howls of frustration followed me, echoing into the chamber beyond.

The view that awaited me there was not much better than the one I had left. The chamber was smaller, and completely empty except for its two occupants.

Ramuell and an angel I had never seen before were, well . . . getting busy. It was disgusting beyond imagining to see a creature of light copulating willingly with the nephilim. At least, I'm pretty sure it was willing. She was making a lot of screeching noises but they seemed to be noises of pleasure. She had the same ethereal beauty as the other angels I had seen—the pale skin, the blond curls, the white, feathery wings. But her beauty was tainted by the horror that she willingly touched.

The nephilim was behind her and they both faced me, but the angel's eyes were closed. While his skin still looked shredded and burned from our last encounter, some of Ramuell's wounds had begun to scab over. He saw me and stopped mid-stroke, pulling out of the angel and roaring. I covered my eyes with my hands.

"Oh, my fucking lord, I am blind," I said, and felt bile in my throat. "That was *gross*. Gross, gross, gross."

I pulled my hands from my face as Ramuell pounded across the cavern toward me, giving me just enough time to shoot into the air and avoid a deadly swipe. My magic surged up, practically forgotten in the horror and strangeness of the last few hours. I gave Ramuell a blast of nightfire and flew higher, staying away from his deadly claws. The nephilim screamed in fury but he could not touch me.

There was a tinkle of familiar laughter a few feet away from me, and I turned from Ramuell to see a pair of blazing green eyes.

"Hello, Ariell," I said to the angel who hovered before me.

She gave a little half bow, a smirk on her perfect pink lips, and then she shot a bolt of lightning straight at my heart.

21

I DODGED OUT OF THE WAY AND THE LIGHTNING SIZ-
zled across my upper arm instead. Ariell's magic smelled
kind of peppery, not the cinnamon that I associated with
angelic powers. I gritted my teeth at the pain in my arm
and sent a blast of blue nightfire at her.

She blocked my magic easily, her tinkling laughter
echoing throughout the chamber. Her laugh was getting on
my nerves. It was the laugh of the head cheerleader in high
school, the one who was so perfect and popular and smug
about it that you wanted to kick her. Or, at least, *I* wanted
to kick her.

"Is that the best you can do, Azazel's daughter?"

"I've got a few tricks up my sleeve," I said. I did have a
few tricks—I just didn't know how to use them on her. But
she didn't need to know that. I gave her another quick blast
of nightfire and she dodged me again, shooting a string of

lightning bolts at me so that I was forced to retreat rather than attack.

Ramuell grew excited by the violence and paced frantically beneath us. He swiped at my heels if I drifted too low and I was careful to stay out of his reach. I wondered why the nephilim didn't use blasts of magic on me the way he had when he fought Gabriel at Clark and Belmont. Maybe the binding that controlled the nephilim limited their powers here in the Valley of Sorrows. If their powers weren't bound, perhaps they could blast themselves out of their restraints.

I tried to concentrate, to think about ways I could hurt Ariell, but it was hard to focus on my abilities when I was trying not to get killed. She launched another bolt at me and I did the flying equivalent of a scurry as part of the rock wall behind me was blasted apart. Ariell giggled.

"You are as weak as your mother," she said.

I felt the magic inside me bubble with anger. She had been responsible for the death of my mother. She had set a nephilim on Katherine and trapped her soul inside a monster for all eternity. There was no way this bitch was leaving the cavern in one piece.

I looked at the rock wall, and at Ariell, smirking in midair. And then I sent a blast of nightfire at the ceiling above her. She wasn't expecting that.

Huge chunks of rock tumbled out of the ceiling and she wasn't able to avoid all of them. One of them smashed into her left wing and sent her spiraling to Earth with a heavy thud. A few more rocks tumbled on top of her and she cried out in anger and pain.

The nephilim hurried to her side like a dog to its master. Ariell brushed Ramuell away as she struggled to her feet.

"Get off me!" she shouted, striking him as he attempted to help her.

Ramuell growled in response. "Be careful, angel."

Ariell glared at the nephilim. "You be careful, monster. Remember, Samiel can re-bind you at any time."

Samiel. That must be Ramuell's other son. I wondered where he was.

I saw Ramuell's claws curve into his palms and thought that Ariell had better watch herself. Whatever power she thought she had over the nephilim would be moot if Ramuell lost his temper and mutilated her.

Still, now would be a good time for some of those handy magical abilities, or maybe some assistance from Evangeline. Since Great-grandma seemed to have disappeared, time for a dose of magical concentration.

I thought of the match flame inside me, and of the electricity that I'd used on Antares. And just like that, my magic responded. It probably wouldn't have worked if I hadn't had a few seconds to think, but Ariell considered me such a weak opponent that she could essentially turn her back on me while she argued with her—*ick, ick, ick*—lover. My hands shot out, crackling electricity, and I caught Ariell by surprise.

She screamed as the electricity danced through her body, over muscle, into bone, under skin. Some of her feathers caught fire and she slammed herself frantically into the walls of the cavern, trying to put out the flames.

Ramuell stumbled away from her and I blasted him, too. The nephilim roared in pain, writhing in the dirt, and an answering cry came from its brethren in the next chamber.

"Yes," I said, and blasted her again. Her screams became louder and more terrified, and I kept on hitting her with the same spell. "Yes."

I started to laugh, and as I laughed and hit Ariell again

and again I felt something twist inside me. I knew it wasn't me that gloried in the terror of another.

"Show yourself, Evangeline," I said, and curled my hands into fists, trying to stop the maniacal flow of magic.

She deserves to suffer for what she has done, Evangeline said, and her voice was inside my head, my blood, my muscles and bones. My fists uncurled of their own volition and magic flowed through me, from me, to torture Ariell. The angel arched on the floor and screamed as electricity burned her up from the inside. She clawed at her skin, just as Antares had done, and the flesh fell away in thin ribbons as she tried to get the magic out.

"Stop it!" I shouted. I was nothing but a puppet to Evangeline. "You have no right to murder her for your own vengeance."

It is your vengeance as well, Granddaughter. She is responsible for the death of your mother, of your friend.

She was right, and part of me did want to kill Ariell and Ramuell for that. But defending yourself in battle wasn't the same as cold-blooded murder. Like I'd told Gabriel, I was supposed to be the good guy.

Ramuell started to rise and white fire poured out of my palms, setting the nephilim aflame. He screamed in torment and the cavern was filled with the stench of his cooking flesh.

"We can't kill them!" I cried out desperately. "It's wrong!"

Wrong? Evangeline's voice was cold and furious. *Wrong? It is wrong to punish those who took me from Lucifer, who would have murdered his children in cold blood for their own aims, their own petty lust for power? It is wrong to punish those responsible for the deaths of my grandchildren, who destroyed my direct line so utterly*

*that you are the last survivor? It is wrong to punish those
who murdered your mother and who would murder you
the same way? No, my granddaughter. It is not wrong. It is
wrong to show them mercy.*

I struggled to close my fists, to shut off the flow of
magic. I wanted to capture Ariell, to have her brought to
Azazel for her crimes. I didn't want to be an instrument
of murder.

But Ramuell, I thought to myself. *Ramuell, I wouldn't
mind killing. If I killed him, Katherine might be set free.*

"No," I said out loud, and as the conviction in me grew I
felt Evangeline in my mind, grasping for control. "No. I'm
not like them. I won't be a monster."

And then I heard Beezle's voice in my head saying,
"Concentrate, concentrate," and I did. I thought of the little
match flame inside me, the one that was blazing like a bonfire at the moment. I thought of Evangeline, lurking in my
blood. I knew I wouldn't be able to shut off the flow of
magic while she was inside me. But Gabriel had said my
will was strong. That was how I'd overcome the spell he'd
put on me, the one to make me compliant.

So instead of trying to shut off the flow of magic, I used
my will and my strength to turn it inside, to find Evangeline
inside me and chase her out. The electricity that sparked
from my fingertips reversed course, flowing back through
my veins. I screamed in agony as it tripped through my
blood, a hunter seeking its prey. I could no longer keep
myself aloft and I fell to Earth in a tumble of wings and
bones. I heard something crunch in my leg and nearly went
blind from the pain.

Evangeline screamed, *Granddaughter, what are you
doing?*

I could feel her inside me, shrinking away from my

power, trying to make herself smaller and smaller. The electricity burned through every inch of me, leaving no cell unturned as it searched for Evangeline.

She burrowed into a corner of my mind, but my magic wanted only one thing. I heard her screaming as it came for her, and her screams were my screams as the magic devoured me to find her.

Then I felt something in my head pop, and a moment later a gush of blood came from my recently broken nose. My magic cut off in an instant. The bonfire lowered to a match flame again, and I opened my eyes to see Evangeline standing before me, not as a ghost or a memory, but a corporeal being. Her face was alight with fury.

"How dare you?" she shrieked, pulling at her hair like a madwoman. "How dare you? I have waited eons for vengeance, waited eons for a vessel with the strength that you have."

I sat up and swiped at my nose with the sleeve of my sweater. I could taste the tang of dirt and my own blood in my mouth. "Yeah, well, I'm not your fucking vessel, am I? I'm Madeline Black, daughter of Azazel, and of Katherine Black, and I will not be used by anyone, not even you, Grandma."

She howled in frustration, scraped her nails along her cheeks and left rivulets of blood. I rolled my eyes at her and assessed the latest damage to my very-human form.

Every part of me hurt. I flapped my wings and used them to level myself to a standing position, floating a few feet above the ground. I didn't want to put any pressure on my left ankle, as it was definitely broken.

The smell of rotten barbecue permeated my abused nose and I spun in a circle, suddenly remembering Ariell and Ramuell. They were both unconscious. Ariell's skin looked boiled, but her chest rose and fell in shallow breaths. Most of her wings were burned off. There were just a few white feathers, gray now from smoke, clinging to a twisted cartilage frame. This, more than anything, made me feel sorry for her. She looked so small and pathetic without her wings.

Ramuell was a shapeless, blackened hulk. It seemed he had tried to curl himself into a ball to put out the flames and more or less melted in that position. Somehow the monstrous thing still breathed.

So, I had my two villains—and one crazy Lost Mother—and no way to contact anyone or to transport them to Azazel. Well, I did have my cell phone, but it was in my jacket pocket at the bottom of the underground path. And I doubted I could get a cell signal in the Forbidden Lands anyway.

"Hey," I called to Evangeline, who had fallen to the ground and was pounding it with her fists. "Hey, crazy lady. I need you for a second."

She looked up at me, eyes red-rimmed and insane. "And why should I help you, betrayer of my blood?"

"Cut the drama," I snapped. "I've got to get in touch with someone to pick up these two losers, and I don't know how to do it. You've been manipulating my magic all this time, so you probably know how to do some long-distance communication, right?"

Her eyes widened, and then she started to laugh, a mad witch's cackle.

"Okay, whatever," I said, and that was when Ramuell tore out my heart.

I didn't have any time to feel pain. My soul snapped its tether and floated away from my shell the instant the nephilim's claws burst through my ribs. I saw my broken body thrown aside. The nephilim screamed in triumph and ate my still-beating heart while I watched. Then he went to Evangeline, scooped her from the ground and bit off her head. I heard her soul fall screaming into his gaping maw.

I floated up and up. I felt so light, so free. No earthly body to bind me. No earthly cares to chain me. No angel wars, no souls to collect, no demons chasing me. No confusing attractions or unwanted fiancés. Just me, a dust mote in the universe.

Ramuell stalked across the cavern and tore Ariell in half with his claws. Apparently not sated by his last little snack, he started to eat her. I felt a little twinge of conscience. I should do something, probably. Ramuell was roaming free and no one knew about it except me. He wouldn't stay here for long. He would find some way to get to a human population and then he would start eating his way through every man, woman and child he could find.

But what can I do, really? I thought as I drifted. *I'm dead. An Agent should be coming for me soon, to take me to the Door.*

Just because you're dead doesn't mean that your magic is gone.

Yes, but I'm tired. Really tired of being chased around by monsters.

Your magic comes from inside you, from your soul. Your magic is still with you even though your shell is gone.

I just want to rest, to be free.

You have a destiny to fulfill, a monster to destroy.

I couldn't run away. I wouldn't run away. I wouldn't let Ramuell defeat me. I wouldn't let innocent lives be lost because I was a coward. And whatever the future brought me, I would face it, because I was a child of Lucifer and Evangeline, of Azazel and Katherine, because all their best powers and purposes had aligned in me. I had been raised to understand my duty, and I wouldn't shirk from it now.

And as I thought this, I felt my magic in a way that I never had before. I felt it flow through me, a part of me, not a thing that I kept locked away in a small corner and took out only when I needed it. It was always there, always alive within me, and it wasn't a match flame. It blazed like the heart of the sun.

I went to my poor shell, and I slid back inside it, and the sun within me burned hotter and brighter. All my broken bones reknit, and my skin sealed up without a scratch. But my heart . . . Where my heart had been I could feel a dark core, like a stone, and I realized that I was less human than I had been before.

I came to my feet, flexing my fingers, my hands, my wings. I felt shiny and new, and my magic was a gentle thing that skimmed the surface of my blood. Then I smiled.

"Hey," I called to Ramuell. "You're going to have to do a lot better than that."

The nephilim ceased crunching away at Ariell and turned to me, mouth agape. I didn't wait for it to attack or to banter. I let my magic flow through me and out, and the room was filled with the light of the sun.

Ramuell screamed, throwing his arms over his eyes. I waited serenely, warmed by the light, and watched as Ramuell began to disappear.

It wasn't like he was melting, precisely, because there was no residue dripping to the floor. It was like bits of him were being burned away, molecule by molecule. First skin, then muscle, then bone and blood. And finally, when there was nothing of Ramuell remaining, there was a burst of light and a pop, and all the souls that had been trapped inside him were before me.

There was my mother, smiling with pride, and Patrick giving me a goofy grin and a thumbs-up. There was the woman who'd been eaten in front of the Starbucks. And there was . . .

"Evangeline."

The voice filled the cavern, and I turned, and my own light dimmed beside the glory of the one who stood there. His face was perfection, his eyes were like two stars, and his wings were as black and glossy as the deepest part of night. But it was not his beauty that had me choking back sobs. It was the look of love on his face, a look that had always been for her, only for her, his Evangeline.

The Morningstar held his arms out to her and she came to him, and he enfolded her in his wings and murmured words of love.

After a few moments he held her away from him, and his eyes gleamed brighter than before. She nodded, and he opened a portal in front of her. Inside the portal was the Door, and Michael was waiting, beckoning to all the lost souls.

The souls slowly filed through the portal, Patrick waving to me, my mother blowing me a kiss. I didn't have time to go to her, to tell her all the things that were in my heart. The little girl inside me cried to see my mommy going away again. The Agent in me knew that she had died a long time ago, and this was the best way. The longer she stayed, the harder it would be for her to leave.

Then Lucifer reluctantly released Evangeline, and she turned to go. Just as she was about to enter the portal, she glanced back at me and gave me a small nod. I returned the gesture, and she disappeared, the portal closing behind her.

Then Lucifer turned his starlight eyes on me and said, "Granddaughter," and held out his arms to me as he had to Evangeline.

I felt compelled to run to him, to embrace him, to feel the warm glow of his approval on me, to kneel to him and call him my lord. This last impulse checked me. I might be his granddaughter, but I was also—as I had told Evangeline—my own self. I was Madeline Black, and I kneeled to no one.

I walked to him sedately, and put my hands in his. He kissed each one of my cheeks and the magic in my blood sang out in recognition of its kin. The room grew brighter, filled with the light of two suns, and I heard a gasp.

I looked toward the bend in the cavern and saw Azazel, Gabriel and—ugh—Nathaniel. My father looked like he was about to bust open with pride, but I had no eyes for him. It was Gabriel I was concerned with, Gabriel who was smiling at me. I felt relief bloom in my chest. He was alive. He was safe.

Then I met Nathaniel's astonished gaze—he was the one who had gasped—and gave him a nod of thanks. His head bobbed up and down in response but I think he was a little shell-shocked at the idea that his betrothed was related to Lucifer. ·

"My granddaughter," Lucifer said, and I turned my gaze back to his. "Tell me what has happened here."

So I told him, about Ariell and Ramuell, about the plot to overthrow him that started with Evangeline and their children and continued even as Ariell was the last conspirator to survive Evangeline's wrath. I told him of Evangeline's decision to go with Michael, and of her attempts to kill Ariell through me. I told him of Antares and his attacks upon me. I told him that Ramuell had eaten Ariell, and torn my heart from my body. I told him that I had returned to life and killed the nephilim with the light of the sun. I didn't mention Ariell's child. I didn't want to draw

Lucifer's attention to half-nephilim children with Gabriel standing right there. He might decide to change his mind about the stay of execution he'd granted so many years ago on Gabriel's life.

Lucifer said nothing as I recited my tale, only kept my hands grasped in his and his eerie starlit eyes fixed on my face. When I was finished I was a little hoarse, and very tired. My injuries were gone but it took a lot out of a girl, coming back from the dead to defeat evil.

"I'm kind of thirsty," I said. Lucifer said something in a language I didn't understand, and a bottle of water appeared in the air. "Hey, neat trick."

"You have killed my firstborn son," Lucifer said. "This is a crime in the law of my kingdom."

I felt something inside me go still and cold. After all of this, was I going to be killed simply because I had destroyed the nephilim?

"However, in doing so you freed Evangeline's soul from this Earth, and for that I am grateful. So I have decided to grant clemency in this matter, and you will be forgiven publicly for your crime."

"Hey, great," I said, speaking without thinking. "I just couldn't sleep tonight if I didn't have your approval."

There was another gasp from Nathaniel and I could practically hear Gabriel rolling his eyes in frustration. I thought for a minute that Lucifer might rescind his offer of clemency and have my head chopped off right there, but he surprised me. He laughed, and his laugh was such lovely music that I had to laugh with him while the other three gaped in wonder.

"You are my own granddaughter," he said. "Your spirit does me proud. However . . ."

I felt the cold sting of dread again.

"You have been granted clemency, but you still owe me a boon for the death of my son. I will be calling on you sometime in the future for the repayment of this favor," he said, and his fingers tightened on mine in a way that made me understand this favor was nonnegotiable.

"And what makes you think," I said, but very softly, so only he could hear, "you can make me do anything that I don't want to do?"

He smiled, and his smile was not the beautiful smile of the first and most glorious angel that he was. It was the smile of the devil, and I felt my bravado shrink a little.

Lucifer leaned forward so that his mouth was at my ear. "I can make you do whatever I like, Granddaughter. There is a secret in your heart that I know, and if you want to protect his life, you will obey me."

He leaned back to look in my face and then slanted his eyes toward Gabriel. My blood pumped faster and my hands grew cold, but I said nothing. How did Lucifer know? To admit that I loved him would condemn Gabriel to death in an instant. I lifted my chin and matched him stare for stare.

"This secret that you think you know—how would you discover the truth of such a thing?"

"Perhaps a little bird, so recently close to your heart, whispered it in my ear."

Evangeline. That bitch.

"Perhaps the little bird was mistaken," I said.

"Be careful, Granddaughter. You are the last child of my heart, but it is my kingdom in which you tread," Lucifer said, and he kissed me again on the cheek. This time his kiss was as cold as stone. "I will see you soon, Granddaughter."

He pulled away from me and clapped his hands. The

other three were at his side in an instant. "And now, to return home."

Lucifer opened a portal filled with swirling mist. "Thrall, you will return as Madeline's bodyguard for the present time."

"Of course, my lord," Gabriel said, and knelt before Lucifer.

The Morningstar met my eyes and I arched an eyebrow at him. I knew why he sent Gabriel back with me, and it wasn't for my protection. It was to remind me every day of what I would lose if I disobeyed Lucifer's wishes.

Gabriel entered the portal before me. I had started to follow when Nathaniel grasped my hand.

"Madeline," he said, and his eyes were very earnest. All the haughtiness had fled. He seemed overwhelmed. I felt a little sorry for him, although not enough to want to continue this farce of an engagement. "I . . . I will see you in fourteen days' time, in Azazel's court."

"Okay," I said, and let him kiss my hand. It seemed like the thing to do. I nodded at Azazel and Lucifer and stepped backward into the portal, more than ready to go home.

Just as the portal was about to close, I saw a flash of movement in the cavern. For a moment I thought I saw green eyes lashed with fury.

Samiel, I thought, and then he was gone, and the portal closed.

We stepped out of the portal into the intersection at Clark and Belmont, and I realized that Lucifer had somehow known exactly where I wanted to be at that moment. It made me wonder about the full extent of his powers and, therefore, about the full extent of mine.

Most of the intersection was still roped off with yellow crime scene tape, and it was almost eerily quiet. There was still a faint and lingering stink of sulfur in the air.

"Why are we here and not at your home?" Gabriel asked, frowning.

"There's something I forgot to do," I said, and flapped my arms at him. "Go stand over there."

"I am not to leave your side," Gabriel said.

"Just go stand over on that corner," I said. "I'm going to sit on this bench right here. You'll be able to see me the whole time."

"I am not certain that Lord Lucifer . . ." he began.

"Look, can we just follow the spirit of the law right now? I need to be alone for a minute."

Indecision warred in his eyes, and then he relented. "All right, Madeline. For now."

I plopped on a bench in front of the donut shop and waved at Gabriel as he took up a post directly across the street. My wings emerged, and I winked out of sight.

I had to wait only a few moments. He'd been expecting me.

"Hello, James," I said, as a young man with floppy blond bangs and almond-shaped eyes sat down beside me.

"You said you wouldn't let the monster eat me," he said.

"And I didn't."

"It almost ate you."

I thought of staring into Ramuell's gaping maw, hearing the cries of the dead souls inside him. "Yes."

He shivered and rubbed his ectoplasmic hands over his ectoplasmic arms. "I don't think I want to stay here. Too many bad memories."

I smiled at him. "I know just the place to take you."

* * *

Beezle was furious with me for going on an adventure without telling him. He also had a cut above his eye. It turned out that Nathaniel had knocked Beezle around a little in order to get him to reveal that Gabriel and I had gone to Greenwitch's. Nathaniel's treatment of Beezle killed any pity I had briefly felt for the angel. I redoubled my vow not to marry the jerk under any circumstance whatsoever. Then I popped a double batch of popcorn for Beezle and spent some time cuddling with him on the couch while he ate.

Gabriel disappeared downstairs as soon as we got home. A couple of hours later, after Beezle had returned to his nest on the roof, the half angel knocked on the back door and walked in through the kitchen. I got up from the sofa and put my arms around him, breathing in the apple pie smell of him and wishing he could stay with me forever.

"I am so happy that you're alive," I said into his shoulder.

"As am I," Gabriel murmured. "My heart nearly stopped when you told the tale of your battle with Ramuell."

I held on tight for a few more moments, trying to stretch it out. I knew what was coming. He pulled away from me and kissed my forehead.

"Madeline, we cannot pretend anymore," he began, and I covered his mouth with my fingers.

"Don't," I said lightly. "Just don't say it. I'm Lucifer's granddaughter, after all. Who knows what might change in the future?"

His look told me that he didn't think very much would change at all, but he gave a little shrug and released me, stepping back to the door.

"I'm not giving up on you," I called after him.

"And I," he said, giving me a very small smile, "would not be so foolish as to bet against you."

J.B. came by a few hours later, after I'd showered and napped and was standing in the kitchen contemplating take-out menus. He looked like he'd been through hell. He collapsed in my comfiest chair and tilted his head back, closing his eyes.

"What's the deal?" I said.

"The upper brass don't know what to think. I didn't want to tell them about you and your mission . . ."

"Thanks," I said.

". . . but I did tell them I thought the creatures that attacked the office were demons. They had no other explanation so they accepted it. They've been rushing around researching demons and trying to rebuild the wards."

"J.B., why weren't any of the deaths at the Agency presaged? I figured out why Ramuell's murders weren't, but what about Antares and the other demons? We should have known that Antares and his pals would attack."

He shrugged. "The big guys at the top have been pretty close-lipped about that. Best I can figure is that since our system didn't know about or recognize demons, then the seers couldn't either. I'm not really sure how that works.

"The cleanup has been a total nightmare. We've convinced the city and the press that there was a gas leak that caused hallucinations and explosions, and that it was related to a similar incident on the north side at Clark and Belmont. On the positive side, I've been promoted. It seems the regional manager was eaten by some kind of glob monster, and several of the survivors credited me with heroism during the battle." He smiled grimly, his eyes still closed.

"So you're not my supervisor anymore," I said, not knowing what else to say. It didn't seem appropriate to congratulate J.B. for a promotion that came at the expense of someone's life.

"No," he said, and opened his eyes. "So this means that I can finally ask you out on a date."

My mouth dropped open. In a week of surprises, nothing could have shocked me more than J. B. Bennett asking me out.

He took in my expression, smiled a little and then shifted around to get more comfortable, closing his eyes again. "You can answer me later."

Something occurred to me. "J.B., have you been monitoring Agents with your secret powers?"

He smiled sleepily. "Not all the time. And not all Agents. Just you."

By the time I came out of my stupor, he had fallen asleep. I covered him with a crocheted afghan and brushed a lock of hair away from his forehead.

A movement in the side window caught my eye. I glanced up and saw Antares hanging outside the window like a very ugly suncatcher. He licked the window. The acid on his tongue burned through the glass.

I flipped him the bird. He narrowed his eyes at me and bared his teeth. I deliberately turned my back on him and started to tidy the room. When I looked back, he was gone.

Beezle flew in the front window. "Antares was here," he announced.

"Yep, I caught that," I said.

Five days ago I was just an Agent. Now I was the daughter of a fallen angel, the great-granddaughter of Lucifer himself. My half brother was still running around trying to figure out a way to kill me, and apparently I'd pissed off Ariell's son as well. I was engaged to a total asshole and magically bound to marry him, I was in big-time lust with a man who was forbidden to love me, and my boss had just asked me out. There was only one thing for me to do.

"Want Chinese?" I asked Beezle.

He pumped his tiny fist in the air. "Pork dumplings!"

So we had pork dumplings, and noodles, and stir-fried chicken. Everything else could wait until tomorrow.

Explore the outer reaches
of imagination—don't miss these authors
of dark fantasy and urban noir who take you
to the edge and beyond . . .

Patricia Briggs	Anne Bishop
Simon R. Green	Marjorie M. Liu
Jim Butcher	Jeanne C. Stein
Kat Richardson	Christopher Golden
Karen Chance	Ilona Andrews
Rachel Caine	Anton Strout

M15G0610